I0664819

About this book

Evil Inc is about a corporation run by and for super-villains. Join the CEO (Chief Evil Officer) Evil Atom, a Silver-Age-villain-turned-businessman; Lightning Lady, a recovering supervillainess; Dr. Haynus, a brain-in-a-jar symbiotically joined to a puppy dog; and the rest of the employees who give a new meaning to "punching in" for the day.

Evil Atom is an aging supervillain and the founder of Evil Inc. He founded Evil Inc. on the concept that you could get away with more evil if you did it legally.

As a supervillain, Evil Atom was one of the top bad guys. For a short while, he partnered with a super-villain named Catspaw.

Lightning Lady has the power to generate and control electricity. She is the head receptionist at Evil Inc., answering directly to Evil Atom.

She is living with her boyfriend, Keagan Newborne, a stand-up comedian and former writer for the comic strip, "Greystone Inn."

Miss Match has the ability to generate and control fire.

She is a star employee in the Plots-and-Schemes Department of Evil Inc.

She and Lightning Lady have become fast friends, but she remains very secretive about anything outside of Evil Inc. business.

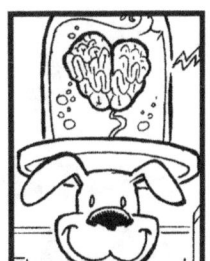

Dr. Haynus, a brilliant evil scientist, was the victim of a lab experiment gone awry. The only way he could be saved was grafting his brain onto his ex-wife's dog, Scruffy.

Scruffy and Haynus live in a symbiotic relationship. Scruffy's brain survived the operation and remains in control of the dog's body. Haynus' brain is sustained by the dog's body, but is unable to control it.

Dr. Muskiday was also the victim of a horrible lab accident. During an experiment with his matter transporter machine, a hapless janitor walked into one of the transporter pods. The janitor's DNA were merged with that of Muskiday's.

Muskiday's head was permanently fused onto the body of the janitor.

Captain Heroic is the top superhero in Fairmont City. He has the ability to fly, super strength and the ability to emit force beams from his gauntlets.

Captain Heroic is also a stay-at-home dad, taking care of his three-year-old son while his wife is at work.

Dr. Haynus has recently become registered as one of Heroic's nemeses.

About the layout

In designing this book, I've taken my daily comic strip — a standard four-panel comic like you're likely to see in your newspaper — and redesigned the panels into a cohesive page structure like you're likely to see in a graphic novel. As a result, several comic strips are used on each page — which means my signature may appear up to four times on the same page. See? It's not an ego thing after all.

Evil Inc can be read Monday through Saturday at ***www.evil-comic.com***

Contents © 2005-06 by Brad J. Guigar.

ISBN: 978-1-4116-8070-8

All rights reserved. No part of this book may be reprinted in any form whatsoever without permission by the author. For any information about this book, this comic strip, and any other publications by this author, use the contact information found on the Web site above.

Chapter 1

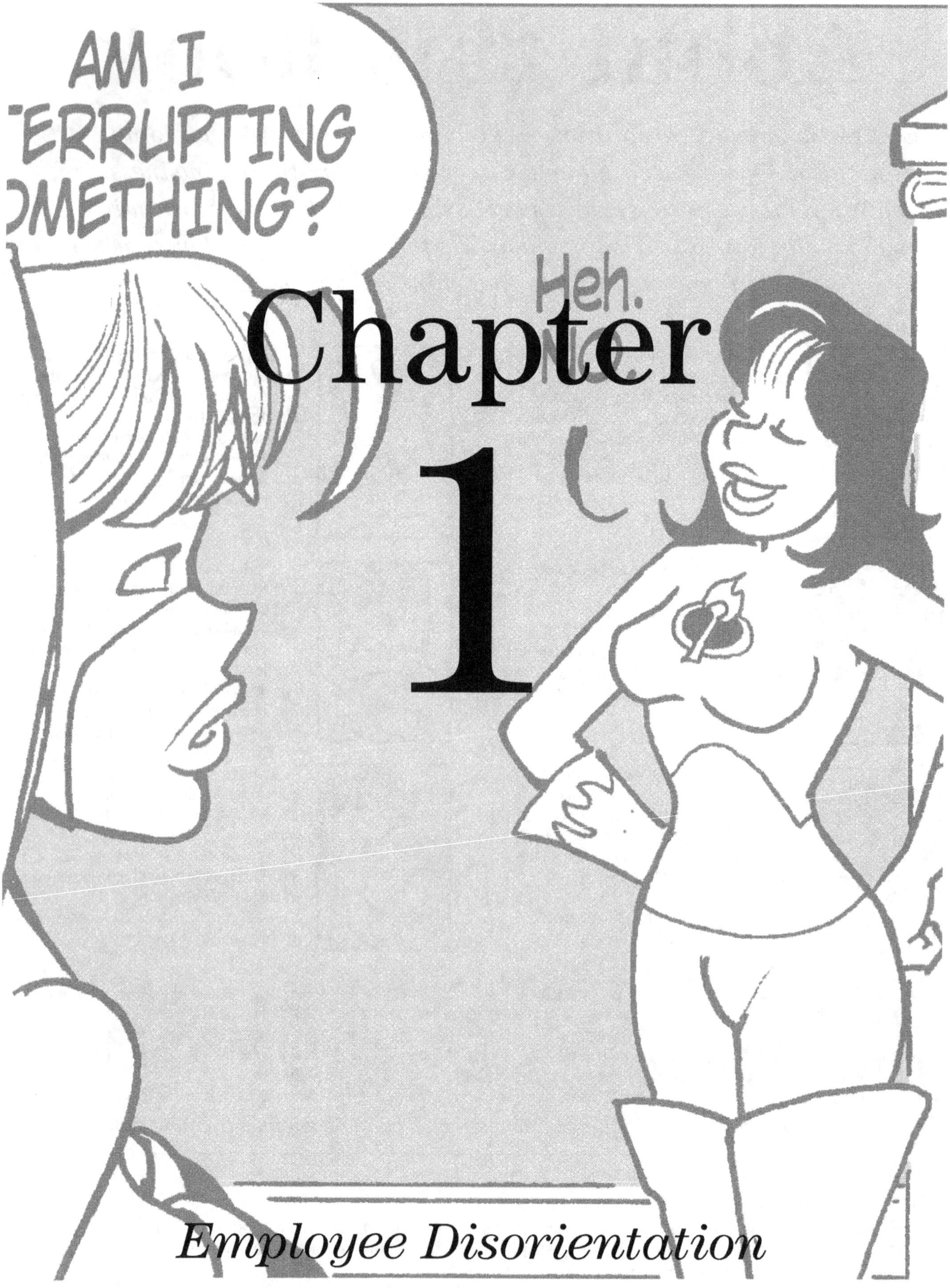
AM I
Heh.

Employee Disorientation

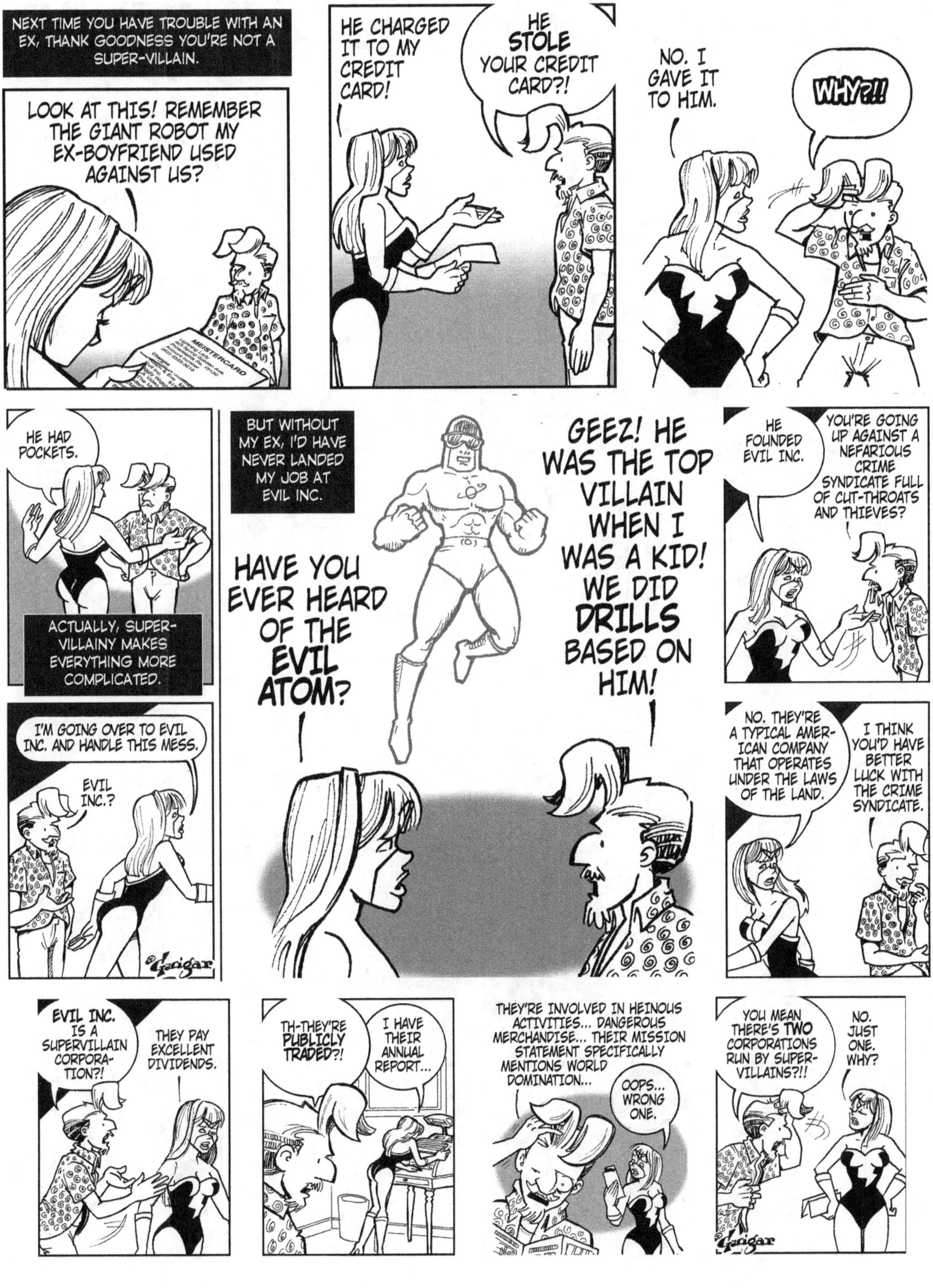
NEXT TIME YOU HAVE TROUBLE WITH AN EX, THANK GOODNESS YOU'RE NOT A SUPER-VILLAIN.
LOOK AT THIS! REMEMBER THE GIANT ROBOT MY EX-BOYFRIEND USED AGAINST US?
MESTERCARD
HE CHARGED IT TO MY CREDIT CARD!
HE STOLE YOUR CREDIT CARD?!
NO. I GAVE IT TO HIM.
WHY?!!
HE HAD POCKETS.
ACTUALLY, SUPER-VILLAINY MAKES EVERYTHING MORE COMPLICATED.
I'M GOING OVER TO EVIL INC. AND HANDLE THIS MESS.
EVIL INC.?
BUT WITHOUT MY EX, I'D HAVE NEVER LANDED MY JOB AT EVIL INC.
HAVE YOU EVER HEARD OF THE EVIL ATOM?
GEEZ! HE WAS THE TOP VILLAIN WHEN I WAS A KID! WE DID DRILLS BASED ON HIM!
HE FOUNDED EVIL INC.
YOU'RE GOING UP AGAINST A NEFARIOUS CRIME SYNDICATE FULL OF CUT-THROATS AND THIEVES?
NO. THEY'RE A TYPICAL AMERICAN COMPANY THAT OPERATES UNDER THE LAWS OF THE LAND.
I THINK YOU'D HAVE BETTER LUCK WITH THE CRIME SYNDICATE.
EVIL INC. IS A SUPERVILLAIN CORPORATION?!
THEY PAY EXCELLENT DIVIDENDS.
TH-THEY'RE PUBLICLY TRADED?!
I HAVE THEIR ANNUAL REPORT...
THEY'RE INVOLVED IN HEINOUS ACTIVITIES... DANGEROUS MERCHANDISE... THEIR MISSION STATEMENT SPECIFICALLY MENTIONS WORLD DOMINATION...
OOPS... WRONG ONE.
YOU MEAN THERE'S TWO CORPORATIONS RUN BY SUPER-VILLAINS?!!
NO. JUST ONE. WHY?
Guigar

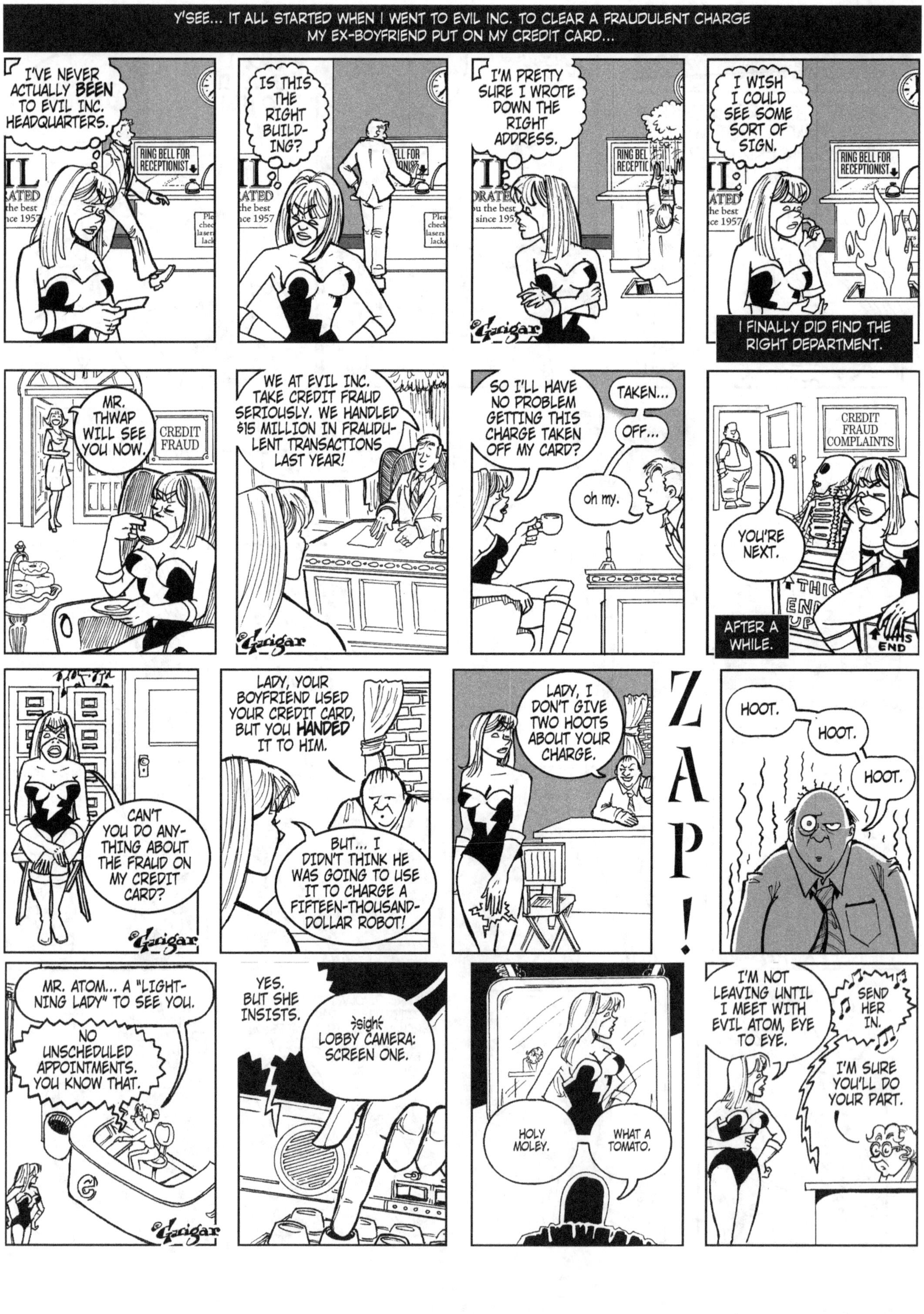

Y'SEE... IT ALL STARTED WHEN I WENT TO EVIL INC. TO CLEAR A FRAUDULENT CHARGE MY EX-BOYFRIEND PUT ON MY CREDIT CARD...
I'VE NEVER ACTUALLY BEEN TO EVIL INC. HEADQUARTERS.
RING BELL FOR RECEPTIONIST
IS THIS THE RIGHT BUILDING?
I'M PRETTY SURE I WROTE DOWN THE RIGHT ADDRESS.
I WISH I COULD SEE SOME SORT OF SIGN.
RING BELL FOR RECEPTIONIST
I FINALLY DID FIND THE RIGHT DEPARTMENT.
MR. THWAP WILL SEE YOU NOW.
CREDIT FRAUD
WE AT EVIL INC. TAKE CREDIT FRAUD SERIOUSLY. WE HANDLED $15 MILLION IN FRAUDULENT TRANSACTIONS LAST YEAR!
SO I'LL HAVE NO PROBLEM GETTING THIS CHARGE TAKEN OFF MY CARD?
TAKEN...
OFF...
oh my.
CREDIT FRAUD COMPLAINTS
YOU'RE NEXT.
AFTER A WHILE.
CAN'T YOU DO ANYTHING ABOUT THE FRAUD ON MY CREDIT CARD?
LADY, YOUR BOYFRIEND USED YOUR CREDIT CARD, BUT YOU HANDED IT TO HIM.
BUT... I DIDN'T THINK HE WAS GOING TO USE IT TO CHARGE A FIFTEEN-THOUSAND-DOLLAR ROBOT!
LADY, I DON'T GIVE TWO HOOTS ABOUT YOUR CHARGE.
ZAP!
HOOT.
HOOT.
HOOT.
MR. ATOM... A "LIGHTNING LADY" TO SEE YOU.
NO UNSCHEDULED APPOINTMENTS. YOU KNOW THAT.
YES. BUT SHE INSISTS.
sigh LOBBY CAMERA: SCREEN ONE.
HOLY MOLEY.
WHAT A TOMATO.
I'M NOT LEAVING UNTIL I MEET WITH EVIL ATOM, EYE TO EYE.
SEND HER IN.
I'M SURE YOU'LL DO YOUR PART.

MR. ATOM'S OFFICE IS AT THE END OF THIS HALL.

WOW!

WE KEEP A NUMBER OF TROPHIES IN HERE... LIKE THIS NEWS PHOTO OF EVIL ATOM BESTING THE AVIAN AVENGER.

I HEARD ABOUT THAT!

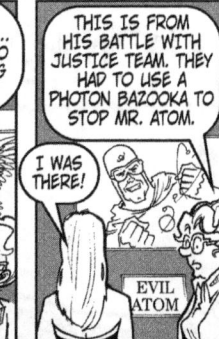

THIS IS FROM HIS BATTLE WITH JUSTICE TEAM. THEY HAD TO USE A PHOTON BAZOOKA TO STOP MR. ATOM.

I WAS THERE!

EVIL ATOM

WOW! I NEVER HEARD ABOUT THIS ONE! DID THEY USE AN AGING FORMULA? A WEIGHT-GAIN RAY?

EVIL ATOM

SHALL I SEND HER IN, SIR?

DO I HAVE A CHOICE?

Y-Y-YOU'RE THE EVIL ATOM?!

YES. WHY?

B-B-BUT... YOU'RE... YOU'RE...

CAREFUL...

...YOU'RE... DENSITY-ADVANCED AND CHRONOLOGICALLY-GIFTED.

SAY! THAT'S CLEVER. WE COULD USE A MIND LIKE YOURS IN OUR MARKETING DEPARTMENT.

REALLY? 'CAUSE I NEED A JOB!

GOOD. YOU'RE HIRED.

AAAAAANND NOW YOU'RE FIRED.

... OR SHOULD I SAY: "EMPLOYMENT DEFICIENT?"

IS THERE AN OPENING FOR ME IN THE MARKETING DEPARTMENT?

OH... THERE'S AN "OPENING"...

Ka-CHUNK

DID YOU REALLY THINK I'D FALL FOR THE OLD "TRAPDOOR" BIT?

NO. THAT'S OUR MARKETING DEPARTMENT.

YOU KEEP YOUR MARKETING DEPARTMENT UNDERGROUND?

AAARRRGGHH!

THE LIGHT! HOW IT BURNS!

IT BURNS STRONGER LONGER!

STOP SHOWING OFF AND GET TO THE CRYPT!

THEY INSIST.

...BUT I REALLY NEED A JOB...

Bzzzz

EXCUSE ME.

SIR... I DID AS YOU ASKED AND SENT THE DOZEN RED ROSES, DIAMOND BRACELET, AND LACY UNDERWEAR TO YOUR WIFE. I INCLUDED THE NOTE THAT SAID, "FROM YOUR LOVE STALLION."

...AND I SENT THE "HAPPY ANNIVERSARY" CARD, HOUSECOAT, AND SLIPPERS TO THAT ADDRESS OF YOUR APARTMENT IN THE CITY.

WELL... I'M LOOKING FOR A NEW SECRETARY...

ARRRGGGHH!

AND THAT'S HOW I ENDED UP THE HEAD RECEPTIONIST AT EVIL INC.

NOT A GLAMOUR JOB, BUT IT SUITS ME FINE.

GOOD NEWS, KEAGAN! I GOT A JOB AT EVIL INC! I'M THE CEO'S SECRETARY AND RECEPTIONIST!

Oops! GOTTA GO... THERE'S A CALL COMING IN ON THE OTHER LINE...

EVIL INCORPORATED... HOW MAY I MISDIRECT YOUR CALL?

I'M SORRY, DR. LIGHT... WE DO NOT OFFER A PRODUCT THAT RESTORES RECOLLECTIONS THAT HAVE BEEN MAGICALLY REMOVED BY HEROES.

BUT WE DO HAVE A CD THAT YOU CAN PLAY WHILE YOU SLEEP. IT INSTILLS GENERIC VILLAINOUS MEMORIES AND SHIPS WITH A BONUS CD OF DIABOLICAL MONOLOGUES.

IT'S $124.99 FOR THE MEMORY UPGRADE... $15.99 FOR THE INSTILLATION FEE.

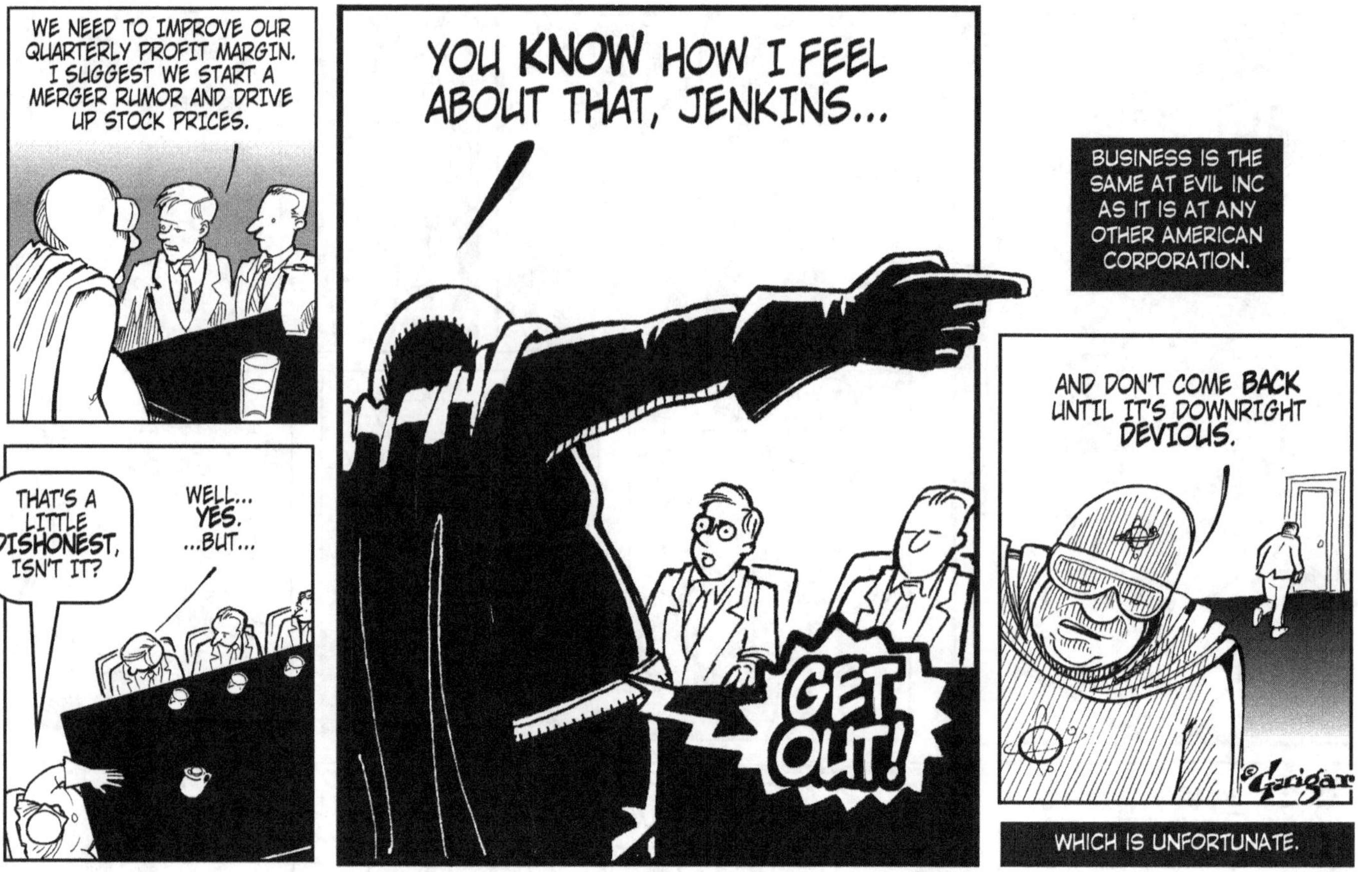
WE NEED TO IMPROVE OUR QUARTERLY PROFIT MARGIN. I SUGGEST WE START A MERGER RUMOR AND DRIVE UP STOCK PRICES.
THAT'S A LITTLE DISHONEST, ISN'T IT?
WELL... YES. ...BUT...
YOU KNOW HOW I FEEL ABOUT THAT, JENKINS...
GET OUT!
BUSINESS IS THE SAME AT EVIL INC AS IT IS AT ANY OTHER AMERICAN CORPORATION.
AND DON'T COME BACK UNTIL IT'S DOWNRIGHT DEVIOUS.
WHICH IS UNFORTUNATE.

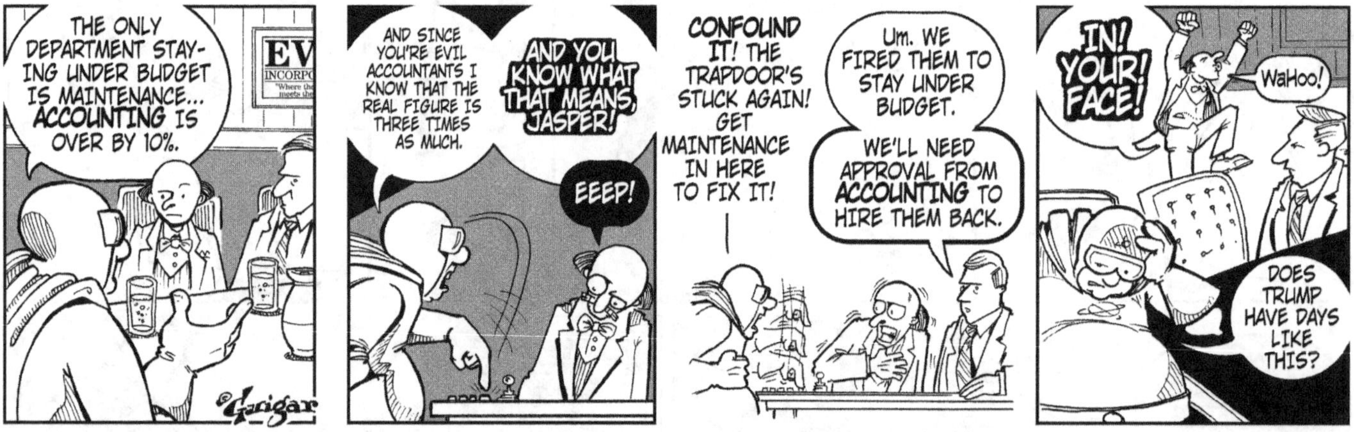
THE ONLY DEPARTMENT STAYING UNDER BUDGET IS MAINTENANCE... ACCOUNTING IS OVER BY 10%.
EVIL INCORPO
AND SINCE YOU'RE EVIL ACCOUNTANTS I KNOW THAT THE REAL FIGURE IS THREE TIMES AS MUCH.
AND YOU KNOW WHAT THAT MEANS, JASPER!
EEEP!
CONFOUND IT! THE TRAPDOOR'S STUCK AGAIN! GET MAINTENANCE IN HERE TO FIX IT!
Um. WE FIRED THEM TO STAY UNDER BUDGET.
WE'LL NEED APPROVAL FROM ACCOUNTING TO HIRE THEM BACK.
IN! YOUR! FACE!
WaHoo!
DOES TRUMP HAVE DAYS LIKE THIS?

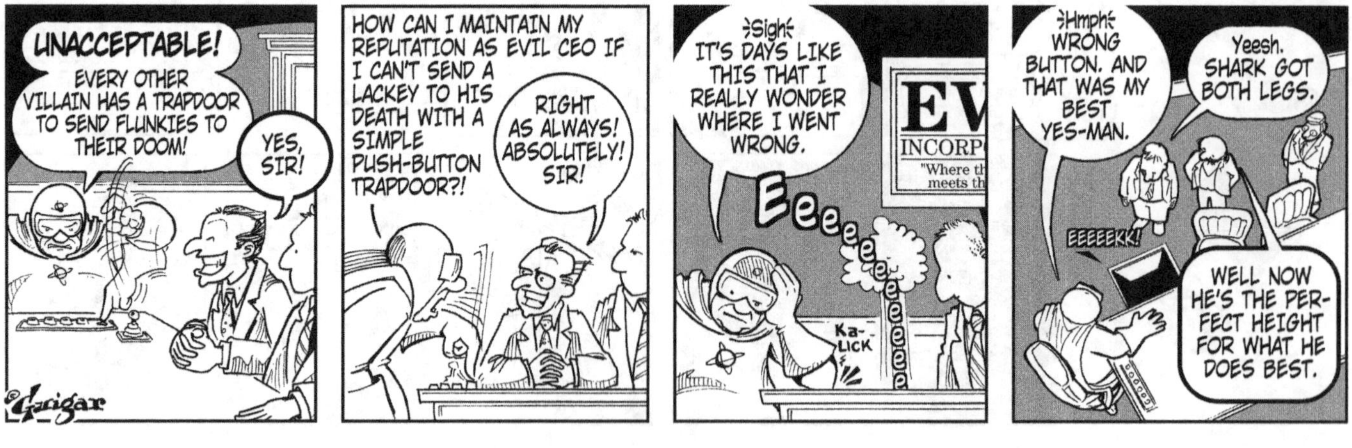
UNACCEPTABLE!
EVERY OTHER VILLAIN HAS A TRAPDOOR TO SEND FLUNKIES TO THEIR DOOM!
YES, SIR!
HOW CAN I MAINTAIN MY REPUTATION AS EVIL CEO IF I CAN'T SEND A LACKEY TO HIS DEATH WITH A SIMPLE PUSH-BUTTON TRAPDOOR?!
RIGHT AS ALWAYS! ABSOLUTELY! SIR!
Sigh
IT'S DAYS LIKE THIS THAT I REALLY WONDER WHERE I WENT WRONG.
EVI INCORPO
Eeeeeeeeeee
Ka-LICK
Hmph
WRONG BUTTON. AND THAT WAS MY BEST YES-MAN.
Yeesh. SHARK GOT BOTH LEGS.
EEEEEKK!
WELL NOW HE'S THE PERFECT HEIGHT FOR WHAT HE DOES BEST.

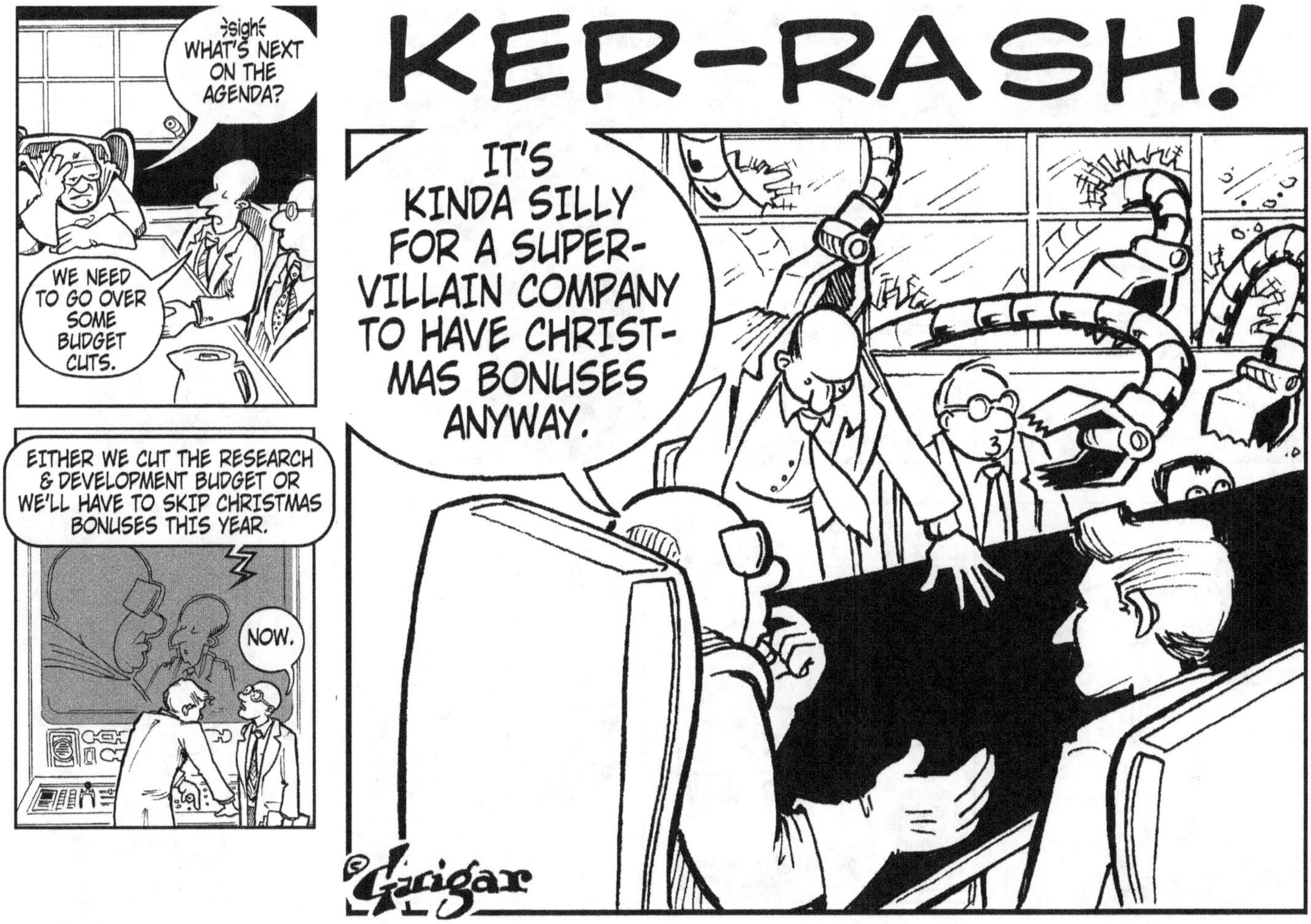
KER-RASH!
-sigh- WHAT'S NEXT ON THE AGENDA?
WE NEED TO GO OVER SOME BUDGET CUTS.
EITHER WE CUT THE RESEARCH & DEVELOPMENT BUDGET OR WE'LL HAVE TO SKIP CHRISTMAS BONUSES THIS YEAR.
NOW.
IT'S KINDA SILLY FOR A SUPER-VILLAIN COMPANY TO HAVE CHRIST-MAS BONUSES ANYWAY.
© Garigar

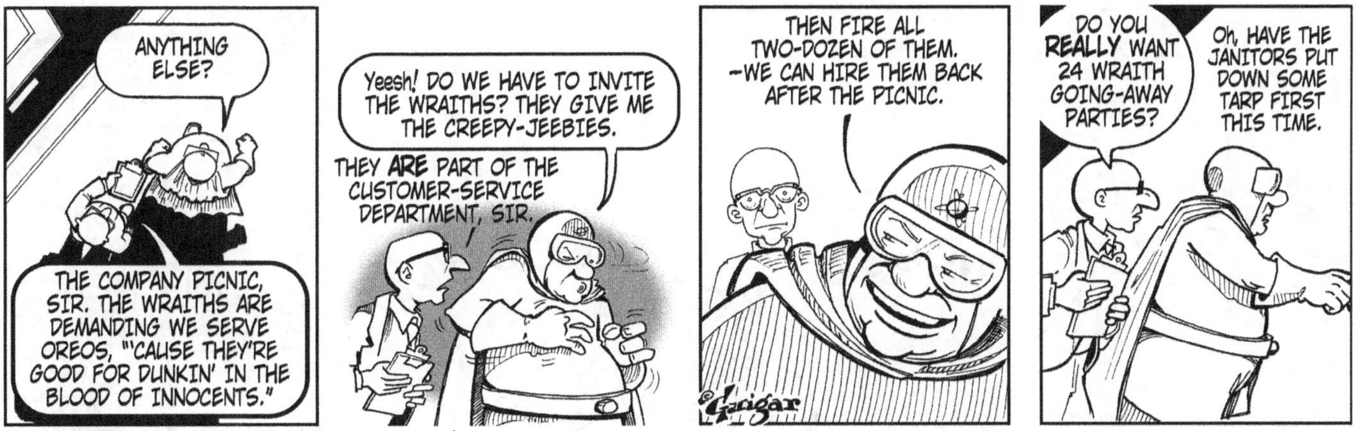
ANYTHING ELSE?
THE COMPANY PICNIC, SIR. THE WRAITHS ARE DEMANDING WE SERVE OREOS, "'CAUSE THEY'RE GOOD FOR DUNKIN' IN THE BLOOD OF INNOCENTS."
Yeesh! DO WE HAVE TO INVITE THE WRAITHS? THEY GIVE ME THE CREEPY-JEEBIES.
THEY ARE PART OF THE CUSTOMER-SERVICE DEPARTMENT, SIR.
THEN FIRE ALL TWO-DOZEN OF THEM. --WE CAN HIRE THEM BACK AFTER THE PICNIC.
© Garigar
DO YOU REALLY WANT 24 WRAITH GOING-AWAY PARTIES?
Oh, HAVE THE JANITORS PUT DOWN SOME TARP FIRST THIS TIME.

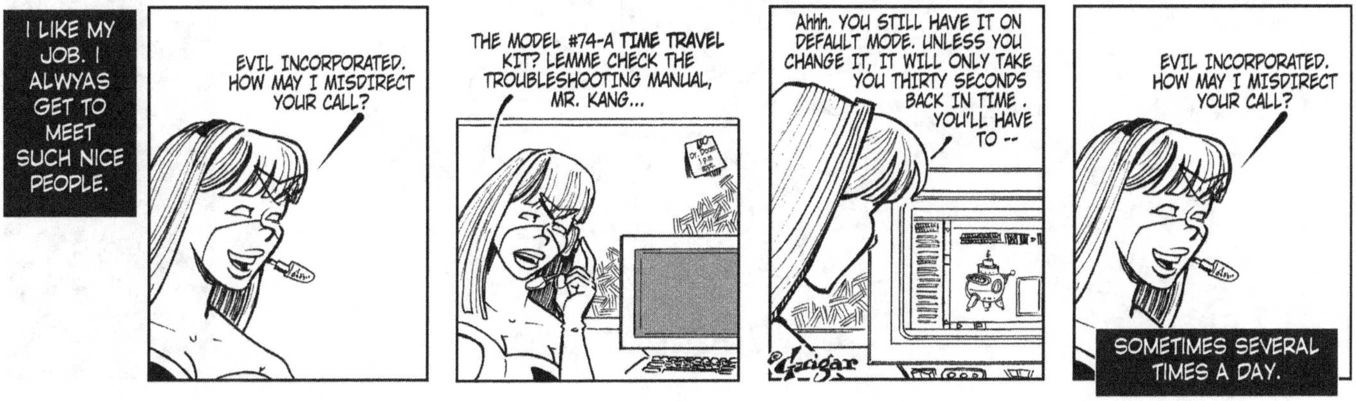
I LIKE MY JOB. I ALWYAS GET TO MEET SUCH NICE PEOPLE.
EVIL INCORPORATED. HOW MAY I MISDIRECT YOUR CALL?
THE MODEL #74-A TIME TRAVEL KIT? LEMME CHECK THE TROUBLESHOOTING MANUAL, MR. KANG...
Ahhh. YOU STILL HAVE IT ON DEFAULT MODE. UNLESS YOU CHANGE IT, IT WILL ONLY TAKE YOU THIRTY SECONDS BACK IN TIME . YOU'LL HAVE TO --
© Garigar
EVIL INCORPORATED. HOW MAY I MISDIRECT YOUR CALL?
SOMETIMES SEVERAL TIMES A DAY.

NOT EVERYBODY AT EVIL INC. IS SO NICE. DOCTOR HAYNUS, FOR INSTANCE... HE'S A BIT OF A HEAD CASE.
I CAN HEAR YOU TWITCH-ING.
EEEP
HOW DID THE BUDGET MEETING GO?
EVIL ATOM'S MAKING SOME CUTS, SIR.
FOOL! THIS COMPANY SHOULD BE IN THE FORTUNE 500! BUT THAT WON'T HAPPEN UNTIL I OUST THAT OLD CRETIN AND ASSUME MY RIGHTFUL POSITION AS PRESIDENT AND CEO OF EVIL INC!
YES SIR. IT'S JUST A MATTER OF TIME BEFORE YOU GET AHEAD.
KEEP CRACKING WISE, WITHER-ING, AND IT JUST MAY BE YOURS.
EVIL ATOM, MY LACKEY INFORMS ME YOU'RE THINKING ABOUT CUTTING MY DEPARTMENT BY TWENTY PERCENT.
WELL, IF YOU'D BEEN AT THE MEETING IN PERSON...
AAAAARRRGGH!
DR. HAYNUS... PERHAPS YOU'D LIKE TO HAVE THIS CONVERSATION AT ANOTHER TIME...
NO! STOP IT! STOP IT, BLAST YOU!
STOP BOUNCING THAT BALL!
IF YOU THINK YOU'RE CUTTING MY DEPART-MENTAL BUDGET BY TWENTY PERCENT, THINK AGAIN! I'LL CRUCIFY YOU AT THE SHARE-HOLDER MEETING AND --
WOGGIDA WOGGIDA WOGGIDA
SQWE
SQWE
GRRRRRRRRRRRRR
ABOUT THE SHAREHOLDER MEETING...?
SHARE
PERCENT
DUCKIE
PLEASE RECONSIDER. I'LL THROW IN A SQUEAKY DUCKIE!
SQWEEKA
SQWEEKA
NO! NO DUCKIE!
DOCTOR HAYNUS WAS THE VICTIM OF A HORRIBLE LAB ACCIDENT. THE ONLY WAY TO SAVE HIM WAS TO GRAFT HIS BRAIN ONTO HIS WIFE'S PET DOG, SCRUFFY.
THEY LIVE IN A WEIRD SYMBIOTIC RELATIONSHIP, STUCK TO EACH OTHER...

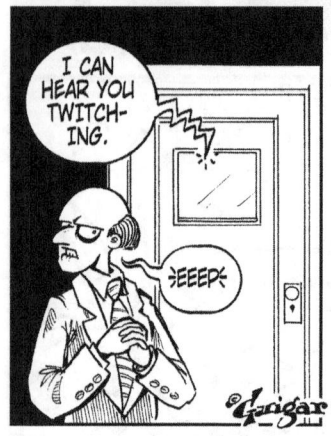

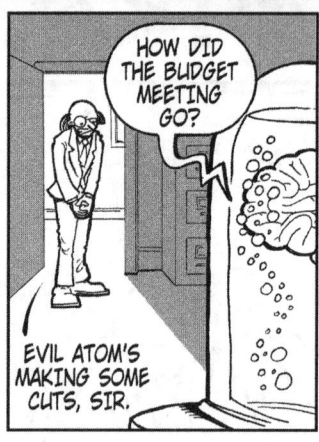

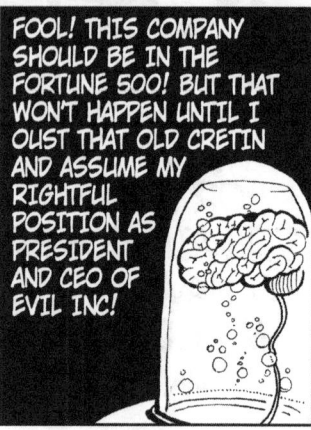

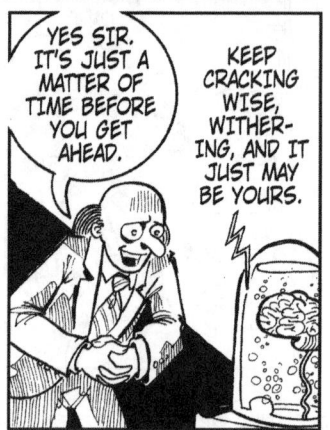

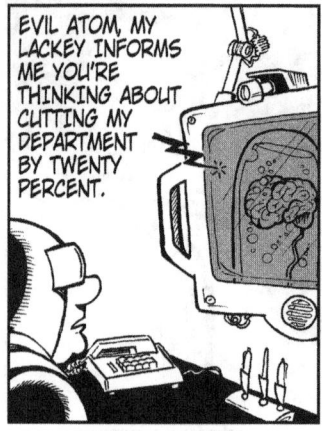

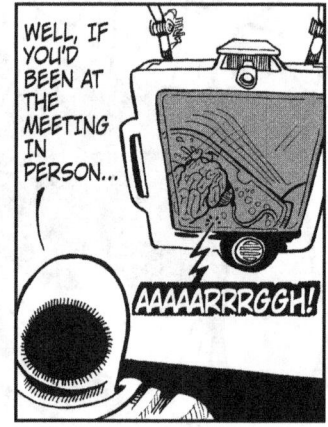

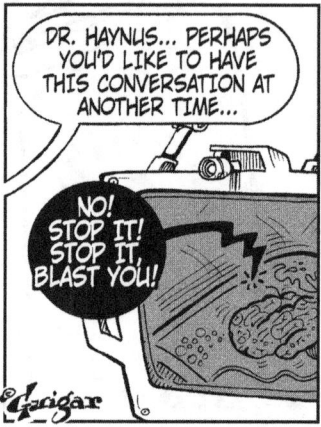

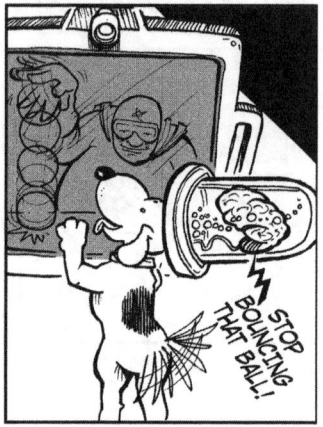

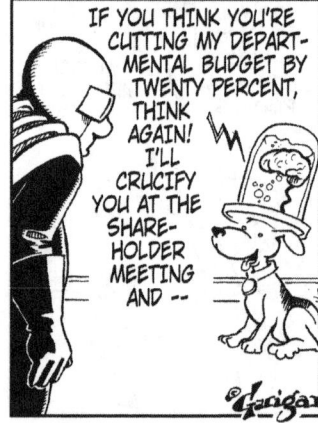

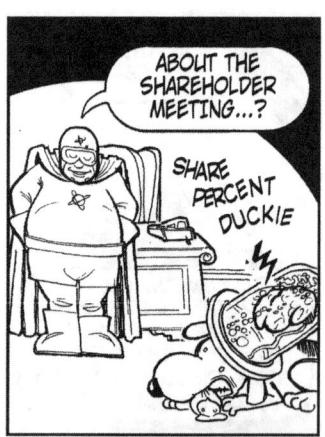

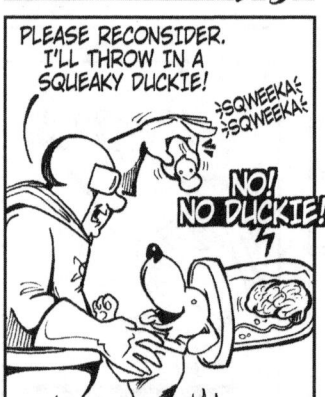

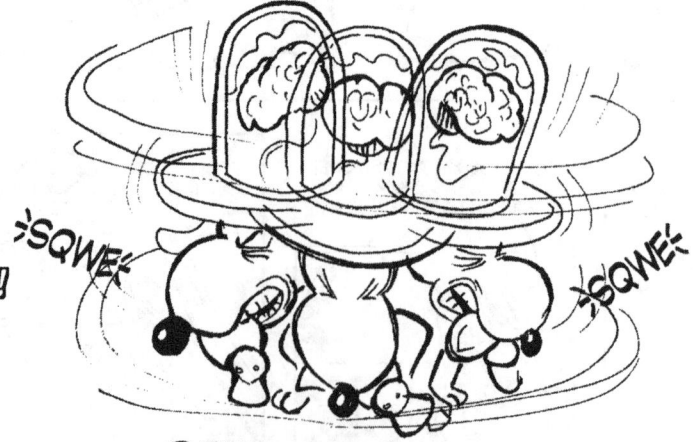

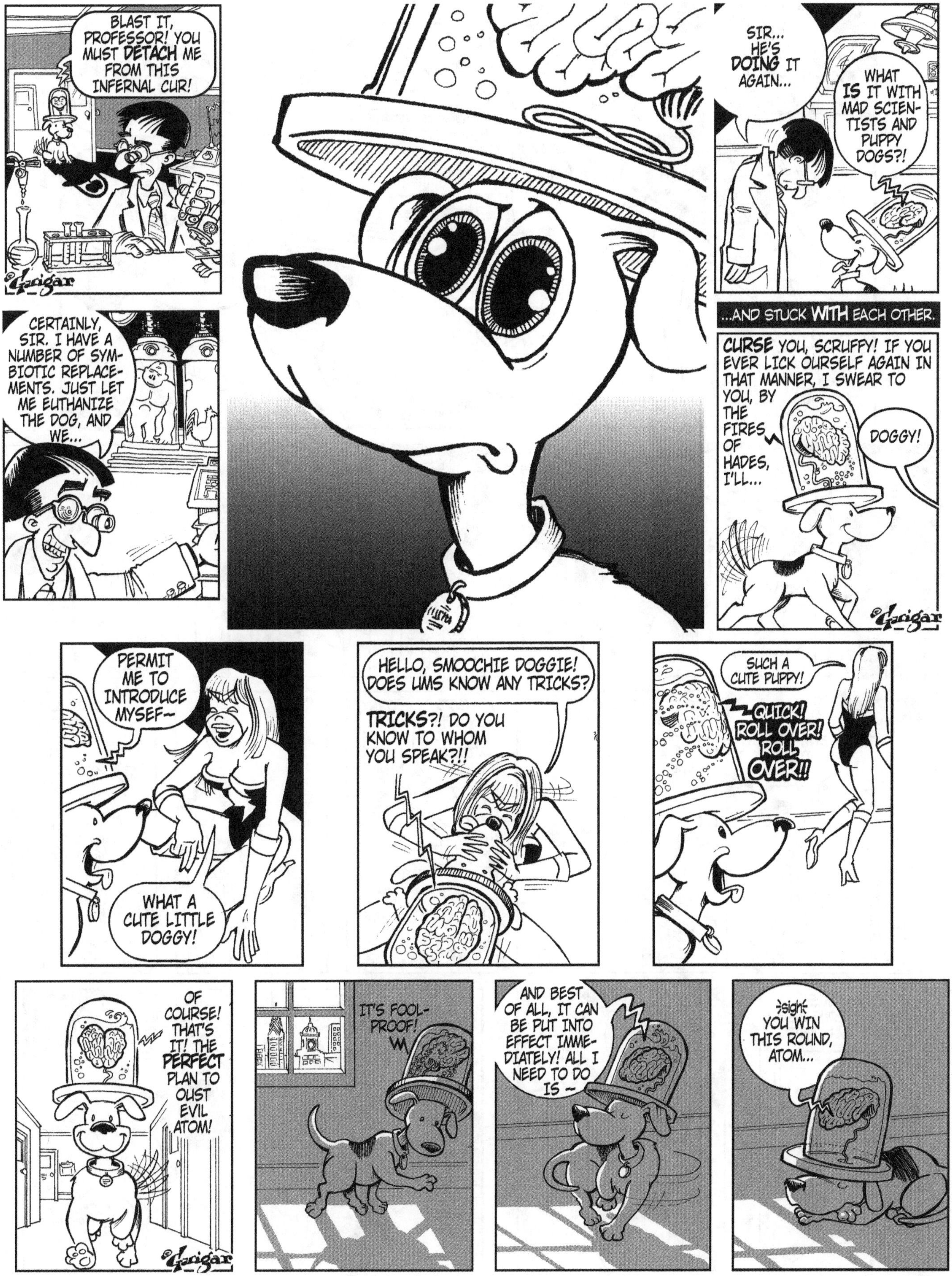

BLAST IT, PROFESSOR! YOU MUST DETACH ME FROM THIS INFERNAL CUR!
SIR... HE'S DOING IT AGAIN...
WHAT IS IT WITH MAD SCIENTISTS AND PUPPY DOGS?!
CERTAINLY, SIR. I HAVE A NUMBER OF SYMBIOTIC REPLACEMENTS. JUST LET ME EUTHANIZE THE DOG, AND WE...
...AND STUCK WITH EACH OTHER.
CURSE YOU, SCRUFFY! IF YOU EVER LICK OURSELF AGAIN IN THAT MANNER, I SWEAR TO YOU, BY THE FIRES OF HADES, I'LL...
DOGGY!
PERMIT ME TO INTRODUCE MYSEF--
WHAT A CUTE LITTLE DOGGY!
HELLO, SMOOCHIE DOGGIE! DOES UMS KNOW ANY TRICKS?
TRICKS?! DO YOU KNOW TO WHOM YOU SPEAK?!!
SUCH A CUTE PUPPY!
QUICK! ROLL OVER! ROLL OVER!!
OF COURSE! THAT'S IT! THE PERFECT PLAN TO OUST EVIL ATOM!
IT'S FOOL-PROOF!
AND BEST OF ALL, IT CAN BE PUT INTO EFFECT IMMEDIATELY! ALL I NEED TO DO IS --
sigh
YOU WIN THIS ROUND, ATOM...

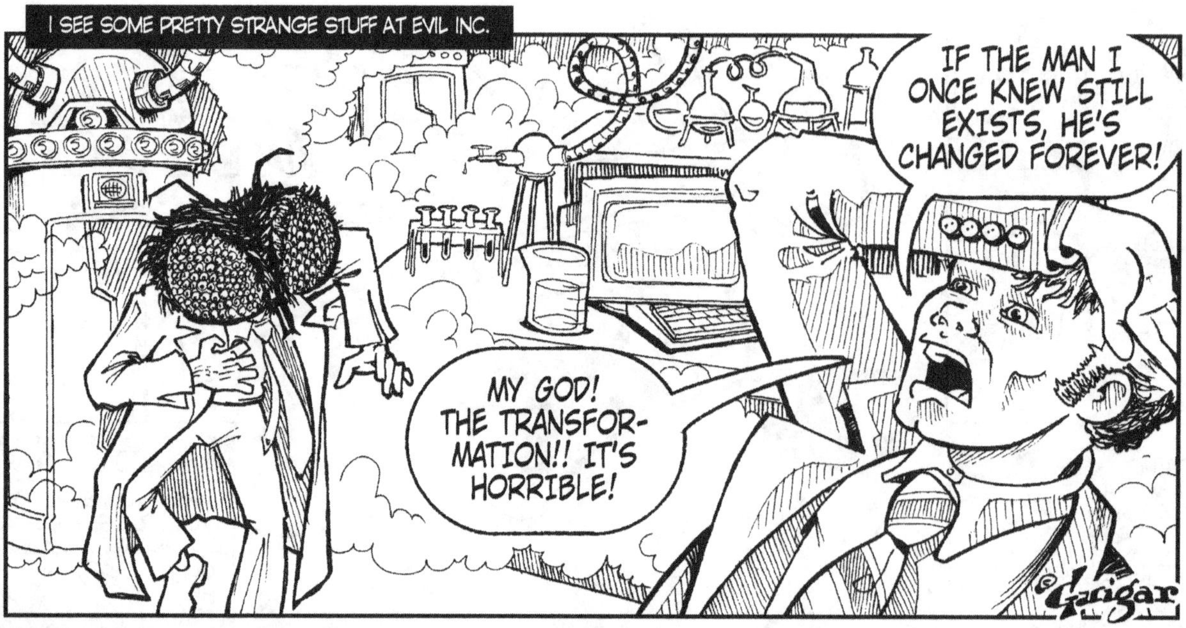
I SEE SOME PRETTY STRANGE STUFF AT EVIL INC.
IF THE MAN I ONCE KNEW STILL EXISTS, HE'S CHANGED FOREVER!
MY GOD! THE TRANSFORMATION!! IT'S HORRIBLE!

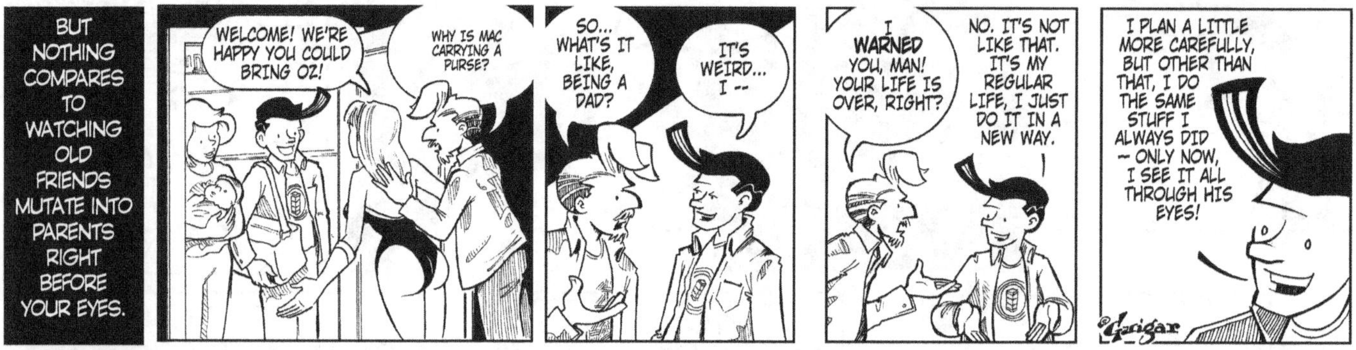
BUT NOTHING COMPARES TO WATCHING OLD FRIENDS MUTATE INTO PARENTS RIGHT BEFORE YOUR EYES.
WELCOME! WE'RE HAPPY YOU COULD BRING OZ!
WHY IS MAC CARRYING A PURSE?
SO... WHAT'S IT LIKE, BEING A DAD?
IT'S WEIRD... I --
I WARNED YOU, MAN! YOUR LIFE IS OVER, RIGHT?
NO. IT'S NOT LIKE THAT. IT'S MY REGULAR LIFE, I JUST DO IT IN A NEW WAY.
I PLAN A LITTLE MORE CAREFULLY, BUT OTHER THAN THAT, I DO THE SAME STUFF I ALWAYS DID -- ONLY NOW, I SEE IT ALL THROUGH HIS EYES!

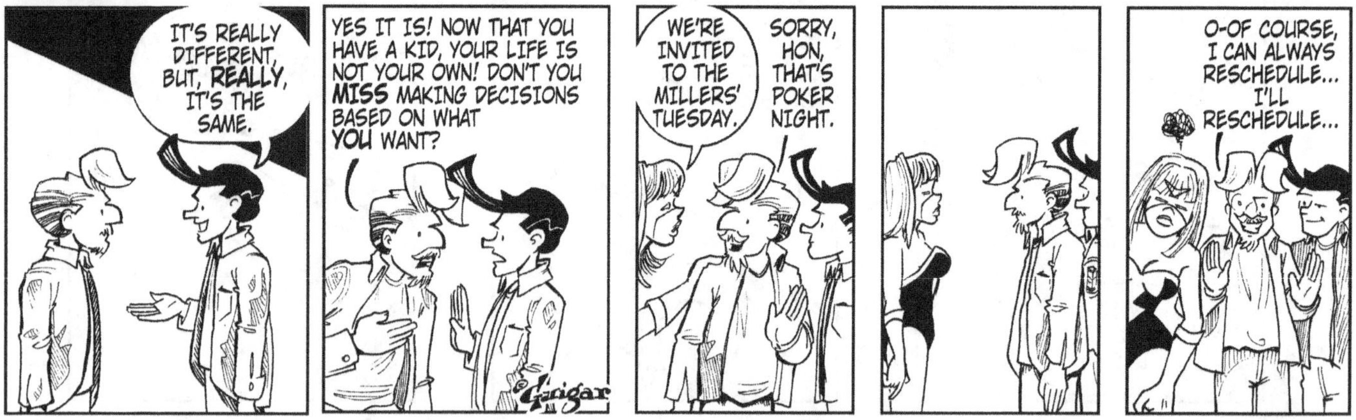
IT'S REALLY DIFFERENT, BUT, REALLY, IT'S THE SAME.
YES IT IS! NOW THAT YOU HAVE A KID, YOUR LIFE IS NOT YOUR OWN! DON'T YOU MISS MAKING DECISIONS BASED ON WHAT YOU WANT?
WE'RE INVITED TO THE MILLERS' TUESDAY.
SORRY, HON, THAT'S POKER NIGHT.
O-OF COURSE, I CAN ALWAYS RESCHEDULE... I'LL RESCHEDULE...

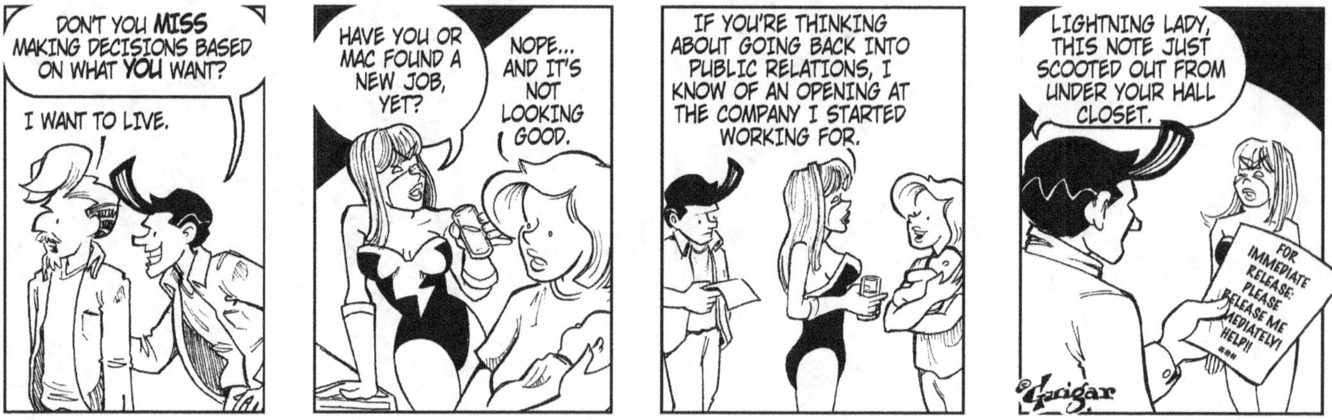
DON'T YOU MISS MAKING DECISIONS BASED ON WHAT YOU WANT?
I WANT TO LIVE.
HAVE YOU OR MAC FOUND A NEW JOB, YET?
NOPE... AND IT'S NOT LOOKING GOOD.
IF YOU'RE THINKING ABOUT GOING BACK INTO PUBLIC RELATIONS, I KNOW OF AN OPENING AT THE COMPANY I STARTED WORKING FOR.
LIGHTNING LADY, THIS NOTE JUST SCOOTED OUT FROM UNDER YOUR HALL CLOSET.
FOR IMMEDIATE RELEASE:
PLEASE RELEASE ME
HELP!!

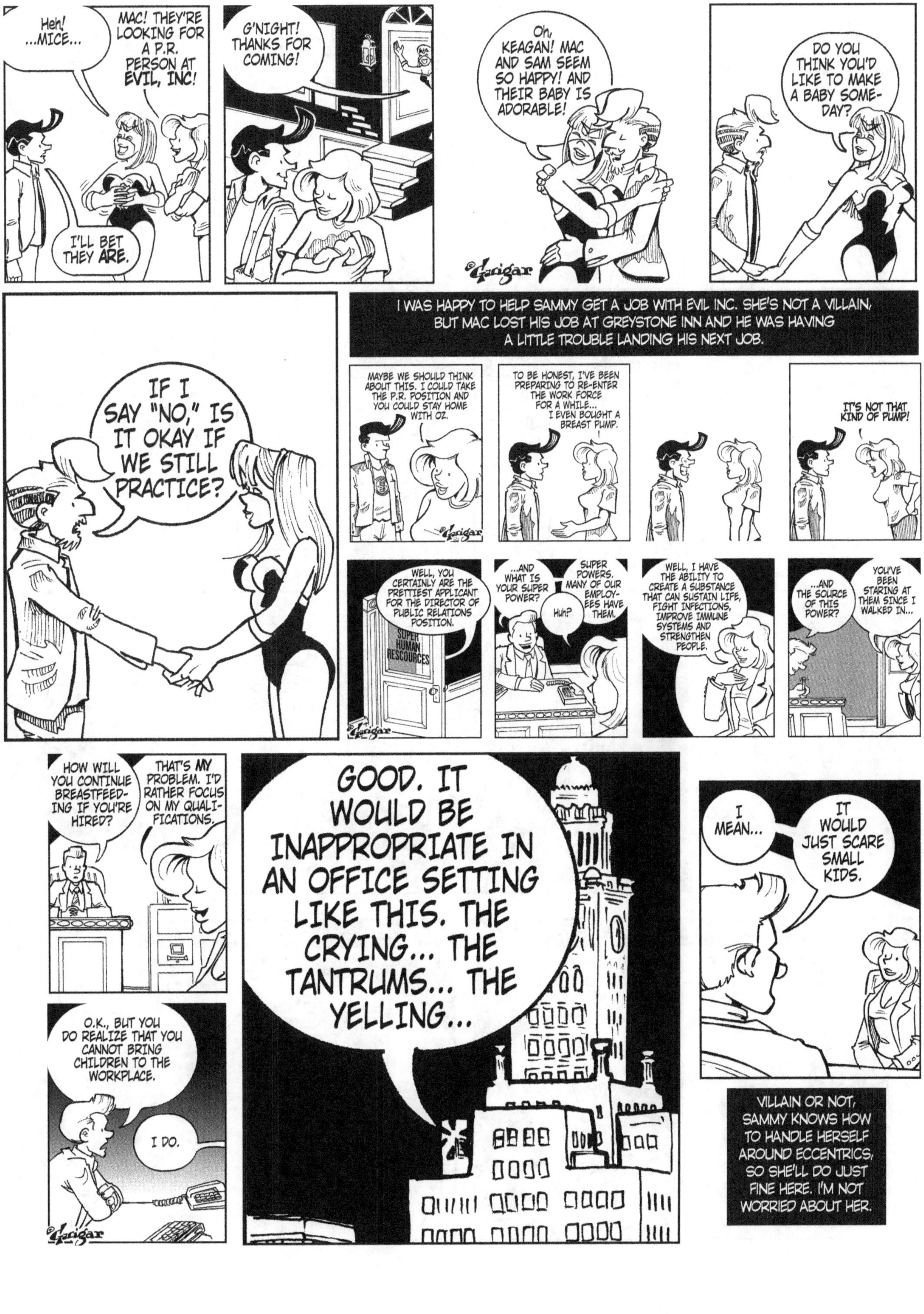
Heh! ...MICE...
MAC! THEY'RE LOOKING FOR A P.R. PERSON AT EVIL, INC!
I'LL BET THEY ARE.
G'NIGHT! THANKS FOR COMING!
Oh, KEAGAN! MAC AND SAM SEEM SO HAPPY! AND THEIR BABY IS ADORABLE!
DO YOU THINK YOU'D LIKE TO MAKE A BABY SOME-DAY?
IF I SAY "NO," IS IT OKAY IF WE STILL PRACTICE?
I WAS HAPPY TO HELP SAMMY GET A JOB WITH EVIL INC. SHE'S NOT A VILLAIN, BUT MAC LOST HIS JOB AT GREYSTONE INN AND HE WAS HAVING A LITTLE TROUBLE LANDING HIS NEXT JOB.
MAYBE WE SHOULD THINK ABOUT THIS. I COULD TAKE THE P.R. POSITION AND YOU COULD STAY HOME WITH OZ.
TO BE HONEST, I'VE BEEN PREPARING TO RE-ENTER THE WORK FORCE FOR A WHILE... I EVEN BOUGHT A BREAST PUMP.
!
IT'S NOT THAT KIND OF PUMP!
WELL, YOU CERTAINLY ARE THE PRETTIEST APPLICANT FOR THE DIRECTOR OF PUBLIC RELATIONS POSITION.
SUPER HUMAN RESOURCES
...AND WHAT IS YOUR SUPER POWER?
SUPER POWERS. MANY OF OUR EMPLOY-EES HAVE THEM.
Huh?
WELL, I HAVE THE ABILITY TO CREATE A SUBSTANCE THAT CAN SUSTAIN LIFE, FIGHT INFECTIONS, IMPROVE IMMUNE SYSTEMS AND STRENGTHEN PEOPLE.
...AND THE SOURCE OF THIS POWER?
YOU'VE BEEN STARING AT THEM SINCE I WALKED IN...
HOW WILL YOU CONTINUE BREASTFEED-ING IF YOU'RE HIRED?
THAT'S MY PROBLEM. I'D RATHER FOCUS ON MY QUALI-FICATIONS.
O.K., BUT YOU DO REALIZE THAT YOU CANNOT BRING CHILDREN TO THE WORKPLACE.
I DO.
GOOD. IT WOULD BE INAPPROPRIATE IN AN OFFICE SETTING LIKE THIS. THE CRYING... THE TANTRUMS... THE YELLING...
I MEAN...
IT WOULD JUST SCARE SMALL KIDS.
VILLAIN OR NOT, SAMMY KNOWS HOW TO HANDLE HERSELF AROUND ECCENTRICS, SO SHE'LL DO JUST FINE HERE. I'M NOT WORRIED ABOUT HER.

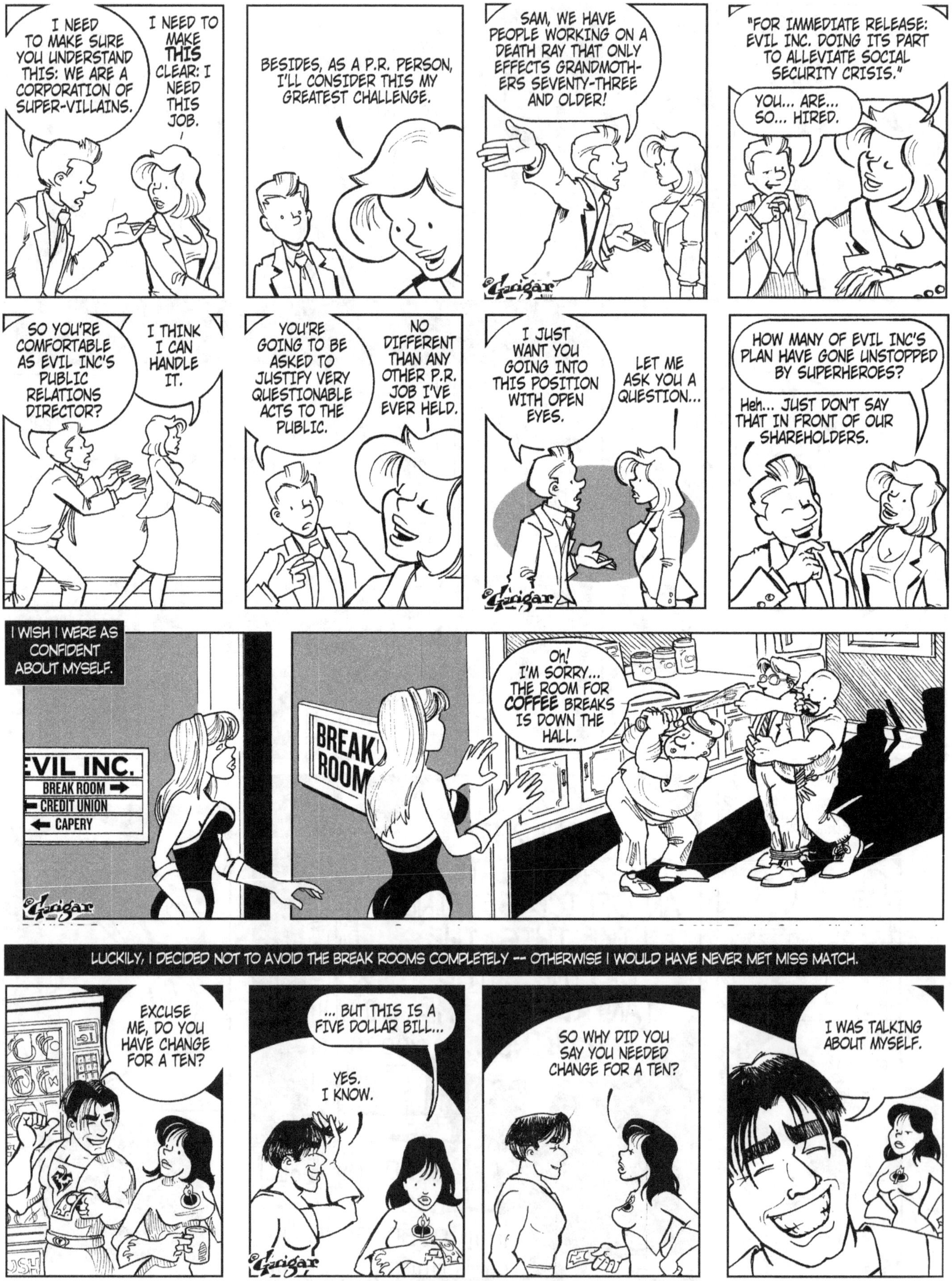
I NEED TO MAKE SURE YOU UNDERSTAND THIS: WE ARE A CORPORATION OF SUPER-VILLAINS.
I NEED TO MAKE THIS CLEAR: I NEED THIS JOB.
BESIDES, AS A P.R. PERSON, I'LL CONSIDER THIS MY GREATEST CHALLENGE.
SAM, WE HAVE PEOPLE WORKING ON A DEATH RAY THAT ONLY EFFECTS GRANDMOTH-ERS SEVENTY-THREE AND OLDER!
"FOR IMMEDIATE RELEASE: EVIL INC. DOING ITS PART TO ALLEVIATE SOCIAL SECURITY CRISIS."
YOU... ARE... SO... HIRED.
SO YOU'RE COMFORTABLE AS EVIL INC'S PUBLIC RELATIONS DIRECTOR?
I THINK I CAN HANDLE IT.
YOU'RE GOING TO BE ASKED TO JUSTIFY VERY QUESTIONABLE ACTS TO THE PUBLIC.
NO DIFFERENT THAN ANY OTHER P.R. JOB I'VE EVER HELD.
I JUST WANT YOU GOING INTO THIS POSITION WITH OPEN EYES.
LET ME ASK YOU A QUESTION...
HOW MANY OF EVIL INC'S PLAN HAVE GONE UNSTOPPED BY SUPERHEROES?
Heh... JUST DON'T SAY THAT IN FRONT OF OUR SHAREHOLDERS.
I WISH I WERE AS CONFIDENT ABOUT MYSELF.
EVIL INC.
BREAK ROOM
CREDIT UNION
CAPERY
BREAK ROOM
Oh! I'M SORRY... THE ROOM FOR COFFEE BREAKS IS DOWN THE HALL.
LUCKILY, I DECIDED NOT TO AVOID THE BREAK ROOMS COMPLETELY -- OTHERWISE I WOULD HAVE NEVER MET MISS MATCH.
EXCUSE ME, DO YOU HAVE CHANGE FOR A TEN?
... BUT THIS IS A FIVE DOLLAR BILL...
YES. I KNOW.
SO WHY DID YOU SAY YOU NEEDED CHANGE FOR A TEN?
I WAS TALKING ABOUT MYSELF.

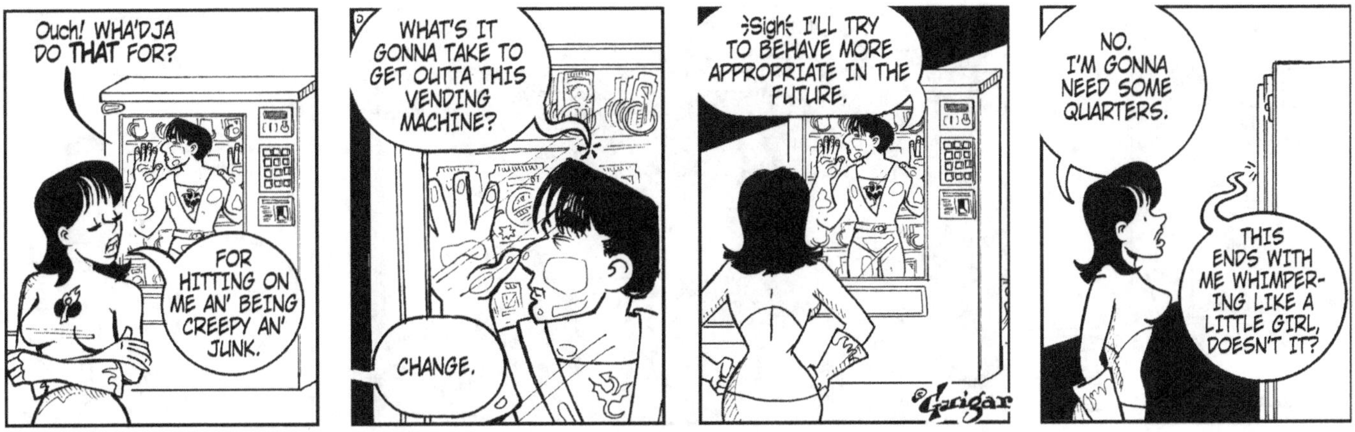

Ouch! WHA'DJA DO THAT FOR?
FOR HITTING ON ME AN' BEING CREEPY AN' JUNK.
WHAT'S IT GONNA TAKE TO GET OUTTA THIS VENDING MACHINE?
CHANGE.
-Sigh- I'LL TRY TO BEHAVE MORE APPROPRIATE IN THE FUTURE.
NO. I'M GONNA NEED SOME QUARTERS.
THIS ENDS WITH ME WHIMPERING LIKE A LITTLE GIRL, DOESN'T IT?
©Garigar

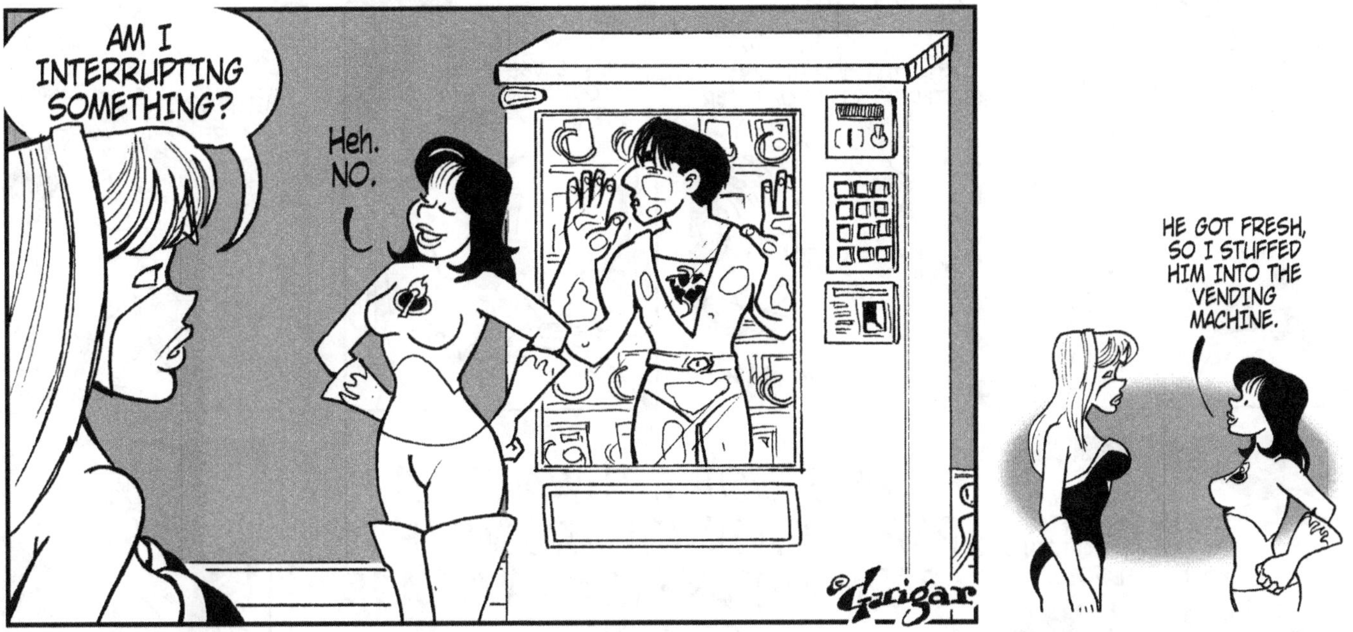

AM I INTERRUPTING SOMETHING?
Heh. NO.
©Garigar
HE GOT FRESH, SO I STUFFED HIM INTO THE VENDING MACHINE.

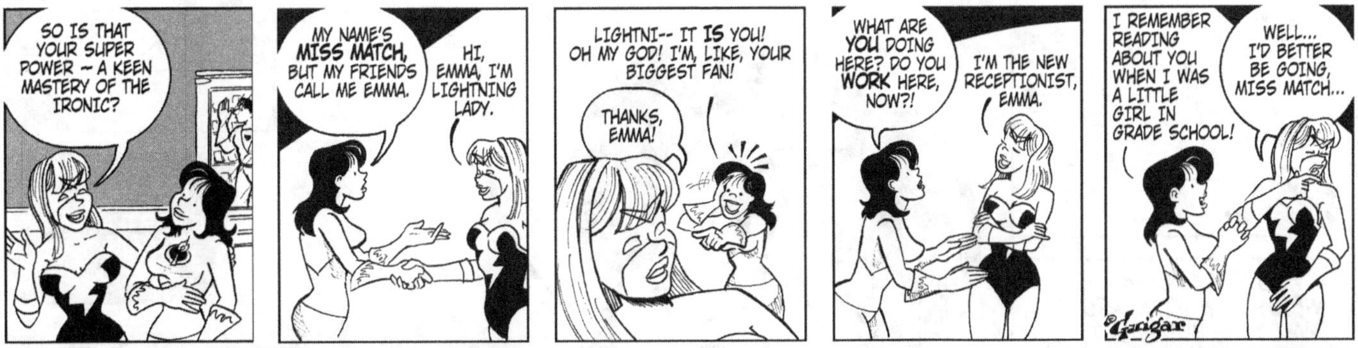

SO IS THAT YOUR SUPER POWER -- A KEEN MASTERY OF THE IRONIC?
MY NAME'S MISS MATCH, BUT MY FRIENDS CALL ME EMMA.
HI, EMMA, I'M LIGHTNING LADY.
LIGHTNI-- IT IS YOU! OH MY GOD! I'M, LIKE, YOUR BIGGEST FAN!
THANKS, EMMA!
WHAT ARE YOU DOING HERE? DO YOU WORK HERE, NOW?!
I'M THE NEW RECEPTIONIST, EMMA.
I REMEMBER READING ABOUT YOU WHEN I WAS A LITTLE GIRL IN GRADE SCHOOL!
WELL... I'D BETTER BE GOING, MISS MATCH...
©Garigar

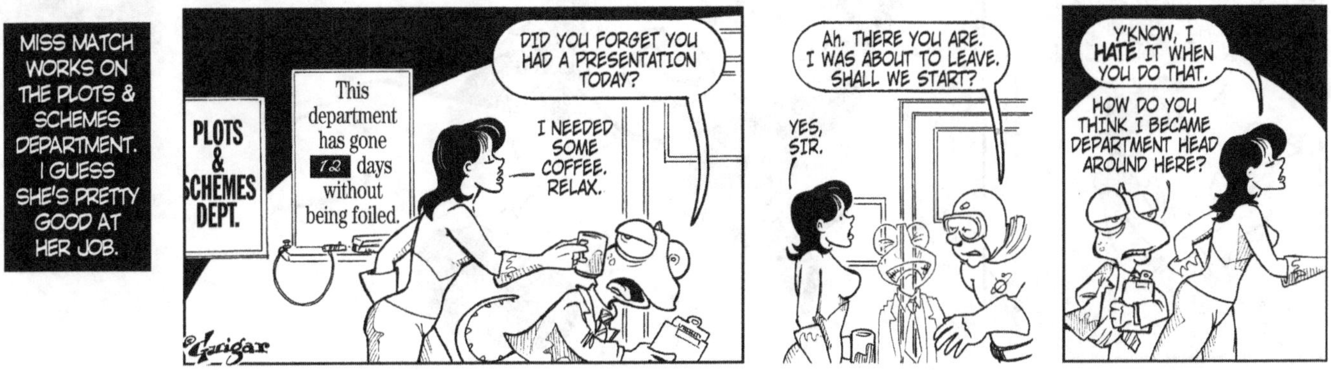

MISS MATCH WORKS ON THE PLOTS & SCHEMES DEPARTMENT. I GUESS SHE'S PRETTY GOOD AT HER JOB.
PLOTS & SCHEMES DEPT.
This department has gone 12 days without being foiled.
DID YOU FORGET YOU HAD A PRESENTATION TODAY?
I NEEDED SOME COFFEE. RELAX.
©Garigar
Ah. THERE YOU ARE. I WAS ABOUT TO LEAVE. SHALL WE START?
YES, SIR.
Y'KNOW, I HATE IT WHEN YOU DO THAT.
HOW DO YOU THINK I BECAME DEPARTMENT HEAD AROUND HERE?

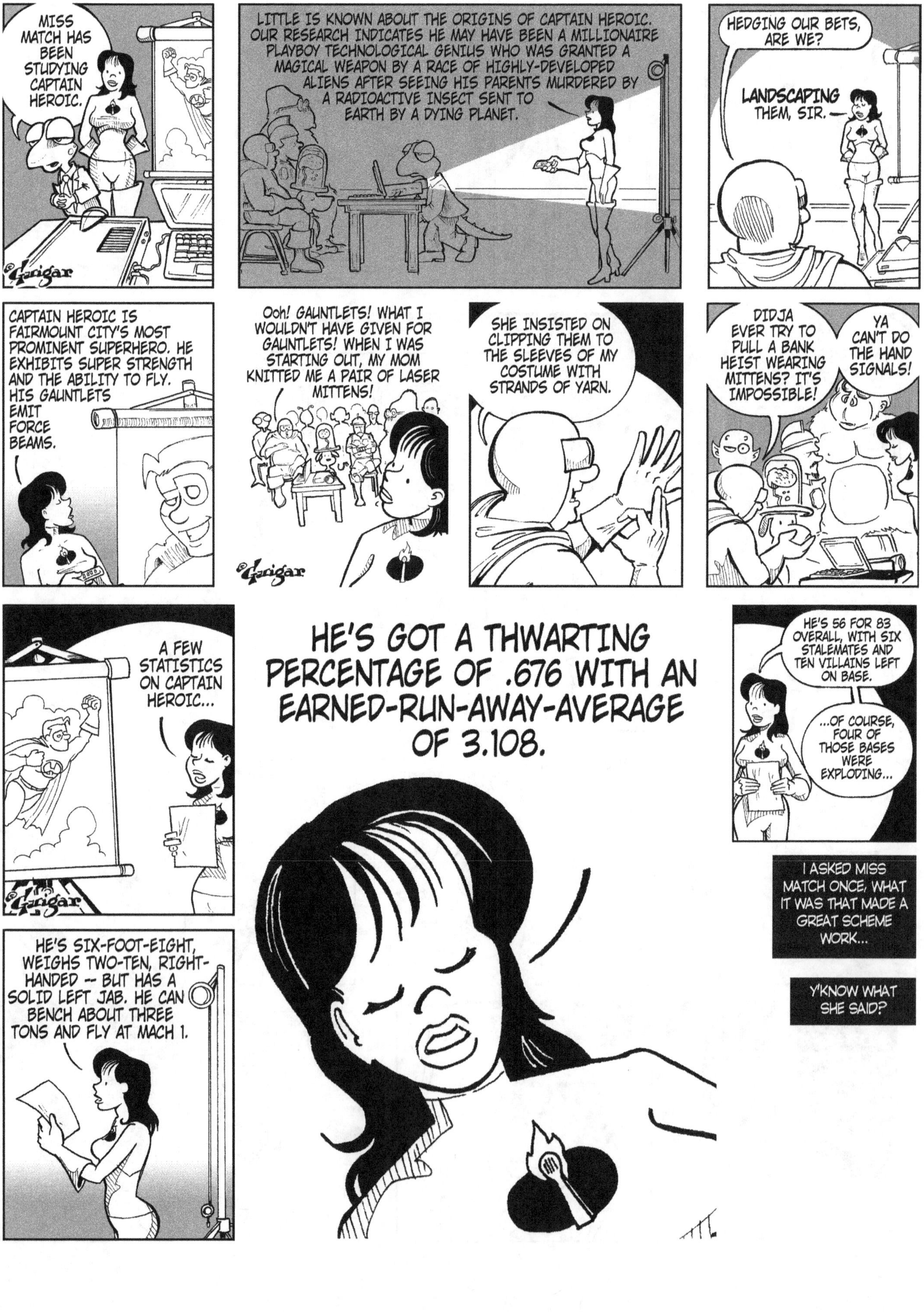
MISS MATCH HAS BEEN STUDYING CAPTAIN HEROIC.
LITTLE IS KNOWN ABOUT THE ORIGINS OF CAPTAIN HEROIC. OUR RESEARCH INDICATES HE MAY HAVE BEEN A MILLIONAIRE PLAYBOY TECHNOLOGICAL GENIUS WHO WAS GRANTED A MAGICAL WEAPON BY A RACE OF HIGHLY-DEVELOPED ALIENS AFTER SEEING HIS PARENTS MURDERED BY A RADIOACTIVE INSECT SENT TO EARTH BY A DYING PLANET.
HEDGING OUR BETS, ARE WE?
LANDSCAPING THEM, SIR.
CAPTAIN HEROIC IS FAIRMOUNT CITY'S MOST PROMINENT SUPERHERO. HE EXHIBITS SUPER STRENGTH AND THE ABILITY TO FLY. HIS GAUNTLETS EMIT FORCE BEAMS.
Ooh! GAUNTLETS! WHAT I WOULDN'T HAVE GIVEN FOR GAUNTLETS! WHEN I WAS STARTING OUT, MY MOM KNITTED ME A PAIR OF LASER MITTENS!
SHE INSISTED ON CLIPPING THEM TO THE SLEEVES OF MY COSTUME WITH STRANDS OF YARN.
DIDJA EVER TRY TO PULL A BANK HEIST WEARING MITTENS? IT'S IMPOSSIBLE!
YA CAN'T DO THE HAND SIGNALS!
A FEW STATISTICS ON CAPTAIN HEROIC...
HE'S SIX-FOOT-EIGHT, WEIGHS TWO-TEN, RIGHT-HANDED -- BUT HAS A SOLID LEFT JAB. HE CAN BENCH ABOUT THREE TONS AND FLY AT MACH 1.
HE'S GOT A THWARTING PERCENTAGE OF .676 WITH AN EARNED-RUN-AWAY-AVERAGE OF 3.108.
HE'S 56 FOR 83 OVERALL, WITH SIX STALEMATES AND TEN VILLAINS LEFT ON BASE.
...OF COURSE, FOUR OF THOSE BASES WERE EXPLODING...
I ASKED MISS MATCH ONCE, WHAT IT WAS THAT MADE A GREAT SCHEME WORK...
Y'KNOW WHAT SHE SAID?

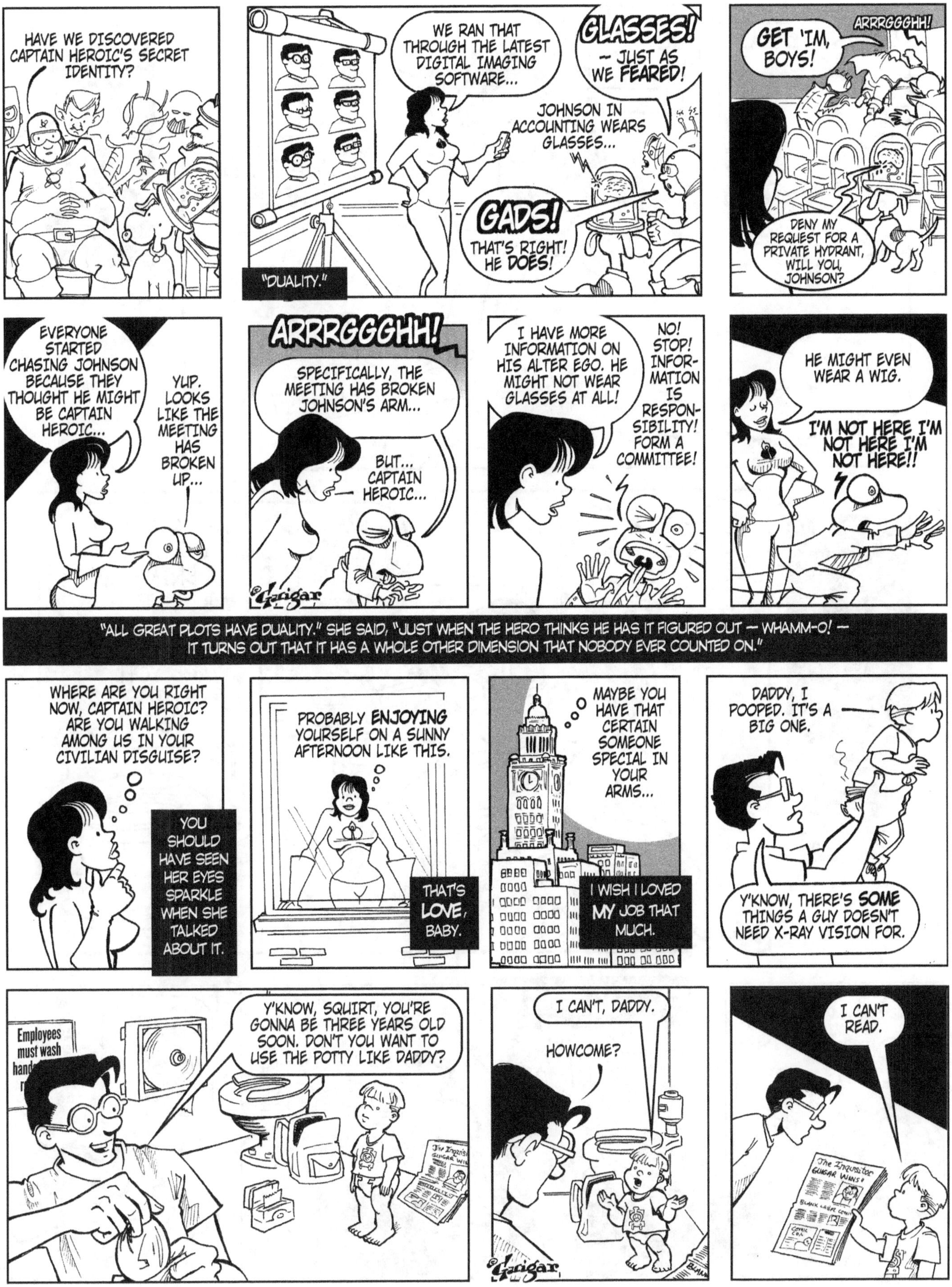
HAVE WE DISCOVERED CAPTAIN HEROIC'S SECRET IDENTITY?
WE RAN THAT THROUGH THE LATEST DIGITAL IMAGING SOFTWARE...
GLASSES! — JUST AS WE FEARED!
JOHNSON IN ACCOUNTING WEARS GLASSES...
GADS! THAT'S RIGHT! HE DOES!
"DUALITY."
GET 'IM, BOYS!
ARRRGGGHH!
DENY MY REQUEST FOR A PRIVATE HYDRANT, WILL YOU, JOHNSON?
EVERYONE STARTED CHASING JOHNSON BECAUSE THEY THOUGHT HE MIGHT BE CAPTAIN HEROIC...
YUP. LOOKS LIKE THE MEETING HAS BROKEN UP...
ARRRGGGHH!
SPECIFICALLY, THE MEETING HAS BROKEN JOHNSON'S ARM...
BUT... CAPTAIN HEROIC...
I HAVE MORE INFORMATION ON HIS ALTER EGO. HE MIGHT NOT WEAR GLASSES AT ALL!
NO! STOP! INFORMATION IS RESPONSIBILITY! FORM A COMMITTEE!
HE MIGHT EVEN WEAR A WIG.
I'M NOT HERE I'M NOT HERE I'M NOT HERE!!
©Gugar
"ALL GREAT PLOTS HAVE DUALITY." SHE SAID, "JUST WHEN THE HERO THINKS HE HAS IT FIGURED OUT — WHAMM-O! — IT TURNS OUT THAT IT HAS A WHOLE OTHER DIMENSION THAT NOBODY EVER COUNTED ON."
WHERE ARE YOU RIGHT NOW, CAPTAIN HEROIC? ARE YOU WALKING AMONG US IN YOUR CIVILIAN DISGUISE?
YOU SHOULD HAVE SEEN HER EYES SPARKLE WHEN SHE TALKED ABOUT IT.
PROBABLY ENJOYING YOURSELF ON A SUNNY AFTERNOON LIKE THIS.
THAT'S LOVE, BABY.
MAYBE YOU HAVE THAT CERTAIN SOMEONE SPECIAL IN YOUR ARMS...
I WISH I LOVED MY JOB THAT MUCH.
DADDY, I POOPED. IT'S A BIG ONE.
Y'KNOW, THERE'S SOME THINGS A GUY DOESN'T NEED X-RAY VISION FOR.
Employees must wash
Y'KNOW, SQUIRT, YOU'RE GONNA BE THREE YEARS OLD SOON. DON'T YOU WANT TO USE THE POTTY LIKE DADDY?
I CAN'T, DADDY.
HOWCOME?
©Gugar
I CAN'T READ.
The Inquisitor
GUGAR WINS

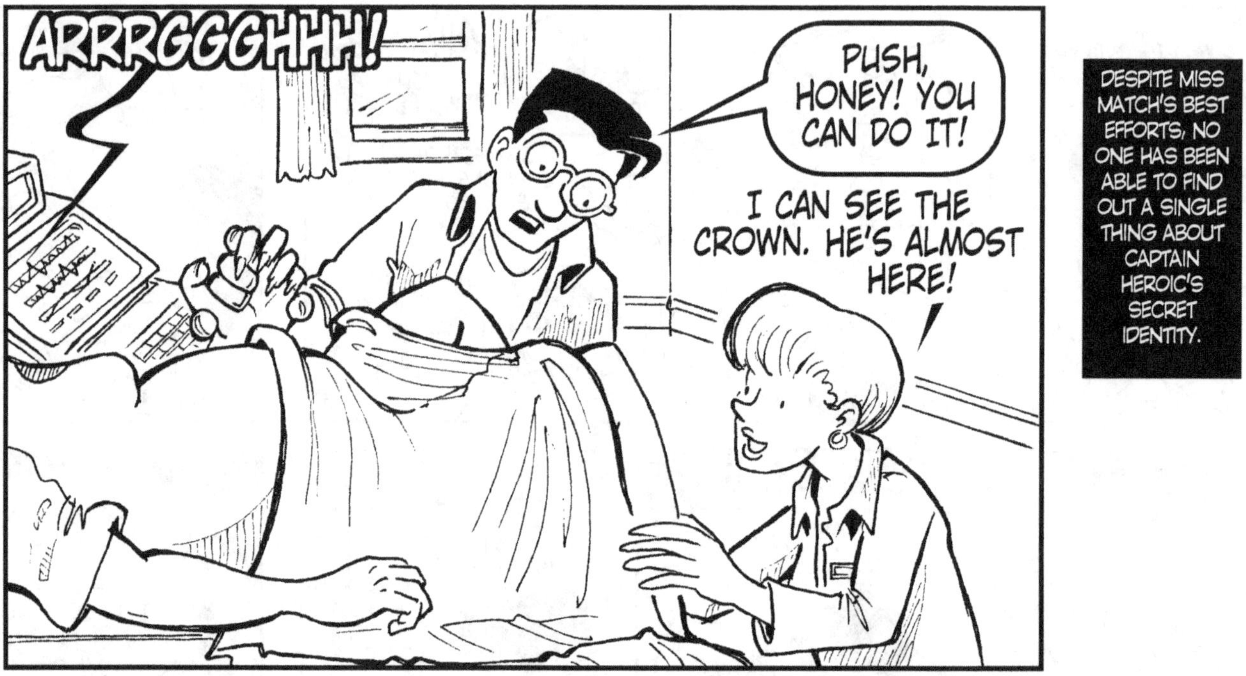

ARRRGGGHHH!
PUSH, HONEY! YOU CAN DO IT!
I CAN SEE THE CROWN. HE'S ALMOST HERE!
DESPITE MISS MATCH'S BEST EFFORTS, NO ONE HAS BEEN ABLE TO FIND OUT A SINGLE THING ABOUT CAPTAIN HEROIC'S SECRET IDENTITY.

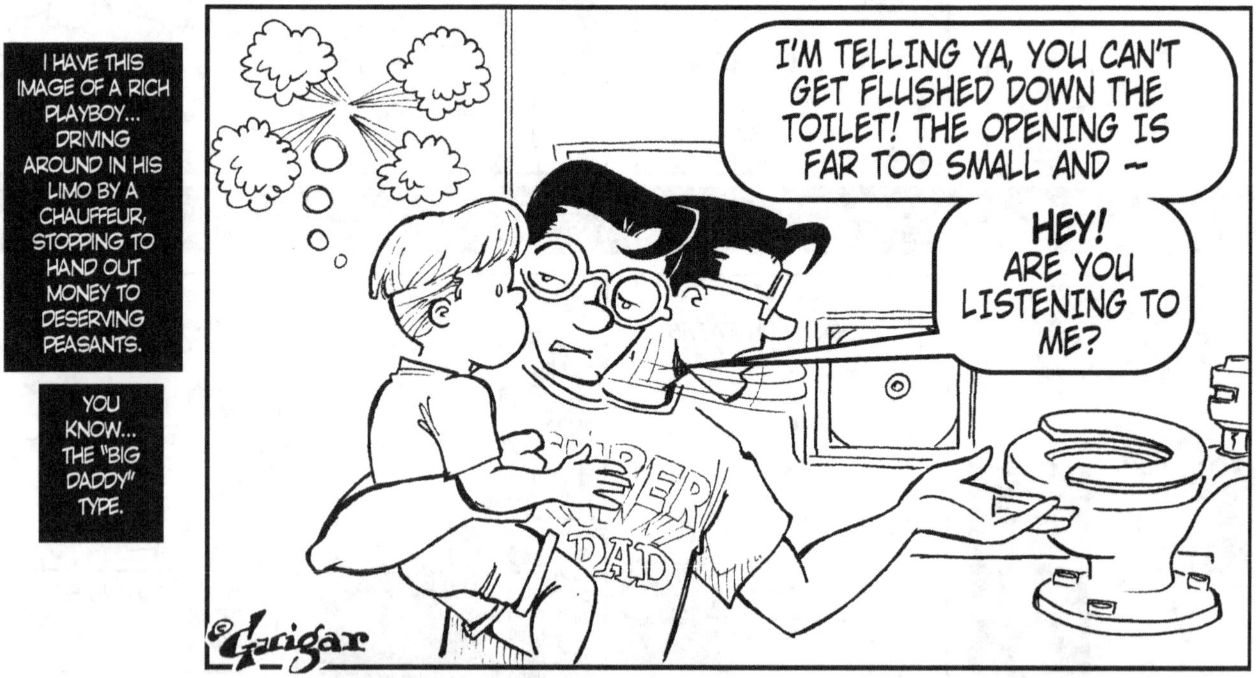

I HAVE THIS IMAGE OF A RICH PLAYBOY... DRIVING AROUND IN HIS LIMO BY A CHAUFFEUR, STOPPING TO HAND OUT MONEY TO DESERVING PEASANTS.
YOU KNOW... THE "BIG DADDY" TYPE.
I'M TELLING YA, YOU CAN'T GET FLUSHED DOWN THE TOILET! THE OPENING IS FAR TOO SMALL AND --
HEY! ARE YOU LISTENING TO ME?
SUPER DAD
© Garigar

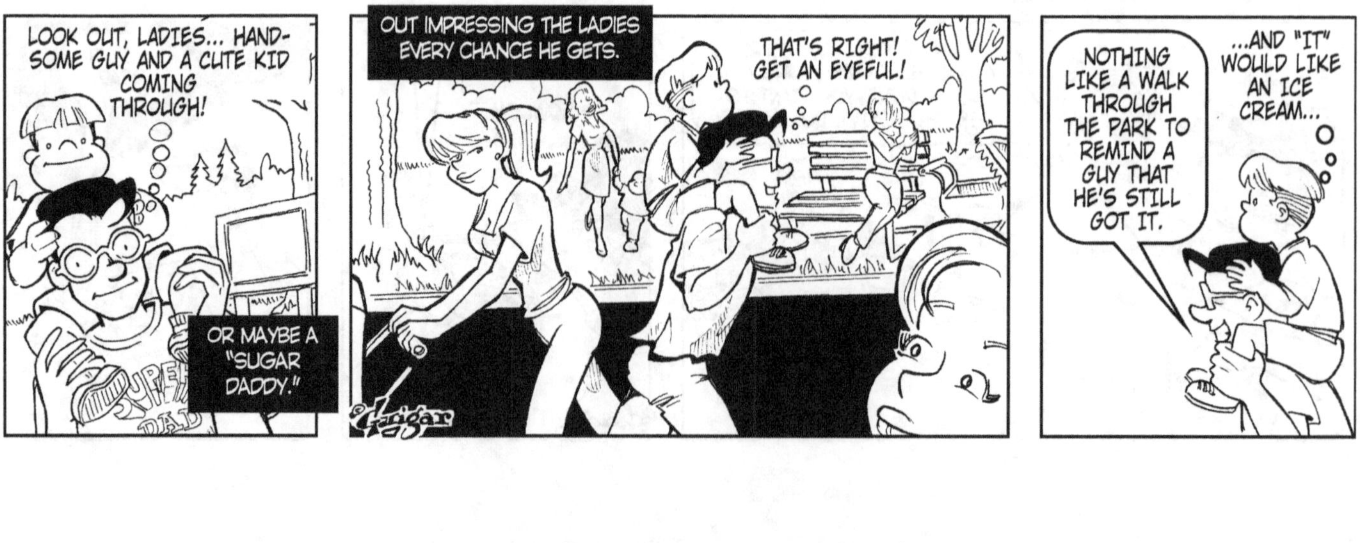

LOOK OUT, LADIES... HANDSOME GUY AND A CUTE KID COMING THROUGH!
OR MAYBE A "SUGAR DADDY."
SUPER DAD
OUT IMPRESSING THE LADIES EVERY CHANCE HE GETS.
THAT'S RIGHT! GET AN EYEFUL!
© Garigar
NOTHING LIKE A WALK THROUGH THE PARK TO REMIND A GUY THAT HE'S STILL GOT IT.
...AND "IT" WOULD LIKE AN ICE CREAM...

Ahem... "PERCY AND THE DRAGON." IT WAS LATE... PERCY WAS ASLEEP...

OR ONE OF THOSE IRONIC ALTER EGOS... THE HEAD OF A CRIME FAMILY.

NO NO NO NO, DADDY. DO IT RIGHT!

Sigh

"PERCY AND THE DRAGON." A BRITT ALCROFT PRODUCTION. BASED ON "THE RAILWAY SERIES" BY THE REV. W. AWDRY. PUBLISHED BY RANDOM HOUSE. PHOTOGRAPHS BY DAVID MITTON AND TERRY PERMANE. FIRST AMERICAN EDITION 1994. COPYRIGHT BY W. HEINEMANN LTD. ALL RESERVED UNDER INTERNATIONAL AND P. AMERICAN RIGHT VENTIONS. LISHED IN BUZZ BOOKS,

YOU SURE KNOW HOW TO DRAW OUT A STORY BEFORE NAPTIME, DON'TCHA?

SO, WHAT DO YOU WANT FOR BREAKFAST, SPORT?

I DON'T KNOW...

ONE THING'S FOR SURE... HE'S SOMETHING IMPORTANT...

Hmmmm... HOW 'BOUT A POPSICLE?

YOU CAN'T EAT POPSICLES FOR BREAKFAST!

REALLY? WHY NOT?

THEY'D MELT IN THE TOASTER.

I-I'M A S--

...LIKE A MOVIE STAR...

CUT!

PRODUCTION NO.: 12
SCENE 2A | TAKE 1 | ROLL 1

I'M A ST-ST-

CUT!

PRODUCTION NO.: 12
SCENE 2A | TAKE 2 | ROLL 1

I.. WELL, YOU COULD SAY THAT I'M...UM...

CUT!

PRODUCTION NO.: 12
SCENE 2A | TAKE 3 | ROLL 1

I'M A ST-ST-STAY-

CUT!

PRODUCTION NO.: 12
SCENE 2A | TAKE 4 | ROLL 1

I'M A STAY-AT-HOME DAD.

GREAT. CAN WE GO OUT AND PLAY NOW?

EVIL INC... HOW MAY I MIS-DIRECT YOUR CALL? OH, HI, DOCTOR DRUID... WHAT? A TYPOGRAPHICAL ERROR IN ONE OF OUR BOOKS?

Evil Inc.

LEMME CALL THE MANUSCRIPT UP. OK... "THE BIG BOOK OF INCANTATIONS." GOT IT. YOU'RE ON CHAPTER TEN? I SEE IT: SUMMONING TWO HUMONGOUS BEASTS... WHAT'S WRONG WITH THAT?

Whooooops... I SEE IT NOW. THERE SHOULDN'T BE AN "R" IN "BEASTS," SHOULD THERE?

WELL, WHAT YOU **DO** WITH THEM IS UP TO YOU. BUT I DON'T THINK THE FOX NETWORK HAS FINALIZED IT'S PRIME TIME LINEUP YET...

...OR A RECEPTIONIST.

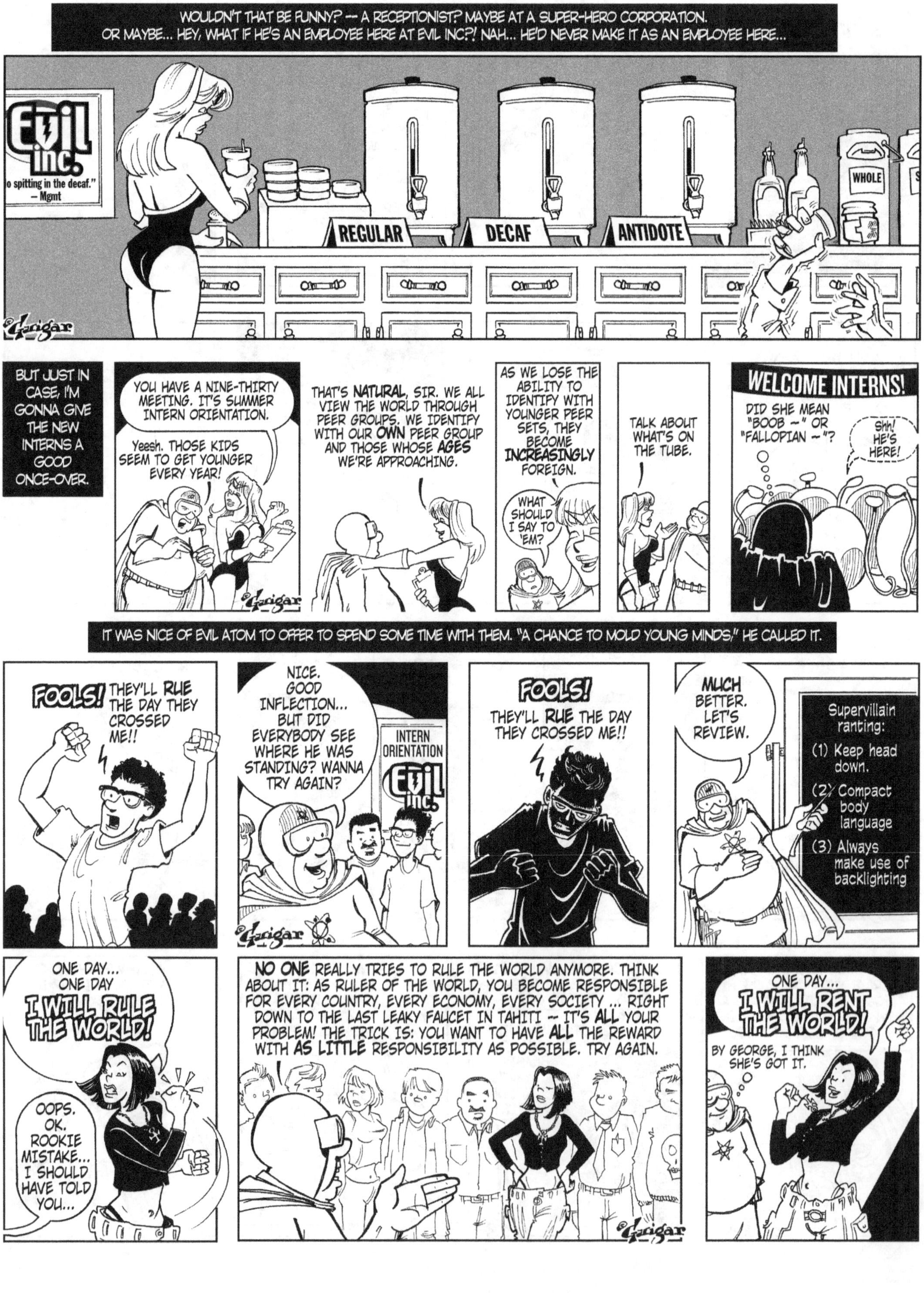

WOULDN'T THAT BE FUNNY? -- A RECEPTIONIST? MAYBE AT A SUPER-HERO CORPORATION.
OR MAYBE... HEY, WHAT IF HE'S AN EMPLOYEE HERE AT EVIL INC.?! NAH... HE'D NEVER MAKE IT AS AN EMPLOYEE HERE...
Evil inc.
o spitting in the decaf." – Mgmt
REGULAR
DECAF
ANTIDOTE
WHOLE
BUT JUST IN CASE, I'M GONNA GIVE THE NEW INTERNS A GOOD ONCE-OVER.
YOU HAVE A NINE-THIRTY MEETING. IT'S SUMMER INTERN ORIENTATION.
Yeesh. THOSE KIDS SEEM TO GET YOUNGER EVERY YEAR!
THAT'S NATURAL, SIR. WE ALL VIEW THE WORLD THROUGH PEER GROUPS. WE IDENTIFY WITH OUR OWN PEER GROUP AND THOSE WHOSE AGES WE'RE APPROACHING.
AS WE LOSE THE ABILITY TO IDENTIFY WITH YOUNGER PEER SETS, THEY BECOME INCREASINGLY FOREIGN.
WHAT SHOULD I SAY TO 'EM?
TALK ABOUT WHAT'S ON THE TUBE.
WELCOME INTERNS!
DID SHE MEAN "BOOB ~" OR "FALLOPIAN ~"?
Shh! HE'S HERE!
IT WAS NICE OF EVIL ATOM TO OFFER TO SPEND SOME TIME WITH THEM. "A CHANCE TO MOLD YOUNG MINDS," HE CALLED IT.
FOOLS! THEY'LL RUE THE DAY THEY CROSSED ME!!
NICE. GOOD INFLECTION... BUT DID EVERYBODY SEE WHERE HE WAS STANDING? WANNA TRY AGAIN?
INTERN ORIENTATION
Evil inc.
FOOLS! THEY'LL RUE THE DAY THEY CROSSED ME!!
MUCH BETTER. LET'S REVIEW.
Supervillain ranting:
(1) Keep head down.
(2) Compact body language
(3) Always make use of backlighting
ONE DAY... ONE DAY I WILL RULE THE WORLD!
OOPS. OK. ROOKIE MISTAKE... I SHOULD HAVE TOLD YOU...
NO ONE REALLY TRIES TO RULE THE WORLD ANYMORE. THINK ABOUT IT: AS RULER OF THE WORLD, YOU BECOME RESPONSIBLE FOR EVERY COUNTRY, EVERY ECONOMY, EVERY SOCIETY ... RIGHT DOWN TO THE LAST LEAKY FAUCET IN TAHITI -- IT'S ALL YOUR PROBLEM! THE TRICK IS: YOU WANT TO HAVE ALL THE REWARD WITH AS LITTLE RESPONSIBILITY AS POSSIBLE. TRY AGAIN.
ONE DAY... I WILL RENT THE WORLD!
BY GEORGE, I THINK SHE'S GOT IT.

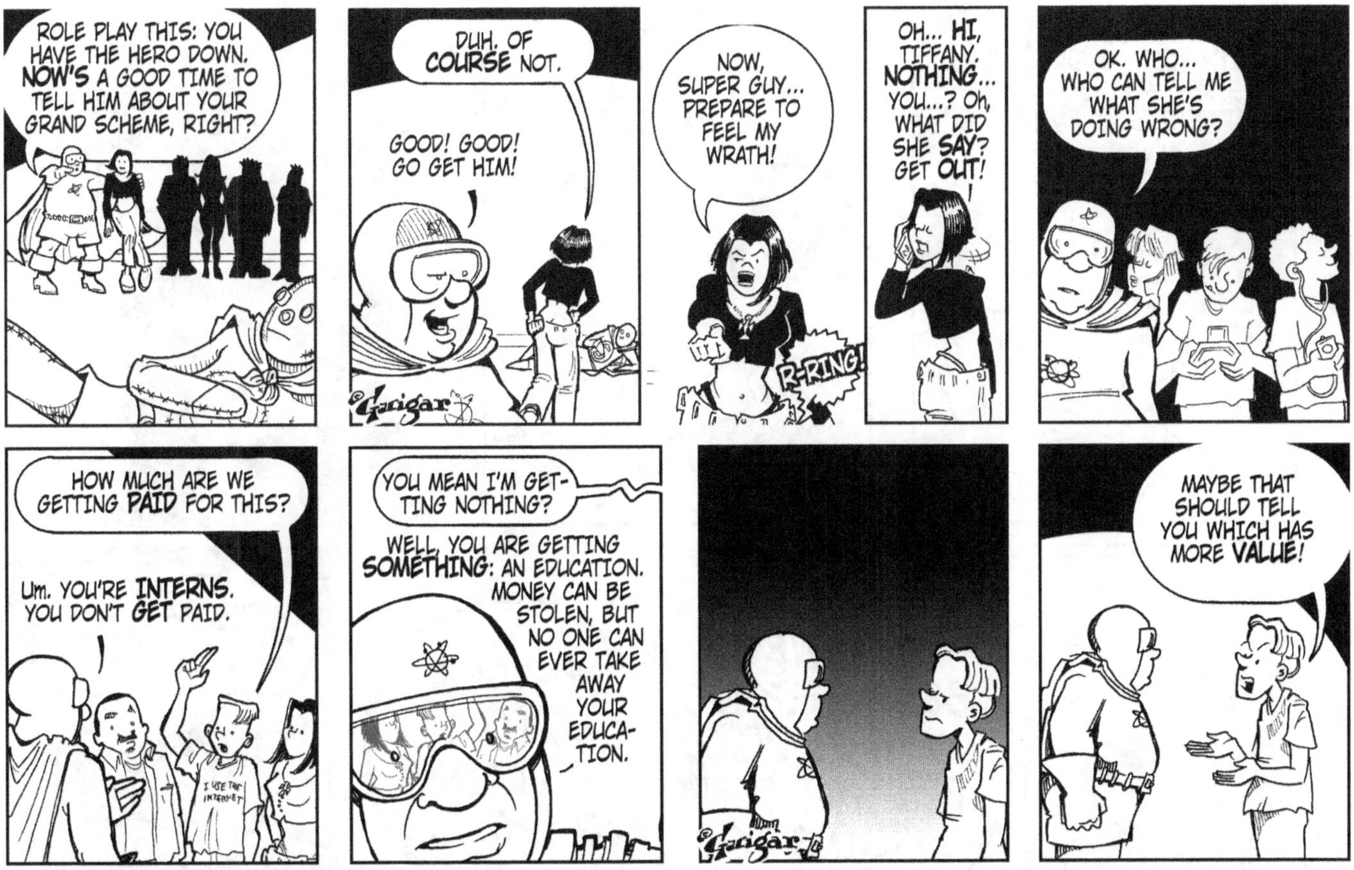
ROLE PLAY THIS: YOU HAVE THE HERO DOWN. NOW'S A GOOD TIME TO TELL HIM ABOUT YOUR GRAND SCHEME, RIGHT?
DUH. OF COURSE NOT.
GOOD! GOOD! GO GET HIM!
NOW, SUPER GUY... PREPARE TO FEEL MY WRATH!
R-RING!
OH... HI, TIFFANY. NOTHING... YOU...? Oh, WHAT DID SHE SAY? GET OUT!
OK. WHO... WHO CAN TELL ME WHAT SHE'S DOING WRONG?
HOW MUCH ARE WE GETTING PAID FOR THIS?
Um. YOU'RE INTERNS. YOU DON'T GET PAID.
YOU MEAN I'M GETTING NOTHING?
WELL, YOU ARE GETTING SOMETHING: AN EDUCATION. MONEY CAN BE STOLEN, BUT NO ONE CAN EVER TAKE AWAY YOUR EDUCATION.
MAYBE THAT SHOULD TELL YOU WHICH HAS MORE VALUE!

JUST WHAT WE NEED. MORE MOLDY MINDS.

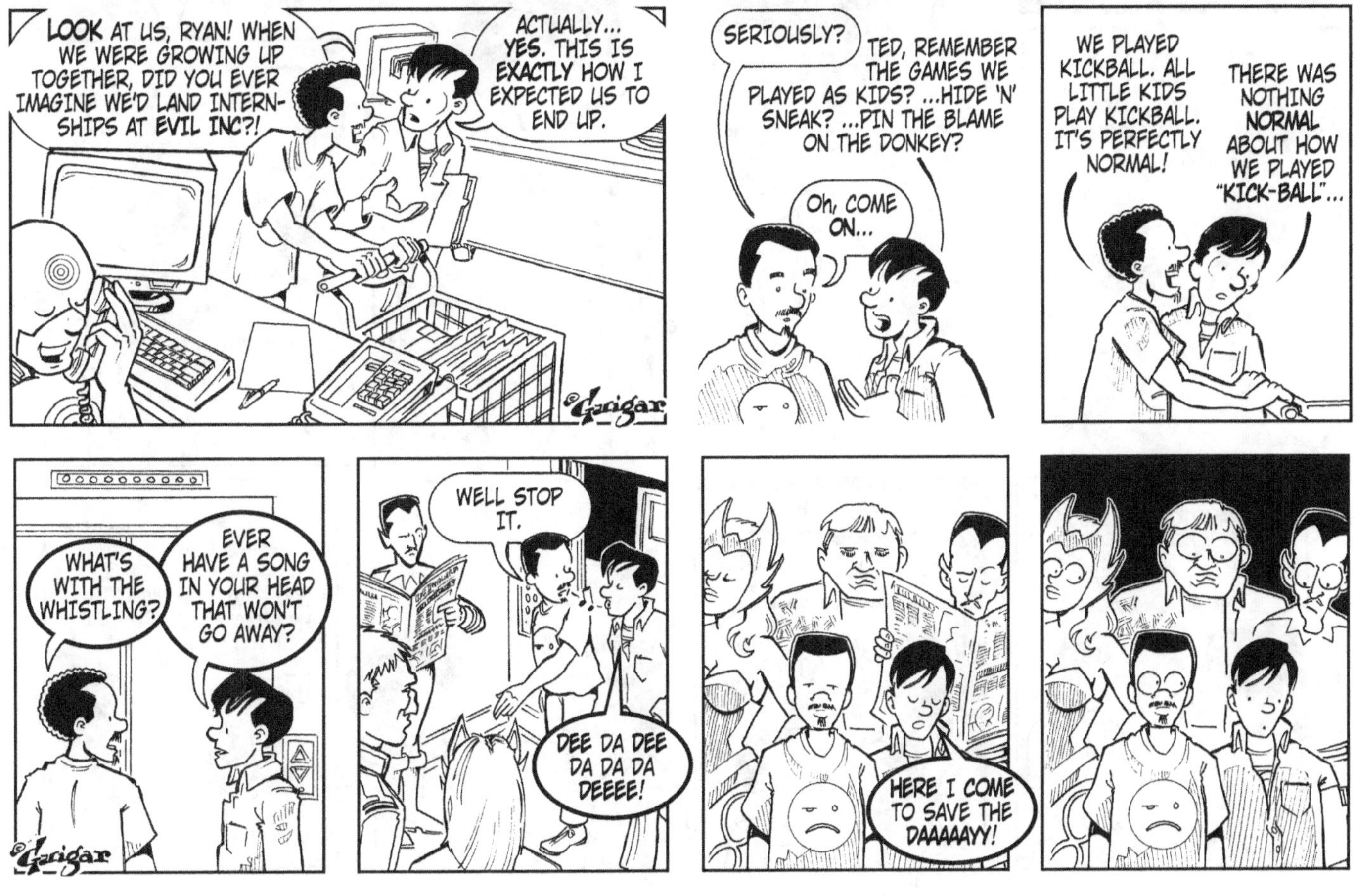
LOOK AT US, RYAN! WHEN WE WERE GROWING UP TOGETHER, DID YOU EVER IMAGINE WE'D LAND INTERNSHIPS AT EVIL INC?!
ACTUALLY... YES. THIS IS EXACTLY HOW I EXPECTED US TO END UP.
SERIOUSLY?
TED, REMEMBER THE GAMES WE PLAYED AS KIDS? ...HIDE 'N' SNEAK? ...PIN THE BLAME ON THE DONKEY?
Oh, COME ON...
WE PLAYED KICKBALL. ALL LITTLE KIDS PLAY KICKBALL. IT'S PERFECTLY NORMAL!
THERE WAS NOTHING NORMAL ABOUT HOW WE PLAYED "KICK-BALL"...
WHAT'S WITH THE WHISTLING?
EVER HAVE A SONG IN YOUR HEAD THAT WON'T GO AWAY?
WELL STOP IT.
DEE DA DEE DA DA DA DEEEE!
HERE I COME TO SAVE THE DAAAAAYY!

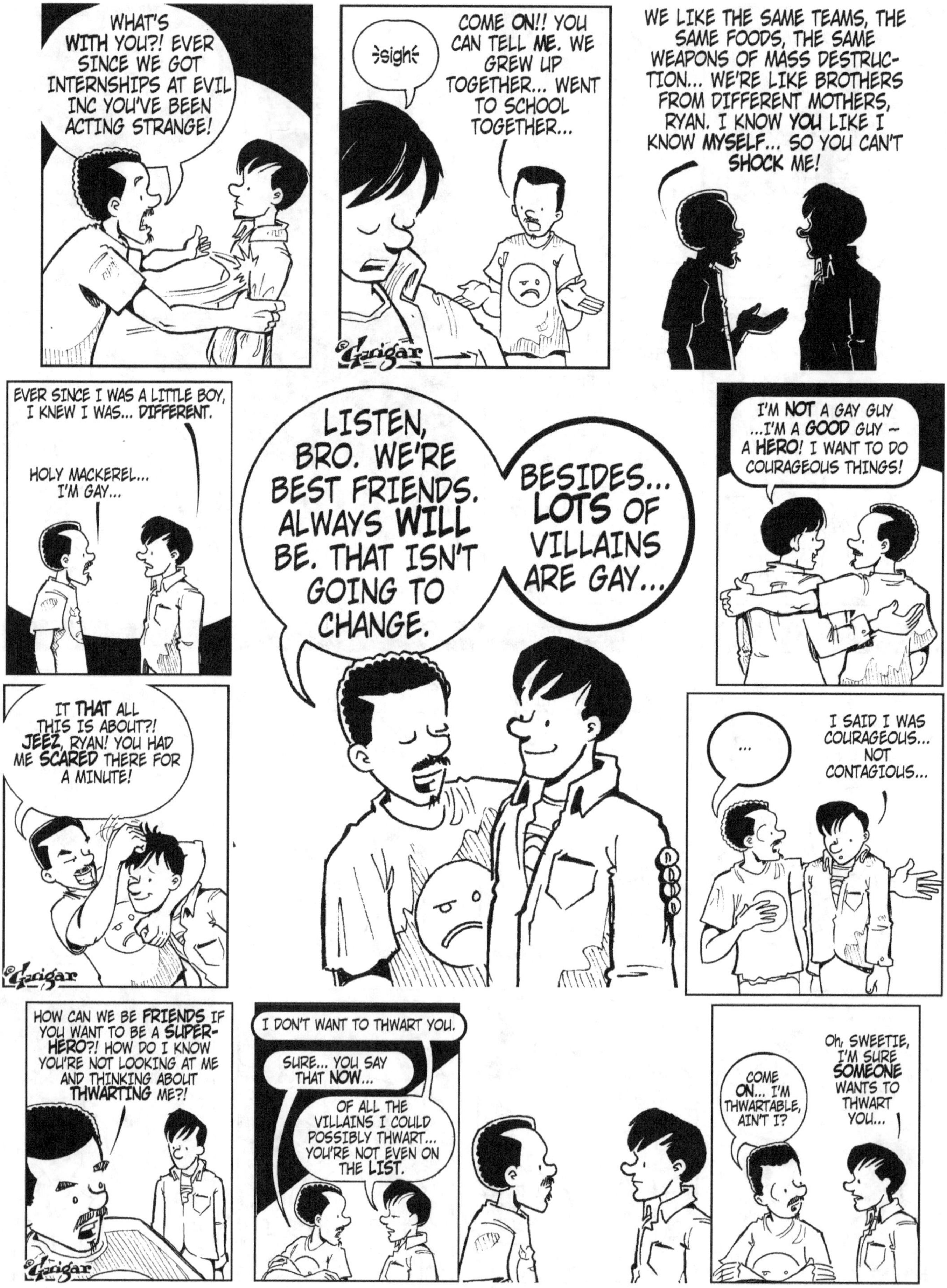
WHAT'S WITH YOU?! EVER SINCE WE GOT INTERNSHIPS AT EVIL INC YOU'VE BEEN ACTING STRANGE!
sigh
COME ON!! YOU CAN TELL ME. WE GREW UP TOGETHER... WENT TO SCHOOL TOGETHER...
WE LIKE THE SAME TEAMS, THE SAME FOODS, THE SAME WEAPONS OF MASS DESTRUCTION... WE'RE LIKE BROTHERS FROM DIFFERENT MOTHERS, RYAN. I KNOW YOU LIKE I KNOW MYSELF... SO YOU CAN'T SHOCK ME!
EVER SINCE I WAS A LITTLE BOY, I KNEW I WAS... DIFFERENT.
HOLY MACKEREL... I'M GAY...
LISTEN, BRO. WE'RE BEST FRIENDS. ALWAYS WILL BE. THAT ISN'T GOING TO CHANGE.
BESIDES... LOTS OF VILLAINS ARE GAY...
I'M NOT A GAY GUY ...I'M A GOOD GUY -- A HERO! I WANT TO DO COURAGEOUS THINGS!
IT THAT ALL THIS IS ABOUT?! JEEZ, RYAN! YOU HAD ME SCARED THERE FOR A MINUTE!
...
I SAID I WAS COURAGEOUS... NOT CONTAGIOUS...
HOW CAN WE BE FRIENDS IF YOU WANT TO BE A SUPER-HERO?! HOW DO I KNOW YOU'RE NOT LOOKING AT ME AND THINKING ABOUT THWARTING ME?!
I DON'T WANT TO THWART YOU.
SURE... YOU SAY THAT NOW...
OF ALL THE VILLAINS I COULD POSSIBLY THWART... YOU'RE NOT EVEN ON THE LIST.
COME ON... I'M THWARTABLE, AIN'T I?
Oh, SWEETIE, I'M SURE SOMEONE WANTS TO THWART YOU...

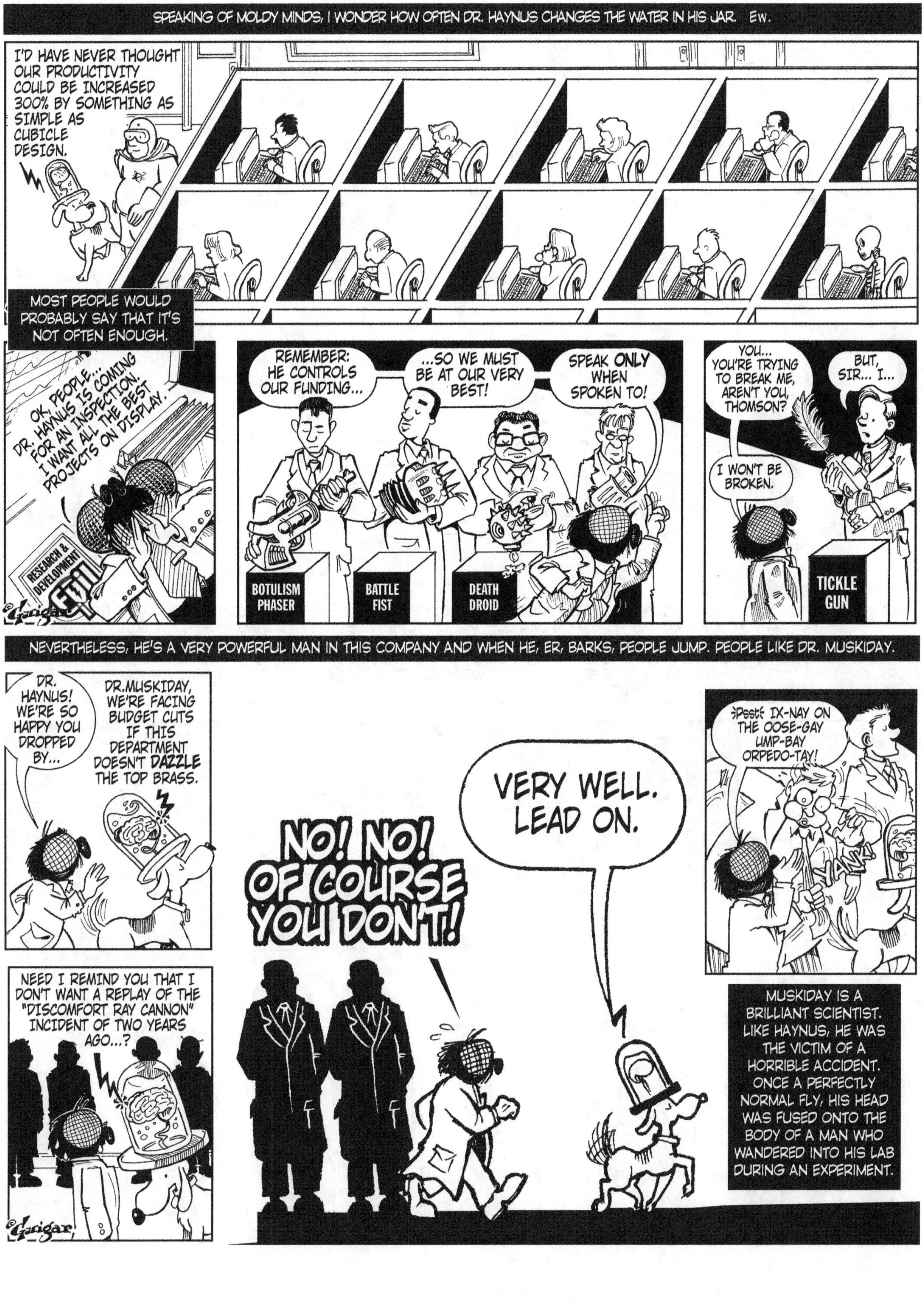
SPEAKING OF MOLDY MINDS, I WONDER HOW OFTEN DR. HAYNUS CHANGES THE WATER IN HIS JAR. Ew.
I'D HAVE NEVER THOUGHT OUR PRODUCTIVITY COULD BE INCREASED 300% BY SOMETHING AS SIMPLE AS CUBICLE DESIGN.
MOST PEOPLE WOULD PROBABLY SAY THAT IT'S NOT OFTEN ENOUGH.
OK, PEOPLE... DR. HAYNUS IS COMING FOR AN INSPECTION. I WANT ALL THE BEST PROJECTS ON DISPLAY.
RESEARCH & DEVELOPMENT
REMEMBER: HE CONTROLS OUR FUNDING...
...SO WE MUST BE AT OUR VERY BEST!
SPEAK ONLY WHEN SPOKEN TO!
BOTULISM PHASER
BATTLE FIST
DEATH DROID
YOU... YOU'RE TRYING TO BREAK ME, AREN'T YOU, THOMSON?
BUT, SIR... I...
I WON'T BE BROKEN.
TICKLE GUN
NEVERTHELESS, HE'S A VERY POWERFUL MAN IN THIS COMPANY AND WHEN HE, ER, BARKS, PEOPLE JUMP. PEOPLE LIKE DR. MUSKIDAY.
DR. HAYNUS! WE'RE SO HAPPY YOU DROPPED BY...
DR.MUSKIDAY, WE'RE FACING BUDGET CUTS IF THIS DEPARTMENT DOESN'T DAZZLE THE TOP BRASS.
NEED I REMIND YOU THAT I DON'T WANT A REPLAY OF THE "DISCOMFORT RAY CANNON" INCIDENT OF TWO YEARS AGO...?
NO! NO! OF COURSE YOU DON'T!
VERY WELL. LEAD ON.
Psst IX-NAY ON THE OOSE-GAY UMP-BAY ORPEDO-TAY!
YANK!
MUSKIDAY IS A BRILLIANT SCIENTIST. LIKE HAYNUS, HE WAS THE VICTIM OF A HORRIBLE ACCIDENT. ONCE A PERFECTLY NORMAL FLY, HIS HEAD WAS FUSED ONTO THE BODY OF A MAN WHO WANDERED INTO HIS LAB DURING AN EXPERIMENT.

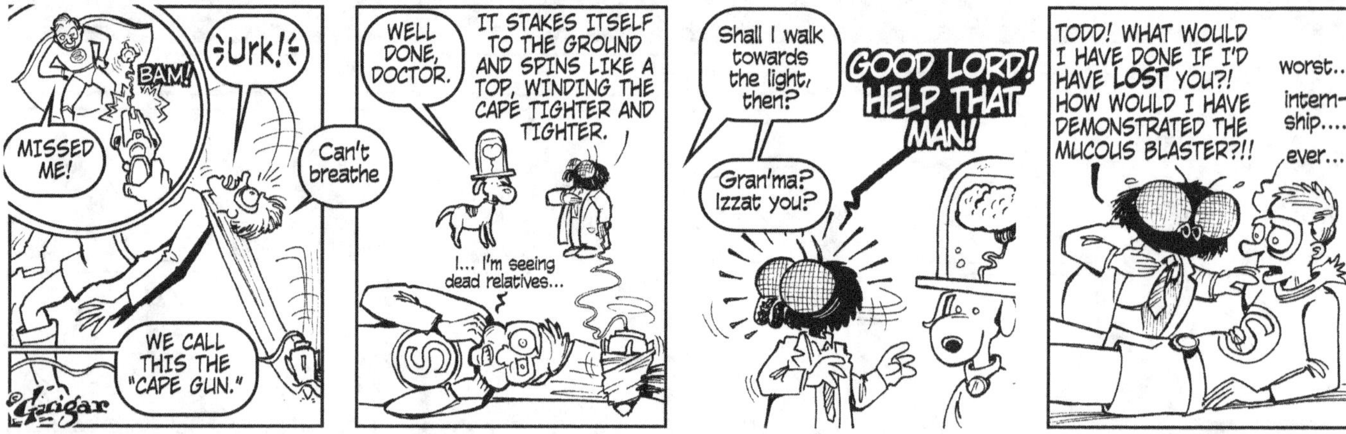
BAM!
MISSED ME!
Urk!
Can't breathe
WE CALL THIS THE "CAPE GUN."
WELL DONE, DOCTOR.
IT STAKES ITSELF TO THE GROUND AND SPINS LIKE A TOP, WINDING THE CAPE TIGHTER AND TIGHTER.
I... I'm seeing dead relatives...
Shall I walk towards the light, then?
Gran'ma? Izzat you?
GOOD LORD! HELP THAT MAN!
TODD! WHAT WOULD I HAVE DONE IF I'D HAVE LOST YOU?! HOW WOULD I HAVE DEMONSTRATED THE MUCOUS BLASTER?!!
worst...
intern-ship....
ever...

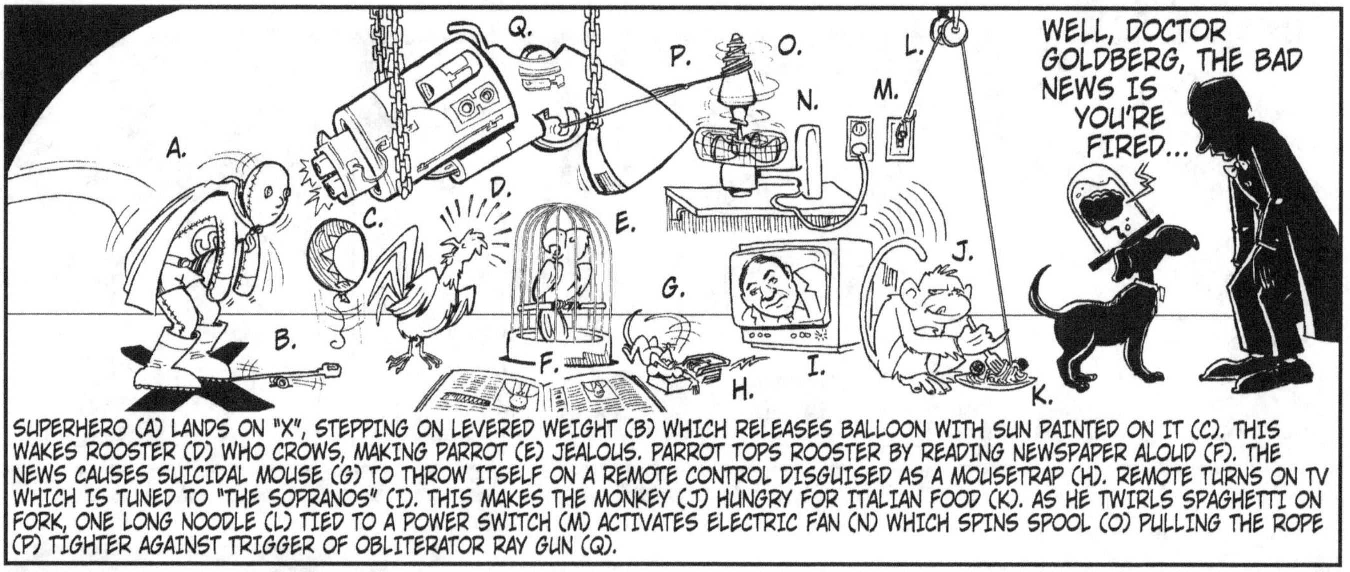
A.
B.
C.
D.
E.
F.
G.
H.
I.
J.
K.
L.
M.
N.
O.
P.
Q.
WELL, DOCTOR GOLDBERG, THE BAD NEWS IS YOU'RE FIRED...
SUPERHERO (A) LANDS ON "X", STEPPING ON LEVERED WEIGHT (B) WHICH RELEASES BALLOON WITH SUN PAINTED ON IT (C). THIS WAKES ROOSTER (D) WHO CROWS, MAKING PARROT (E) JEALOUS. PARROT TOPS ROOSTER BY READING NEWSPAPER ALOUD (F). THE NEWS CAUSES SUICIDAL MOUSE (G) TO THROW ITSELF ON A REMOTE CONTROL DISGUISED AS A MOUSETRAP (H). REMOTE TURNS ON TV WHICH IS TUNED TO "THE SOPRANOS" (I). THIS MAKES THE MONKEY (J) HUNGRY FOR ITALIAN FOOD (K). AS HE TWIRLS SPAGHETTI ON FORK, ONE LONG NOODLE (L) TIED TO A POWER SWITCH (M) ACTIVATES ELECTRIC FAN (N) WHICH SPINS SPOOL (O) PULLING THE ROPE (P) TIGHTER AGAINST TRIGGER OF OBLITERATOR RAY GUN (Q).

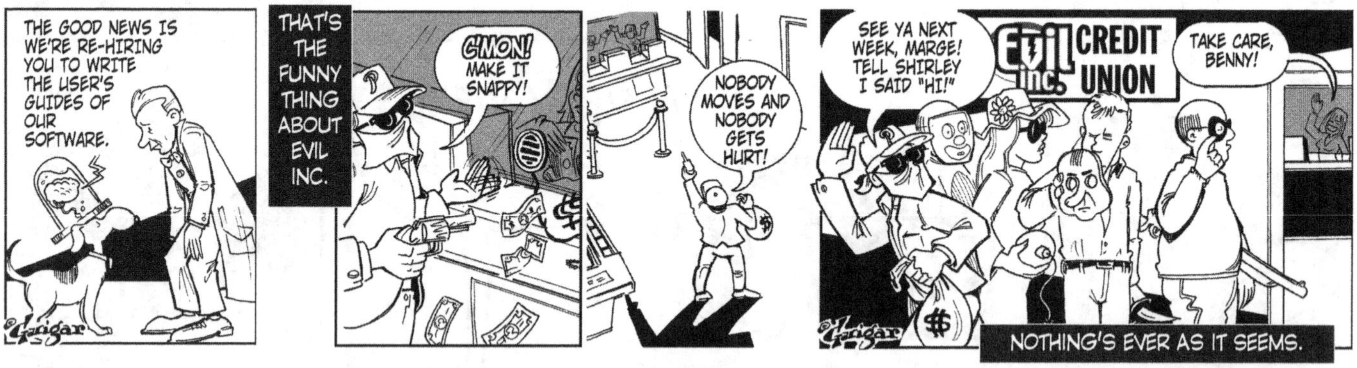
THE GOOD NEWS IS WE'RE RE-HIRING YOU TO WRITE THE USER'S GUIDES OF OUR SOFTWARE.
THAT'S THE FUNNY THING ABOUT EVIL INC.
C'MON! MAKE IT SNAPPY!
NOBODY MOVES AND NOBODY GETS HURT!
SEE YA NEXT WEEK, MARGE! TELL SHIRLEY I SAID "HI!"
EVIL INC. CREDIT UNION
TAKE CARE, BENNY!
NOTHING'S EVER AS IT SEEMS.

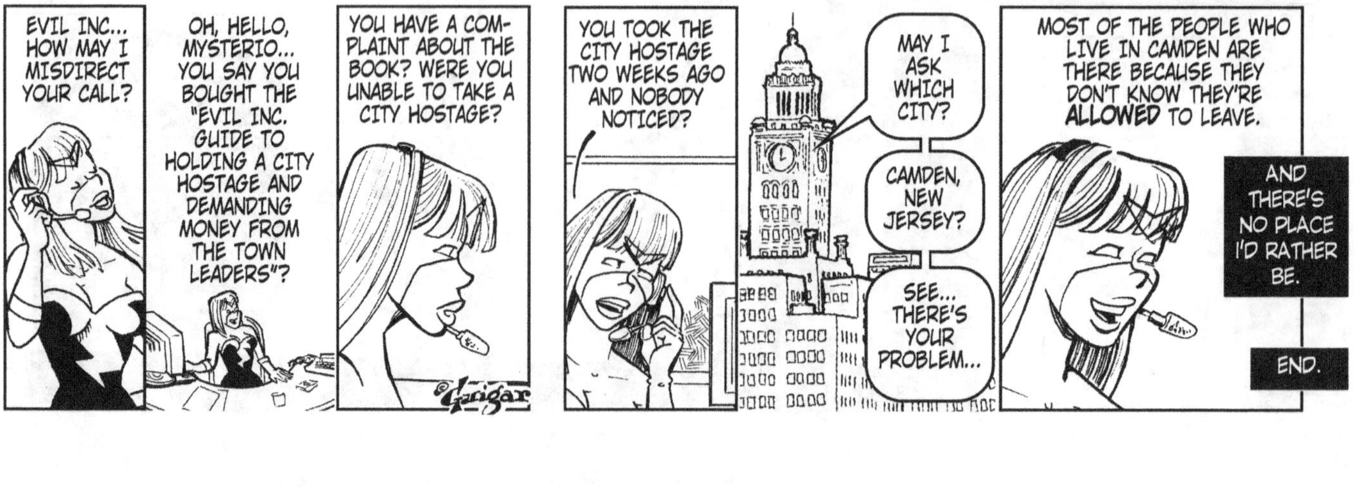
EVIL INC... HOW MAY I MISDIRECT YOUR CALL?
OH, HELLO, MYSTERIO... YOU SAY YOU BOUGHT THE "EVIL INC. GUIDE TO HOLDING A CITY HOSTAGE AND DEMANDING MONEY FROM THE TOWN LEADERS"?
YOU HAVE A COMPLAINT ABOUT THE BOOK? WERE YOU UNABLE TO TAKE A CITY HOSTAGE?
YOU TOOK THE CITY HOSTAGE TWO WEEKS AGO AND NOBODY NOTICED?
MAY I ASK WHICH CITY?
CAMDEN, NEW JERSEY?
SEE... THERE'S YOUR PROBLEM...
MOST OF THE PEOPLE WHO LIVE IN CAMDEN ARE THERE BECAUSE THEY DON'T KNOW THEY'RE ALLOWED TO LEAVE.
AND THERE'S NO PLACE I'D RATHER BE.
END.

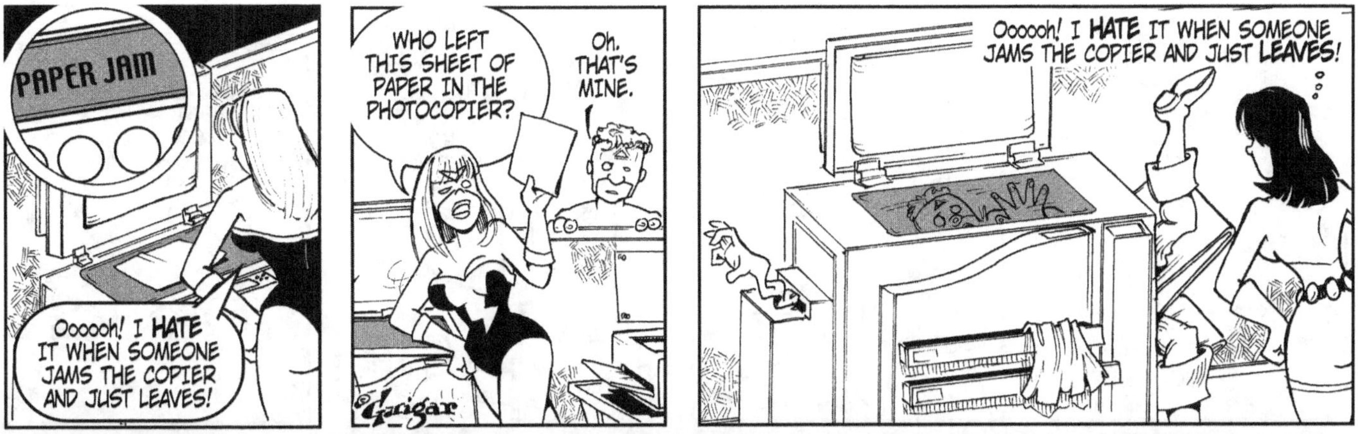
PAPER JAM
Oooooh! I HATE IT WHEN SOMEONE JAMS THE COPIER AND JUST LEAVES!
WHO LEFT THIS SHEET OF PAPER IN THE PHOTOCOPIER?
Oh. THAT'S MINE.
Oooooh! I HATE IT WHEN SOMEONE JAMS THE COPIER AND JUST LEAVES!

MY NAME IS LIGHTNING LADY. I'M A SUPER-VILLAIN. I'M THE HEAD RECEPTIONIST AT EVIL INCORPORATED, A COMPANY RUN BY SUPER-VILLAINS FOR SUPER-VILLAINS.

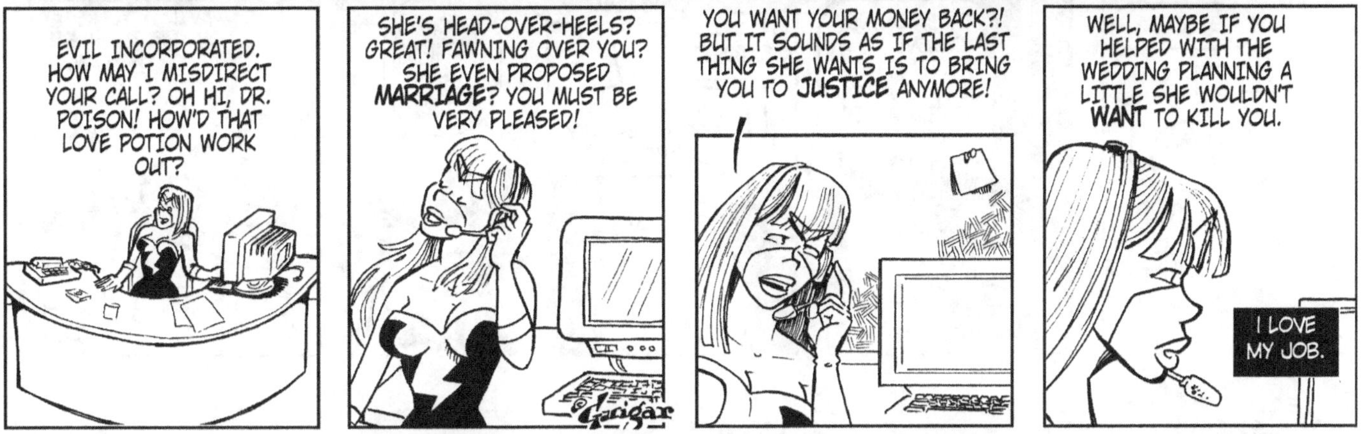
EVIL INCORPORATED. HOW MAY I MISDIRECT YOUR CALL? OH HI, DR. POISON! HOW'D THAT LOVE POTION WORK OUT?
SHE'S HEAD-OVER-HEELS? GREAT! FAWNING OVER YOU? SHE EVEN PROPOSED MARRIAGE? YOU MUST BE VERY PLEASED!
YOU WANT YOUR MONEY BACK?! BUT IT SOUNDS AS IF THE LAST THING SHE WANTS IS TO BRING YOU TO JUSTICE ANYMORE!
WELL, MAYBE IF YOU HELPED WITH THE WEDDING PLANNING A LITTLE SHE WOULDN'T WANT TO KILL YOU.
I LOVE MY JOB.

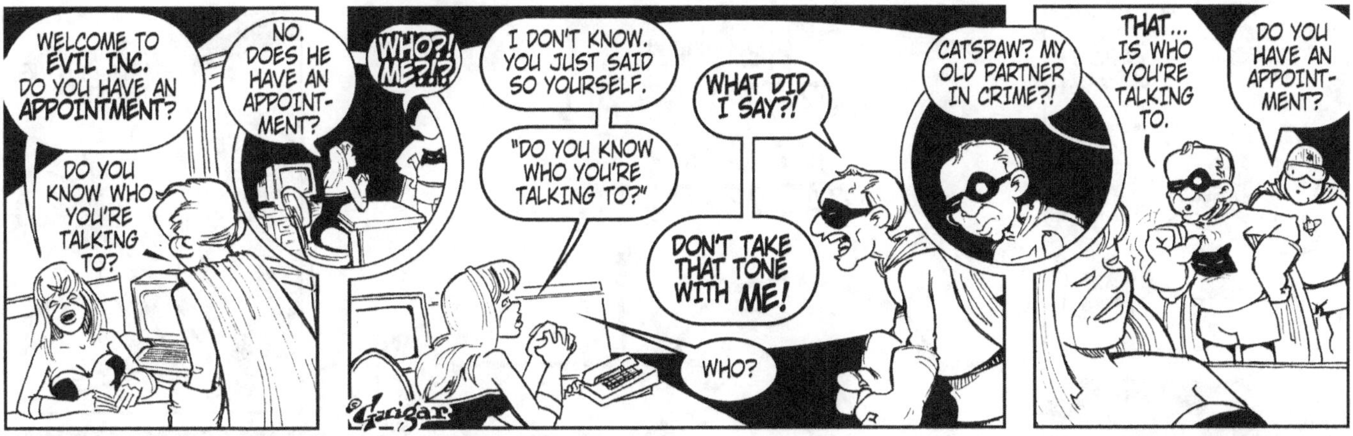
WELCOME TO EVIL INC. DO YOU HAVE AN APPOINTMENT?
DO YOU KNOW WHO YOU'RE TALKING TO?
NO. DOES HE HAVE AN APPOINTMENT?
WHO?! ME?!?
I DON'T KNOW. YOU JUST SAID SO YOURSELF.
"DO YOU KNOW WHO YOU'RE TALKING TO?"
WHAT DID I SAY?!
DON'T TAKE THAT TONE WITH ME!
WHO?
CATSPAW? MY OLD PARTNER IN CRIME?!
THAT... IS WHO YOU'RE TALKING TO.
DO YOU HAVE AN APPOINTMENT?

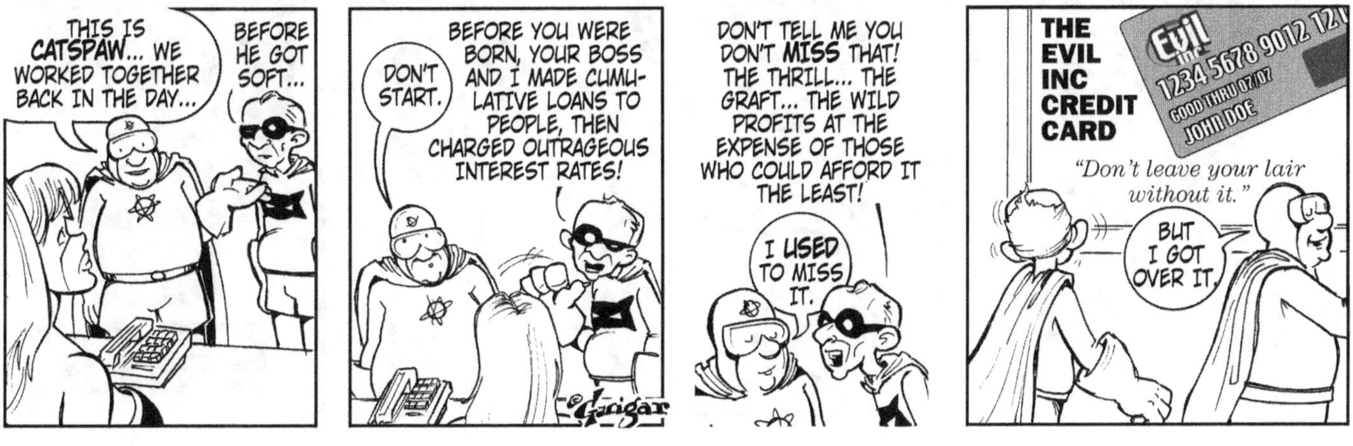
THIS IS CATSPAW... WE WORKED TOGETHER BACK IN THE DAY...
BEFORE HE GOT SOFT...
DON'T START.
BEFORE YOU WERE BORN, YOUR BOSS AND I MADE CUMULATIVE LOANS TO PEOPLE, THEN CHARGED OUTRAGEOUS INTEREST RATES!
DON'T TELL ME YOU DON'T MISS THAT! THE THRILL... THE GRAFT... THE WILD PROFITS AT THE EXPENSE OF THOSE WHO COULD AFFORD IT THE LEAST!
I USED TO MISS IT.
THE EVIL INC CREDIT CARD
Evil Inc
1234 5678 9012 12
GOOD THRU 02/07
JOHN DOE
"Don't leave your lair without it."
BUT I GOT OVER IT.

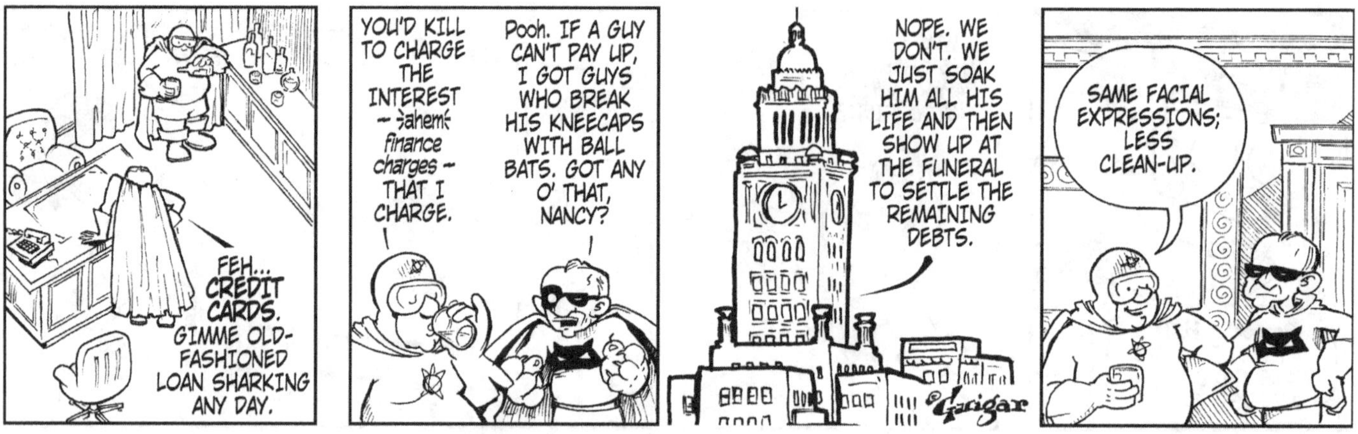

FEH... CREDIT CARDS. GIMME OLD-FASHIONED LOAN SHARKING ANY DAY.
YOU'D KILL TO CHARGE THE INTEREST -- *ahem* finance charges -- THAT I CHARGE.
Pooh. IF A GUY CAN'T PAY UP, I GOT GUYS WHO BREAK HIS KNEECAPS WITH BALL BATS. GOT ANY O' THAT, NANCY?
NOPE. WE DON'T. WE JUST SOAK HIM ALL HIS LIFE AND THEN SHOW UP AT THE FUNERAL TO SETTLE THE REMAINING DEBTS.
SAME FACIAL EXPRESSIONS; LESS CLEAN-UP.

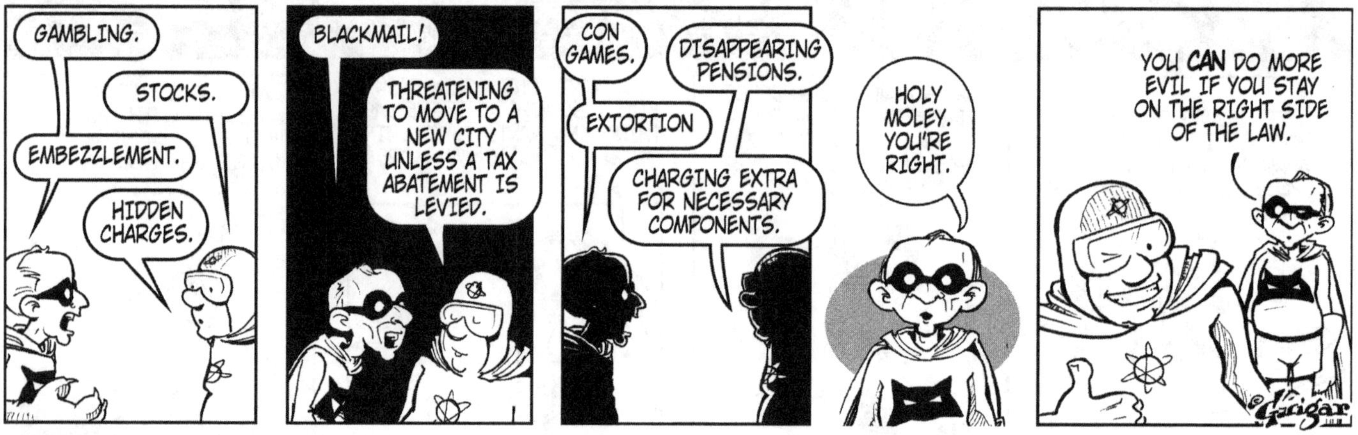

GAMBLING.
STOCKS.
EMBEZZLEMENT.
HIDDEN CHARGES.
BLACKMAIL!
THREATENING TO MOVE TO A NEW CITY UNLESS A TAX ABATEMENT IS LEVIED.
CON GAMES.
DISAPPEARING PENSIONS.
EXTORTION
CHARGING EXTRA FOR NECESSARY COMPONENTS.
HOLY MOLEY. YOU'RE RIGHT.
YOU CAN DO MORE EVIL IF YOU STAY ON THE RIGHT SIDE OF THE LAW.

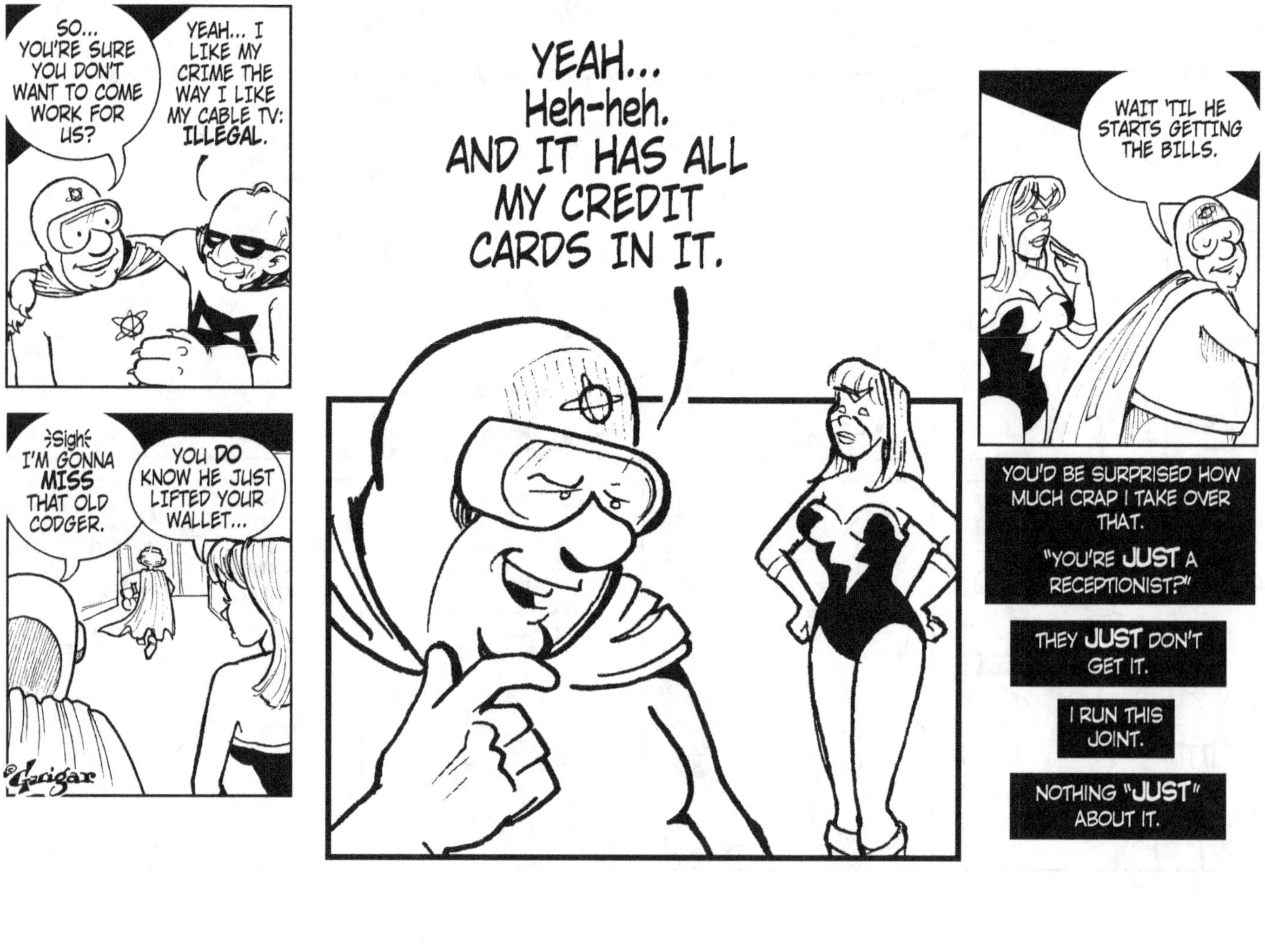

SO... YOU'RE SURE YOU DON'T WANT TO COME WORK FOR US?
YEAH... I LIKE MY CRIME THE WAY I LIKE MY CABLE TV: ILLEGAL.
Sigh I'M GONNA MISS THAT OLD CODGER.
YOU DO KNOW HE JUST LIFTED YOUR WALLET...
YEAH... Heh-heh. AND IT HAS ALL MY CREDIT CARDS IN IT.
WAIT 'TIL HE STARTS GETTING THE BILLS.
YOU'D BE SURPRISED HOW MUCH CRAP I TAKE OVER THAT.
"YOU'RE JUST A RECEPTIONIST?"
THEY JUST DON'T GET IT.
I RUN THIS JOINT.
NOTHING "JUST" ABOUT IT.

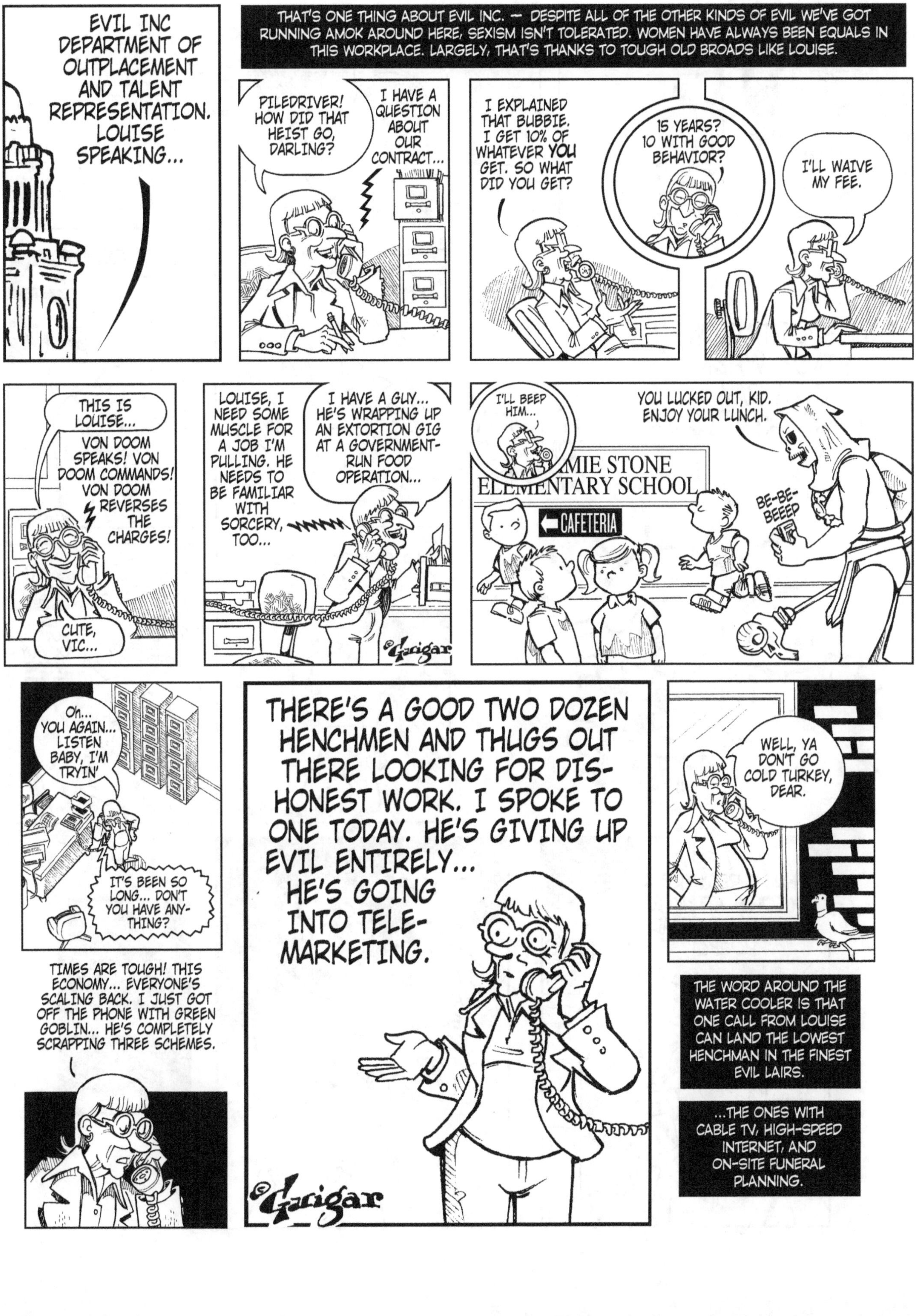
EVIL INC DEPARTMENT OF OUTPLACEMENT AND TALENT REPRESENTATION. LOUISE SPEAKING...
THAT'S ONE THING ABOUT EVIL INC. — DESPITE ALL OF THE OTHER KINDS OF EVIL WE'VE GOT RUNNING AMOK AROUND HERE, SEXISM ISN'T TOLERATED. WOMEN HAVE ALWAYS BEEN EQUALS IN THIS WORKPLACE. LARGELY, THAT'S THANKS TO TOUGH OLD BROADS LIKE LOUISE.
PILEDRIVER! HOW DID THAT HEIST GO, DARLING?
I HAVE A QUESTION ABOUT OUR CONTRACT...
I EXPLAINED THAT BUBBIE. I GET 10% OF WHATEVER YOU GET. SO WHAT DID YOU GET?
15 YEARS? 10 WITH GOOD BEHAVIOR?
I'LL WAIVE MY FEE.
THIS IS LOUISE...
VON DOOM SPEAKS! VON DOOM COMMANDS! VON DOOM REVERSES THE CHARGES!
CUTE, VIC...
LOUISE, I NEED SOME MUSCLE FOR A JOB I'M PULLING. HE NEEDS TO BE FAMILIAR WITH SORCERY, TOO...
I HAVE A GUY... HE'S WRAPPING UP AN EXTORTION GIG AT A GOVERNMENT-RUN FOOD OPERATION...
©Garigar
I'LL BEEP HIM...
YOU LUCKED OUT, KID. ENJOY YOUR LUNCH.
ELEMENTARY SCHOOL
CAFETERIA
BE-BE-BEEEP
Oh... YOU AGAIN... LISTEN BABY, I'M TRYIN'
IT'S BEEN SO LONG... DON'T YOU HAVE ANYTHING?
TIMES ARE TOUGH! THIS ECONOMY... EVERYONE'S SCALING BACK. I JUST GOT OFF THE PHONE WITH GREEN GOBLIN... HE'S COMPLETELY SCRAPPING THREE SCHEMES.
THERE'S A GOOD TWO DOZEN HENCHMEN AND THUGS OUT THERE LOOKING FOR DISHONEST WORK. I SPOKE TO ONE TODAY. HE'S GIVING UP EVIL ENTIRELY... HE'S GOING INTO TELEMARKETING.
©Garigar
WELL, YA DON'T GO COLD TURKEY, DEAR.
THE WORD AROUND THE WATER COOLER IS THAT ONE CALL FROM LOUISE CAN LAND THE LOWEST HENCHMAN IN THE FINEST EVIL LAIRS.
...THE ONES WITH CABLE TV, HIGH-SPEED INTERNET, AND ON-SITE FUNERAL PLANNING.

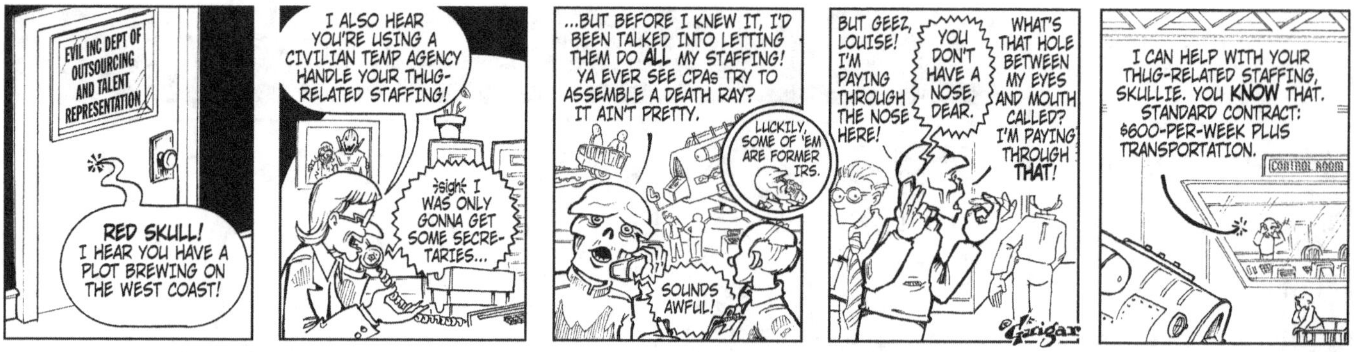
EVIL INC DEPT OF OUTSOURCING AND TALENT REPRESENTATION
RED SKULL! I HEAR YOU HAVE A PLOT BREWING ON THE WEST COAST!
I ALSO HEAR YOU'RE USING A CIVILIAN TEMP AGENCY HANDLE YOUR THUG-RELATED STAFFING!
sigh I WAS ONLY GONNA GET SOME SECRE-TARIES...
...BUT BEFORE I KNEW IT, I'D BEEN TALKED INTO LETTING THEM DO ALL MY STAFFING! YA EVER SEE CPAs TRY TO ASSEMBLE A DEATH RAY? IT AIN'T PRETTY.
LUCKILY, SOME OF 'EM ARE FORMER IRS.
SOUNDS AWFUL!
BUT GEEZ, LOUISE! I'M PAYING THROUGH THE NOSE HERE!
YOU DON'T HAVE A NOSE, DEAR.
WHAT'S THAT HOLE BETWEEN MY EYES AND MOUTH CALLED? I'M PAYING THROUGH THAT!
I CAN HELP WITH YOUR THUG-RELATED STAFFING, SKULLIE. YOU KNOW THAT. STANDARD CONTRACT: $600-PER-WEEK PLUS TRANSPORTATION.
CONTROL ROOM

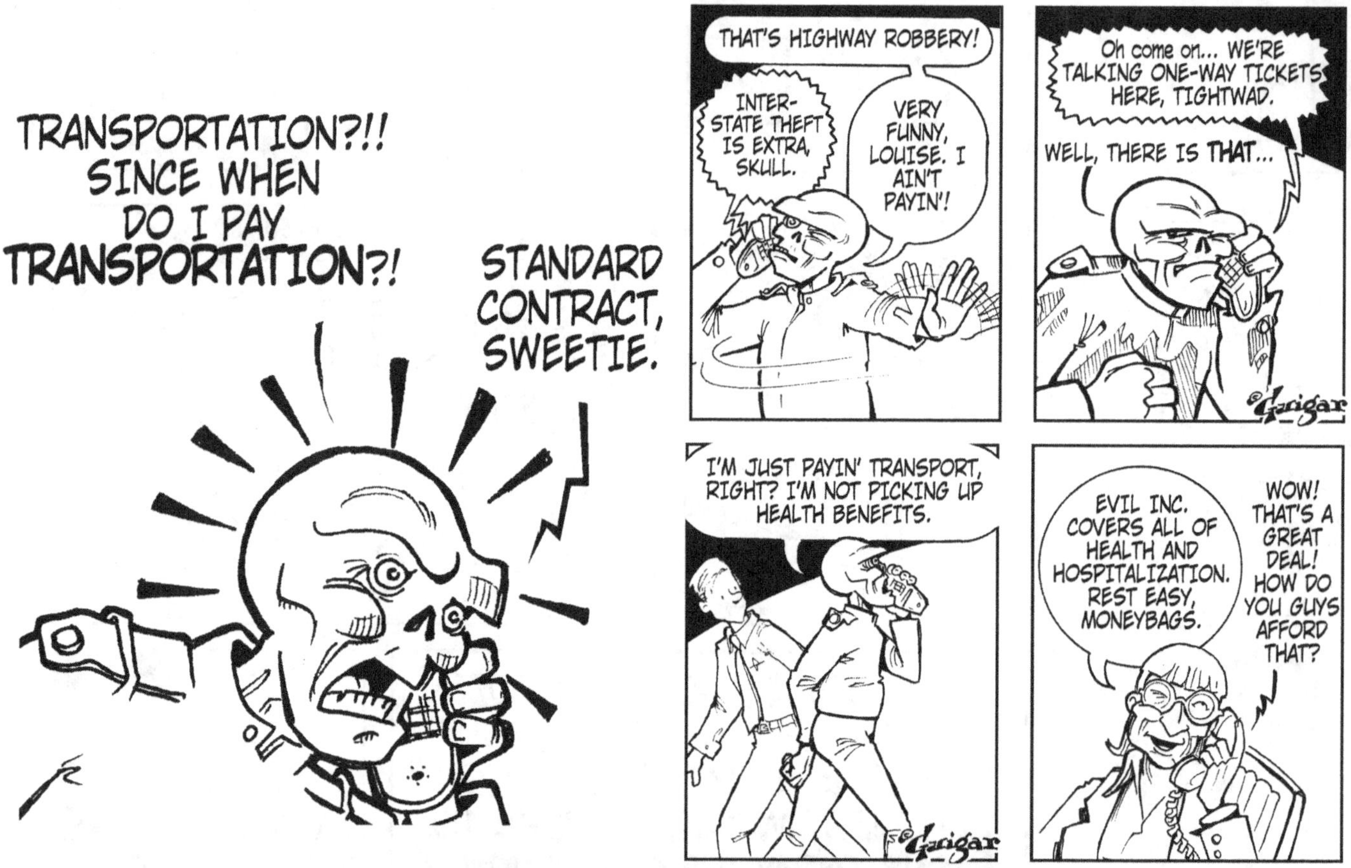
TRANSPORTATION?!! SINCE WHEN DO I PAY TRANSPORTATION?!
STANDARD CONTRACT, SWEETIE.
THAT'S HIGHWAY ROBBERY!
INTER-STATE THEFT IS EXTRA, SKULL.
VERY FUNNY, LOUISE. I AIN'T PAYIN'!
Oh come on... WE'RE TALKING ONE-WAY TICKETS HERE, TIGHTWAD.
WELL, THERE IS THAT...
I'M JUST PAYIN' TRANSPORT, RIGHT? I'M NOT PICKING UP HEALTH BENEFITS.
EVIL INC. COVERS ALL OF HEALTH AND HOSPITALIZATION. REST EASY, MONEYBAGS.
WOW! THAT'S A GREAT DEAL! HOW DO YOU GUYS AFFORD THAT?

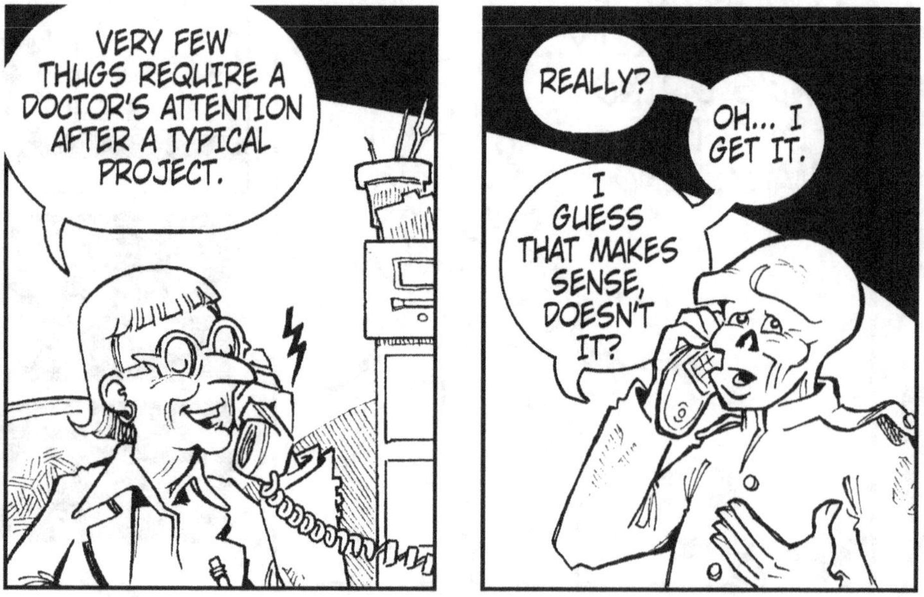
VERY FEW THUGS REQUIRE A DOCTOR'S ATTENTION AFTER A TYPICAL PROJECT.
REALLY?
OH... I GET IT.
I GUESS THAT MAKES SENSE, DOESN'T IT?

YA GOTTA LOVE A LADY WHO CAN GO TOE-TO-TOE WITH A BIG TIME BADDY LIKE RED SKULL.

I MEAN, HE'S ONE OF THE TOP NEMESES IN THE BUSINESS.

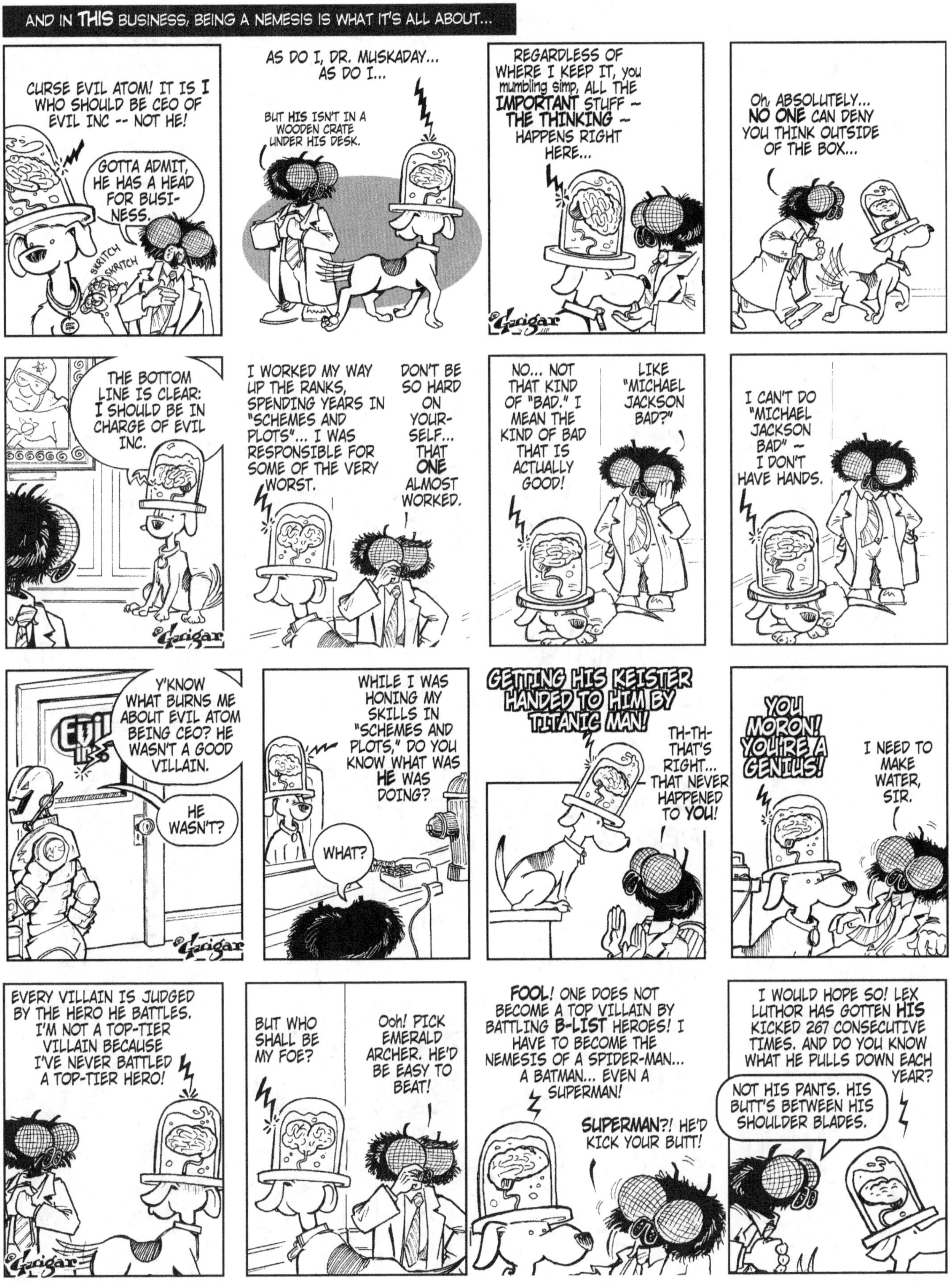
AND IN THIS BUSINESS, BEING A NEMESIS IS WHAT IT'S ALL ABOUT...
CURSE EVIL ATOM! IT IS I WHO SHOULD BE CEO OF EVIL INC -- NOT HE!
GOTTA ADMIT, HE HAS A HEAD FOR BUSI-NESS.
SKRITCH SKRITCH
AS DO I, DR. MUSKADAY... AS DO I...
BUT HIS ISN'T IN A WOODEN CRATE UNDER HIS DESK.
REGARDLESS OF WHERE I KEEP IT, you mumbling simp, ALL THE IMPORTANT STUFF -- THE THINKING -- HAPPENS RIGHT HERE...
Oh, ABSOLUTELY... NO ONE CAN DENY YOU THINK OUTSIDE OF THE BOX...
Garigar
THE BOTTOM LINE IS CLEAR: I SHOULD BE IN CHARGE OF EVIL INC.
I WORKED MY WAY UP THE RANKS, SPENDING YEARS IN "SCHEMES AND PLOTS"... I WAS RESPONSIBLE FOR SOME OF THE VERY WORST.
DON'T BE SO HARD ON YOUR-SELF... THAT ONE ALMOST WORKED.
NO... NOT THAT KIND OF "BAD." I MEAN THE KIND OF BAD THAT IS ACTUALLY GOOD!
LIKE "MICHAEL JACKSON BAD?"
I CAN'T DO "MICHAEL JACKSON BAD" -- I DON'T HAVE HANDS.
Garigar
Y'KNOW WHAT BURNS ME ABOUT EVIL ATOM BEING CEO? HE WASN'T A GOOD VILLAIN.
HE WASN'T?
WHILE I WAS HONING MY SKILLS IN "SCHEMES AND PLOTS," DO YOU KNOW WHAT WAS HE WAS DOING?
WHAT?
GETTING HIS KEISTER HANDED TO HIM BY TITANIC MAN!
TH-TH-THAT'S RIGHT... THAT NEVER HAPPENED TO YOU!
YOU MORON! YOU'RE A GENIUS!
I NEED TO MAKE WATER, SIR.
Garigar
EVERY VILLAIN IS JUDGED BY THE HERO HE BATTLES. I'M NOT A TOP-TIER VILLAIN BECAUSE I'VE NEVER BATTLED A TOP-TIER HERO!
BUT WHO SHALL BE MY FOE?
Ooh! PICK EMERALD ARCHER. HE'D BE EASY TO BEAT!
FOOL! ONE DOES NOT BECOME A TOP VILLAIN BY BATTLING B-LIST HEROES! I HAVE TO BECOME THE NEMESIS OF A SPIDER-MAN... A BATMAN... EVEN A SUPERMAN!
SUPERMAN?! HE'D KICK YOUR BUTT!
I WOULD HOPE SO! LEX LUTHOR HAS GOTTEN HIS KICKED 267 CONSECUTIVE TIMES. AND DO YOU KNOW WHAT HE PULLS DOWN EACH YEAR?
NOT HIS PANTS. HIS BUTT'S BETWEEN HIS SHOULDER BLADES.
Garigar

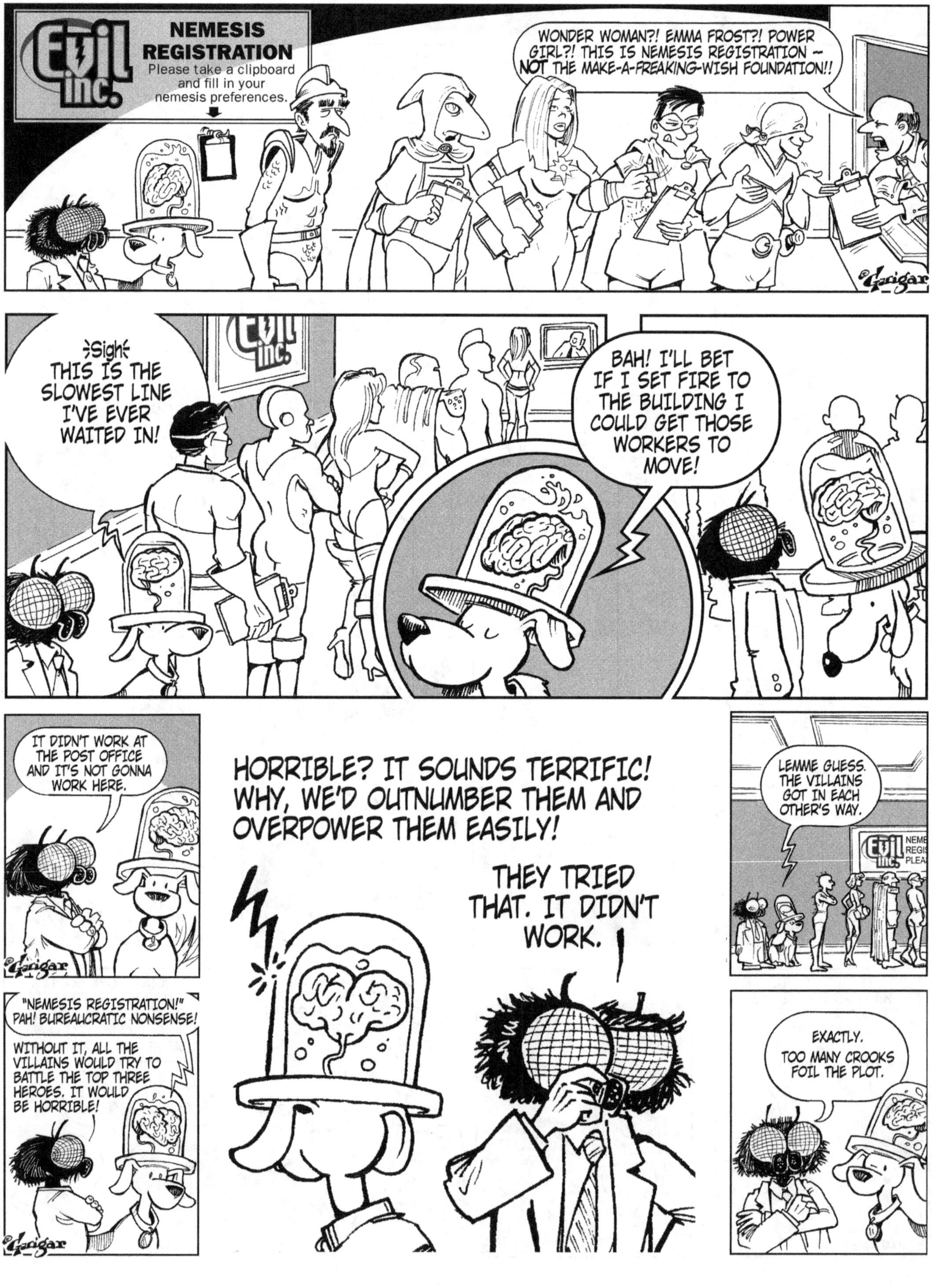

Evil inc.
NEMESIS REGISTRATION
Please take a clipboard and fill in your nemesis preferences.
WONDER WOMAN?! EMMA FROST?! POWER GIRL?! THIS IS NEMESIS REGISTRATION -- NOT THE MAKE-A-FREAKING-WISH FOUNDATION!!
©Garigar
Sigh
THIS IS THE SLOWEST LINE I'VE EVER WAITED IN!
BAH! I'LL BET IF I SET FIRE TO THE BUILDING I COULD GET THOSE WORKERS TO MOVE!
IT DIDN'T WORK AT THE POST OFFICE AND IT'S NOT GONNA WORK HERE.
©Garigar
"NEMESIS REGISTRATION!" PAH! BUREAUCRATIC NONSENSE!
WITHOUT IT, ALL THE VILLAINS WOULD TRY TO BATTLE THE TOP THREE HEROES. IT WOULD BE HORRIBLE!
©Garigar
HORRIBLE? IT SOUNDS TERRIFIC! WHY, WE'D OUTNUMBER THEM AND OVERPOWER THEM EASILY!
THEY TRIED THAT. IT DIDN'T WORK.
LEMME GUESS. THE VILLAINS GOT IN EACH OTHER'S WAY.
EXACTLY. TOO MANY CROOKS FOIL THE PLOT.

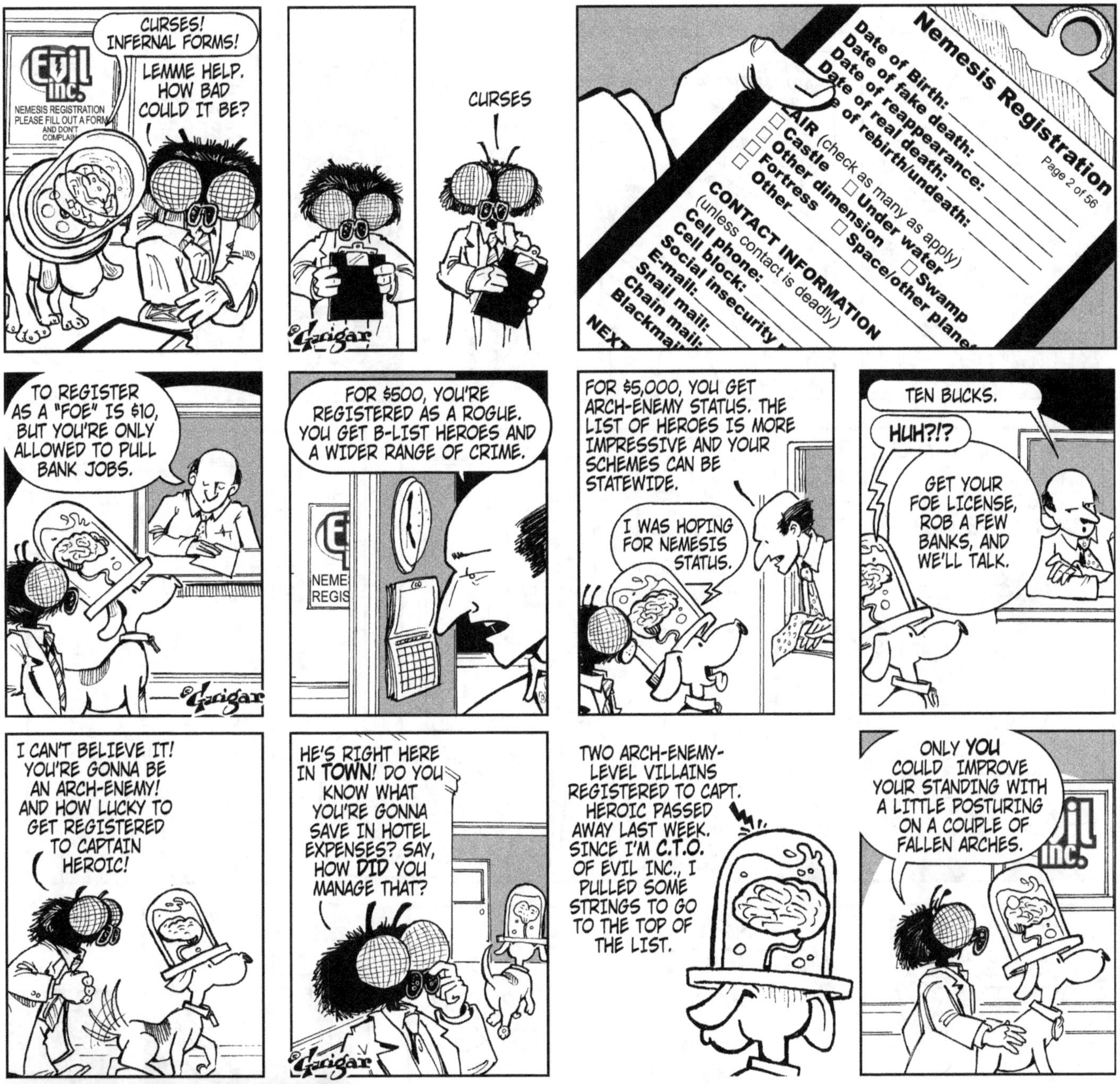
CURSES! INFERNAL FORMS!
LEMME HELP. HOW BAD COULD IT BE?
EVIL INC.
NEMESIS REGISTRATION
PLEASE FILL OUT A FORM AND DON'T COMPLAIN
CURSES
Nemesis Registration
Page 2 of 56
Date of Birth:
Date of fake death:
Date of reappearance:
Date of real death:
e of rebirth/undeath:
AIR (check as many as apply)
Castle
Under water
Swamp
Other dimension
Space/other plane
Fortress
Other
CONTACT INFORMATION
(unless contact is deadly)
Cell phone:
Cell block:
Social insecurity
E-mail:
Snail mail:
Chain mail:
Blackmail:
TO REGISTER AS A "FOE" IS $10, BUT YOU'RE ONLY ALLOWED TO PULL BANK JOBS.
FOR $500, YOU'RE REGISTERED AS A ROGUE. YOU GET B-LIST HEROES AND A WIDER RANGE OF CRIME.
FOR $5,000, YOU GET ARCH-ENEMY STATUS. THE LIST OF HEROES IS MORE IMPRESSIVE AND YOUR SCHEMES CAN BE STATEWIDE.
I WAS HOPING FOR NEMESIS STATUS.
TEN BUCKS.
HUH?!?
GET YOUR FOE LICENSE, ROB A FEW BANKS, AND WE'LL TALK.
I CAN'T BELIEVE IT! YOU'RE GONNA BE AN ARCH-ENEMY! AND HOW LUCKY TO GET REGISTERED TO CAPTAIN HEROIC!
HE'S RIGHT HERE IN TOWN! DO YOU KNOW WHAT YOU'RE GONNA SAVE IN HOTEL EXPENSES? SAY, HOW DID YOU MANAGE THAT?
TWO ARCH-ENEMY-LEVEL VILLAINS REGISTERED TO CAPT. HEROIC PASSED AWAY LAST WEEK. SINCE I'M C.T.O. OF EVIL INC., I PULLED SOME STRINGS TO GO TO THE TOP OF THE LIST.
ONLY YOU COULD IMPROVE YOUR STANDING WITH A LITTLE POSTURING ON A COUPLE OF FALLEN ARCHES.

WELL, THAT'S HOW I HEARD THE STORY.

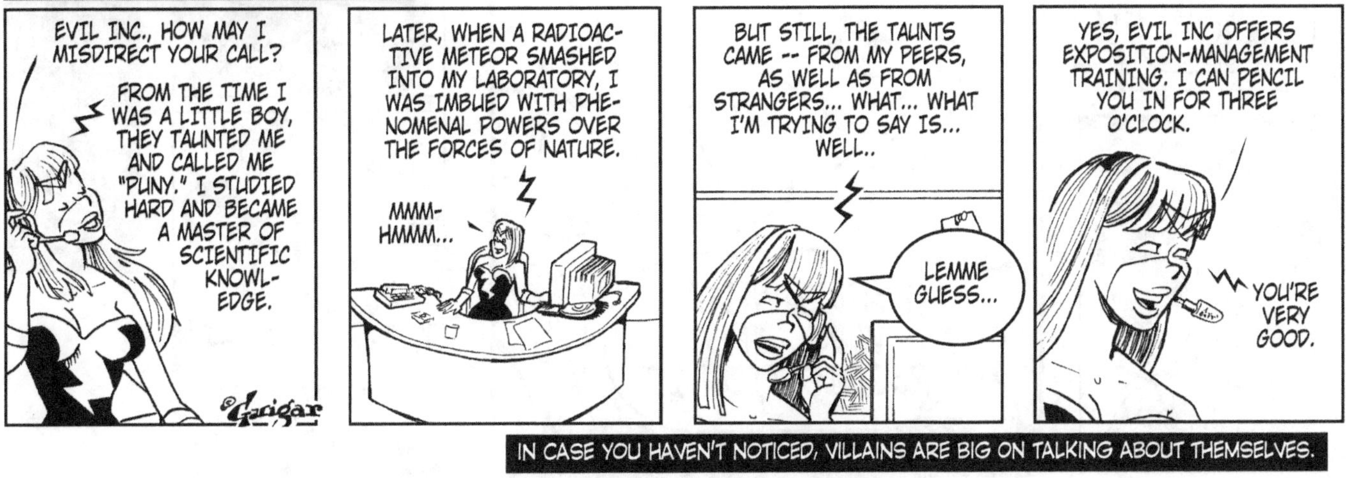
EVIL INC., HOW MAY I MISDIRECT YOUR CALL?
FROM THE TIME I WAS A LITTLE BOY, THEY TAUNTED ME AND CALLED ME "PUNY." I STUDIED HARD AND BECAME A MASTER OF SCIENTIFIC KNOWL-EDGE.
LATER, WHEN A RADIOAC-TIVE METEOR SMASHED INTO MY LABORATORY, I WAS IMBUED WITH PHE-NOMENAL POWERS OVER THE FORCES OF NATURE.
MMM-HMMM...
BUT STILL, THE TAUNTS CAME -- FROM MY PEERS, AS WELL AS FROM STRANGERS... WHAT... WHAT I'M TRYING TO SAY IS... WELL...
LEMME GUESS...
YES, EVIL INC OFFERS EXPOSITION-MANAGEMENT TRAINING. I CAN PENCIL YOU IN FOR THREE O'CLOCK.
YOU'RE VERY GOOD.

IN CASE YOU HAVEN'T NOTICED, VILLAINS ARE BIG ON TALKING ABOUT THEMSELVES.

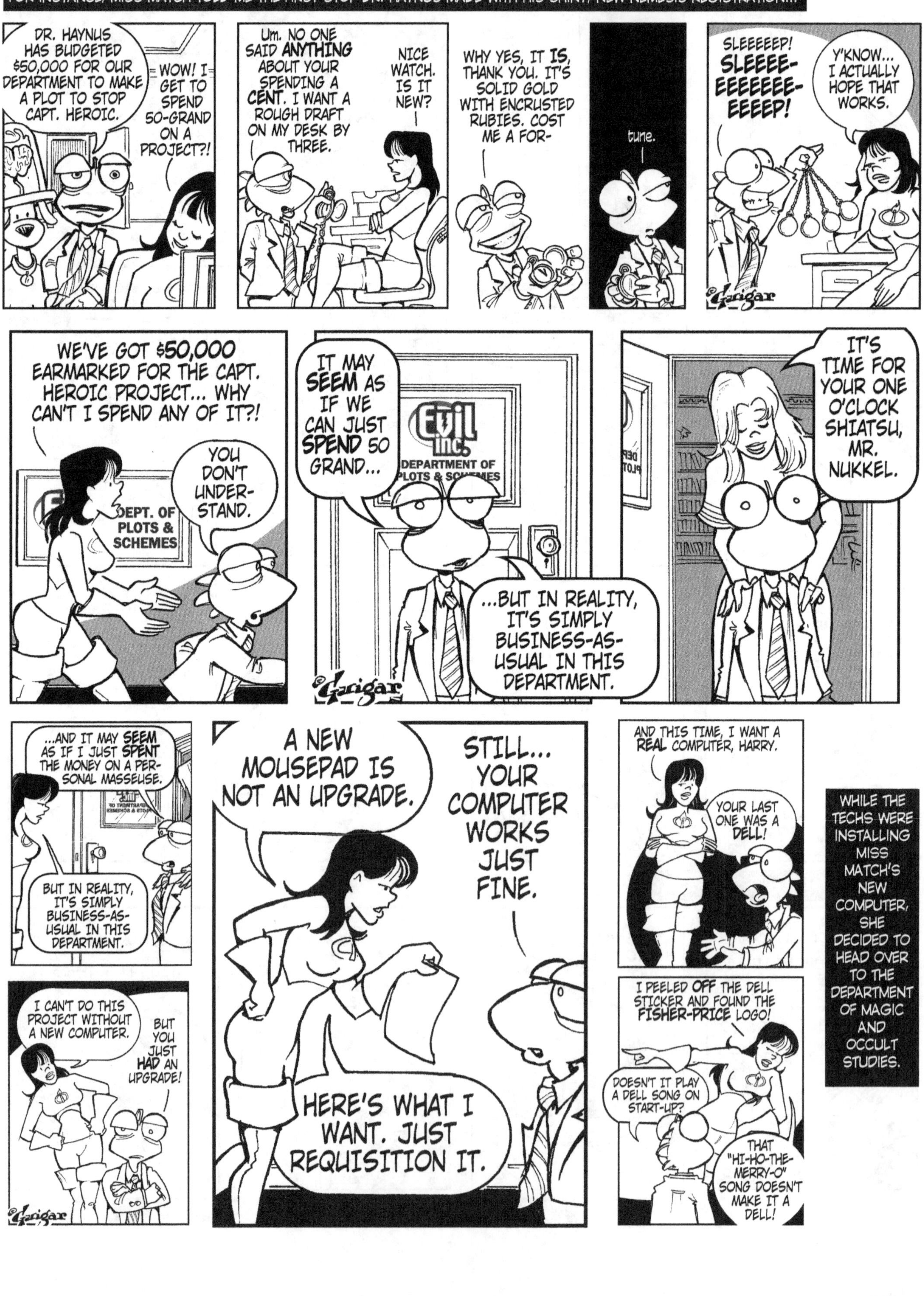
FOR INSTANCE, MISS MATCH TOLD ME THE FIRST STOP DR. HAYNUS MADE WITH HIS SHINY, NEW NEMESIS REGISTRATION...
DR. HAYNUS HAS BUDGETED $50,000 FOR OUR DEPARTMENT TO MAKE A PLOT TO STOP CAPT. HEROIC.
WOW! I GET TO SPEND 50-GRAND ON A PROJECT?!
Um. NO ONE SAID ANYTHING ABOUT YOUR SPENDING A CENT. I WANT A ROUGH DRAFT ON MY DESK BY THREE.
NICE WATCH. IS IT NEW?
WHY YES, IT IS, THANK YOU. IT'S SOLID GOLD WITH ENCRUSTED RUBIES. COST ME A FOR-
tune.
SLEEEEEP! SLEEEE-EEEEEEE-EEEEP!
Y'KNOW... I ACTUALLY HOPE THAT WORKS.
WE'VE GOT $50,000 EARMARKED FOR THE CAPT. HEROIC PROJECT... WHY CAN'T I SPEND ANY OF IT?!
YOU DON'T UNDER-STAND.
DEPT. OF PLOTS & SCHEMES
IT MAY SEEM AS IF WE CAN JUST SPEND 50 GRAND...
Evil inc. DEPARTMENT OF PLOTS & SCHEMES
...BUT IN REALITY, IT'S SIMPLY BUSINESS-AS-USUAL IN THIS DEPARTMENT.
IT'S TIME FOR YOUR ONE O'CLOCK SHIATSU, MR. NUKKEL.
...AND IT MAY SEEM AS IF I JUST SPENT THE MONEY ON A PER-SONAL MASSEUSE.
BUT IN REALITY, IT'S SIMPLY BUSINESS-AS-USUAL IN THIS DEPARTMENT.
I CAN'T DO THIS PROJECT WITHOUT A NEW COMPUTER.
BUT YOU JUST HAD AN UPGRADE!
A NEW MOUSEPAD IS NOT AN UPGRADE.
STILL... YOUR COMPUTER WORKS JUST FINE.
HERE'S WHAT I WANT. JUST REQUISITION IT.
AND THIS TIME, I WANT A REAL COMPUTER, HARRY.
YOUR LAST ONE WAS A DELL!
I PEELED OFF THE DELL STICKER AND FOUND THE FISHER-PRICE LOGO!
DOESN'T IT PLAY A DELL SONG ON START-UP?
THAT "HI-HO-THE-MERRY-O" SONG DOESN'T MAKE IT A DELL!
WHILE THE TECHS WERE INSTALLING MISS MATCH'S NEW COMPUTER, SHE DECIDED TO HEAD OVER TO THE DEPARTMENT OF MAGIC AND OCCULT STUDIES.

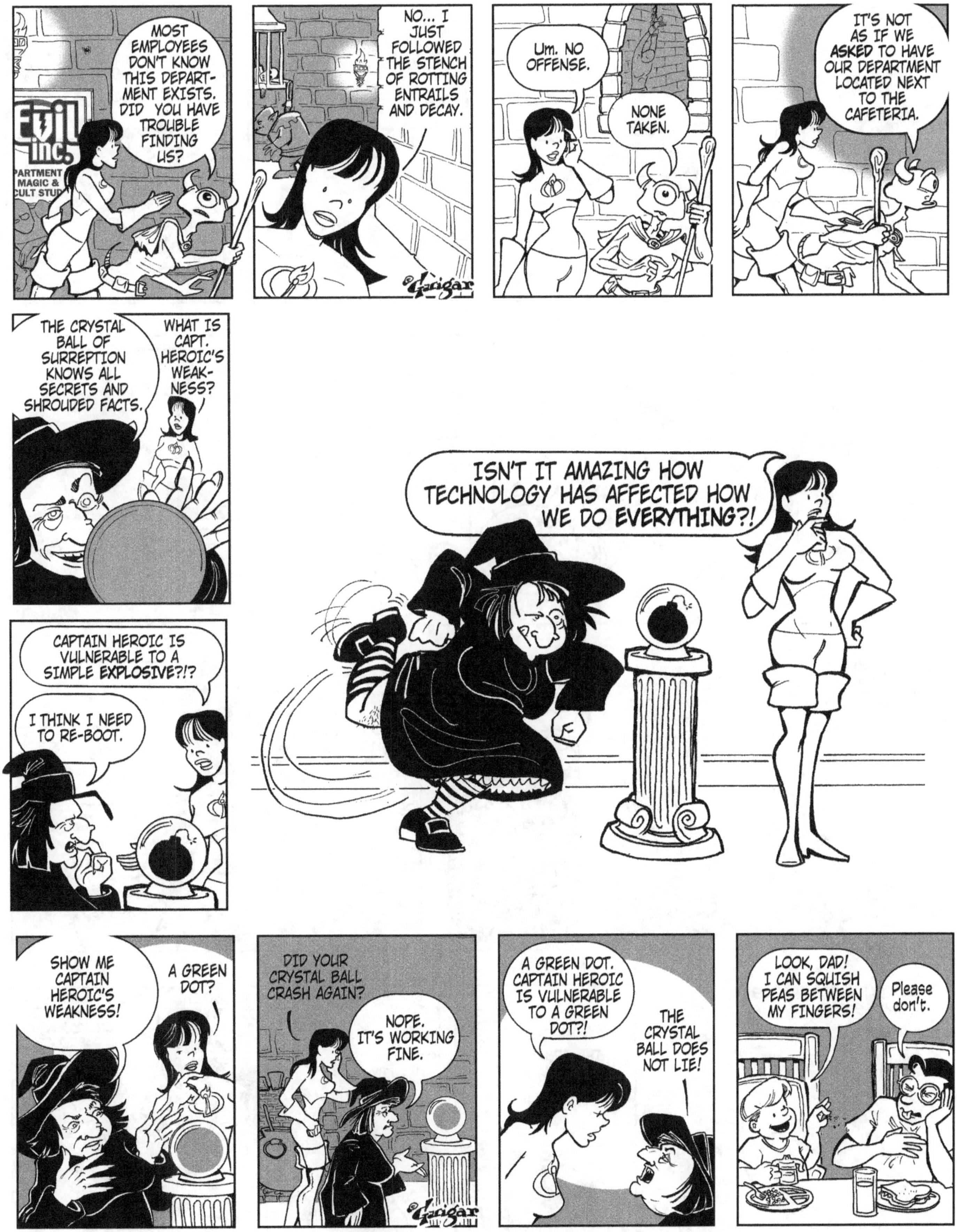

Evil inc.
PARTMENT MAGIC & CULT STUD
MOST EMPLOYEES DON'T KNOW THIS DEPARTMENT EXISTS. DID YOU HAVE TROUBLE FINDING US?
NO... I JUST FOLLOWED THE STENCH OF ROTTING ENTRAILS AND DECAY.
Um. NO OFFENSE.
NONE TAKEN.
IT'S NOT AS IF WE ASKED TO HAVE OUR DEPARTMENT LOCATED NEXT TO THE CAFETERIA.
THE CRYSTAL BALL OF SURREPTION KNOWS ALL SECRETS AND SHROUDED FACTS.
WHAT IS CAPT. HEROIC'S WEAKNESS?
CAPTAIN HEROIC IS VULNERABLE TO A SIMPLE EXPLOSIVE?!?
I THINK I NEED TO RE-BOOT.
ISN'T IT AMAZING HOW TECHNOLOGY HAS AFFECTED HOW WE DO EVERYTHING?!
SHOW ME CAPTAIN HEROIC'S WEAKNESS!
A GREEN DOT?
DID YOUR CRYSTAL BALL CRASH AGAIN?
NOPE. IT'S WORKING FINE.
A GREEN DOT. CAPTAIN HEROIC IS VULNERABLE TO A GREEN DOT?!
THE CRYSTAL BALL DOES NOT LIE!
LOOK, DAD! I CAN SQUISH PEAS BETWEEN MY FINGERS!
Please don't.

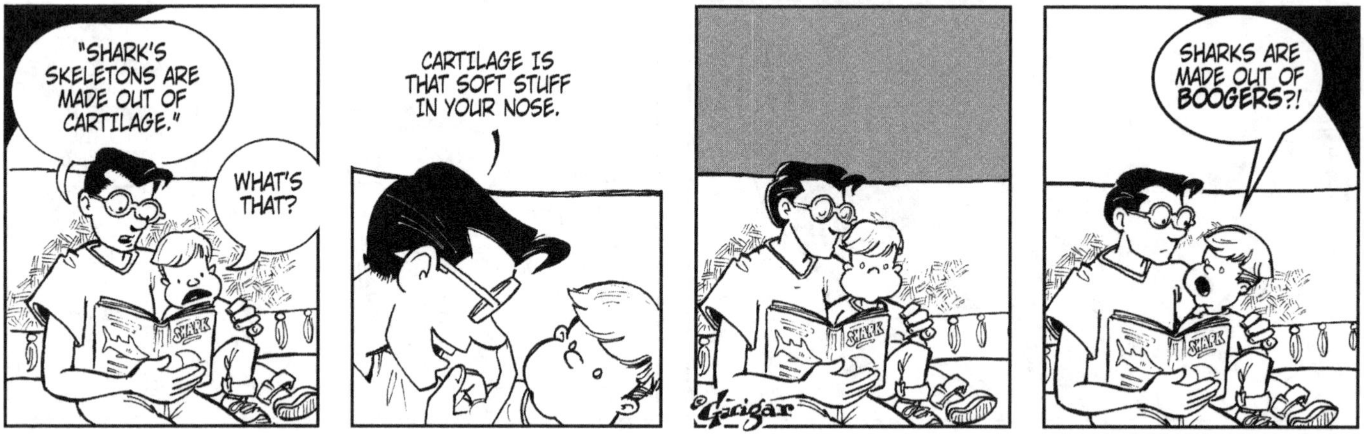
"SHARK'S SKELETONS ARE MADE OUT OF CARTILAGE."
WHAT'S THAT?
SHARK
CARTILAGE IS THAT SOFT STUFF IN YOUR NOSE.
SHARKS ARE MADE OUT OF **BOOGERS**?!

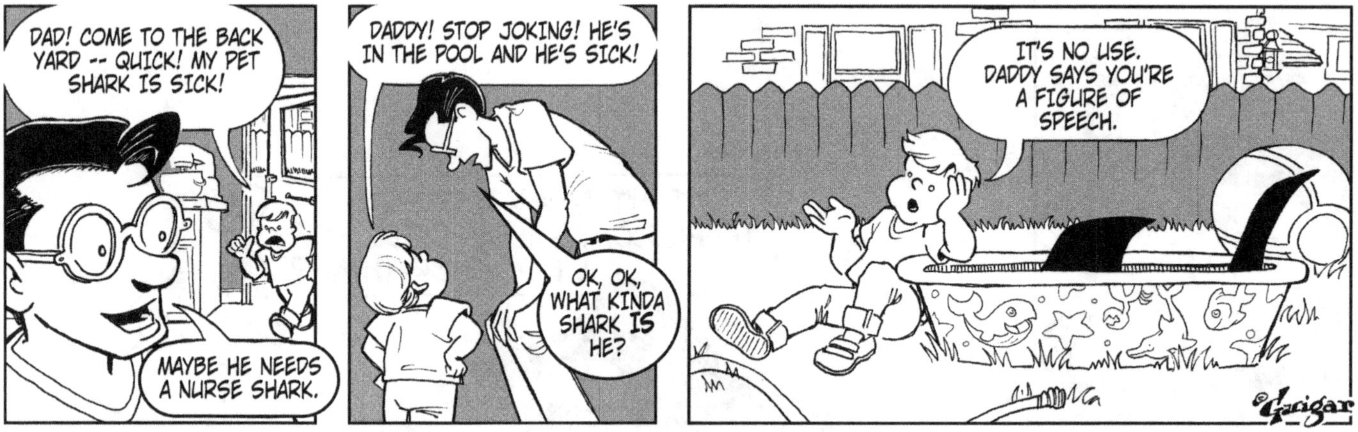
DAD! COME TO THE BACK YARD -- QUICK! MY PET SHARK IS SICK!
MAYBE HE NEEDS A NURSE SHARK.
DADDY! STOP JOKING! HE'S IN THE POOL AND HE'S SICK!
OK, OK, WHAT KINDA SHARK **IS** HE?
IT'S NO USE. DADDY SAYS YOU'RE A FIGURE OF SPEECH.

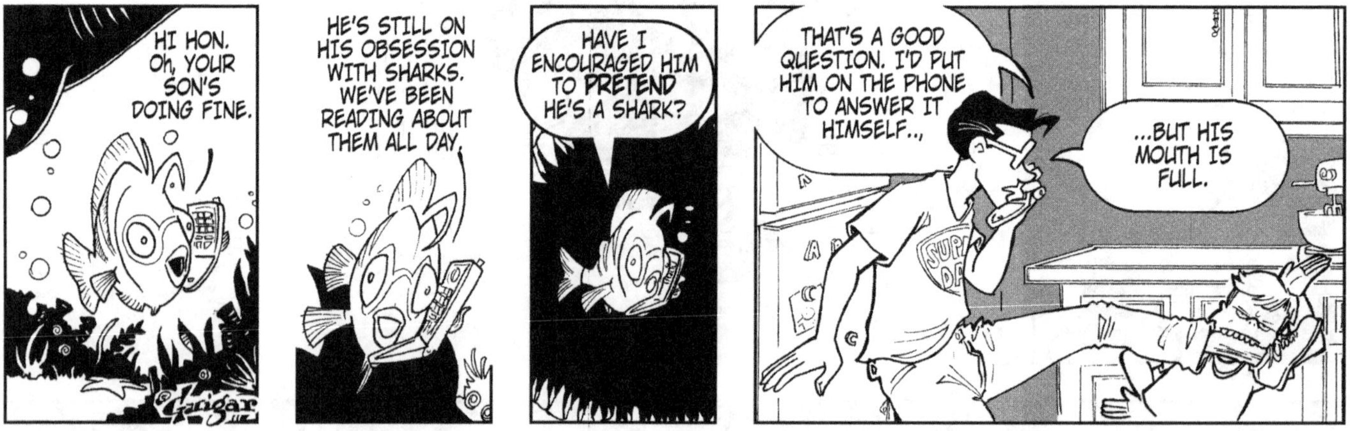
HI HON. Oh, YOUR SON'S DOING FINE.
HE'S STILL ON HIS OBSESSION WITH SHARKS. WE'VE BEEN READING ABOUT THEM ALL DAY.
HAVE I ENCOURAGED HIM TO **PRETEND** HE'S A SHARK?
THAT'S A GOOD QUESTION. I'D PUT HIM ON THE PHONE TO ANSWER IT HIMSELF...,
...BUT HIS MOUTH IS FULL.

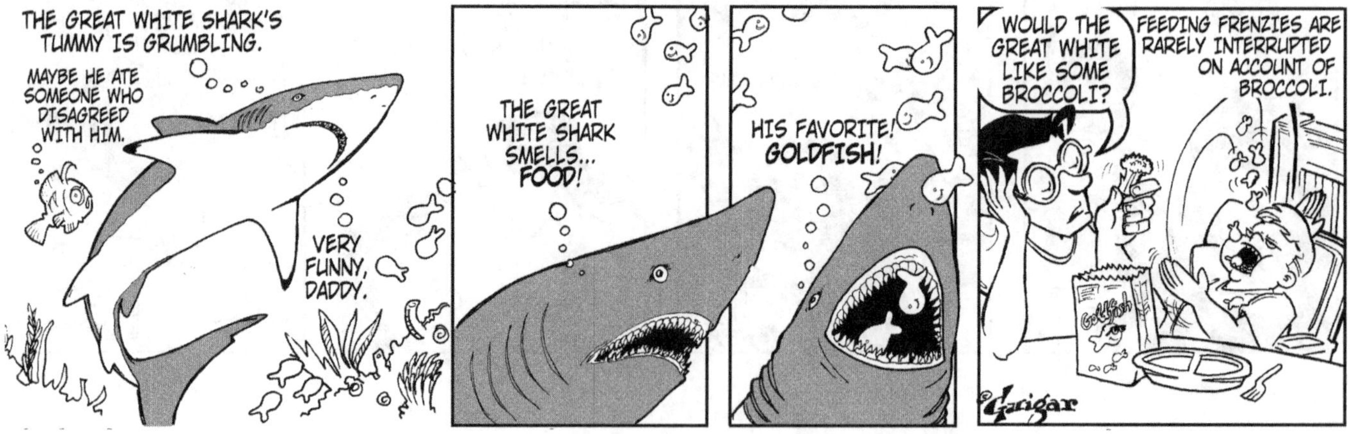
THE GREAT WHITE SHARK'S TUMMY IS GRUMBLING.
MAYBE HE ATE SOMEONE WHO DISAGREED WITH HIM.
VERY FUNNY, DADDY.
THE GREAT WHITE SHARK SMELLS... **FOOD**!
HIS FAVORITE! **GOLDFISH**!
WOULD THE GREAT WHITE LIKE SOME BROCCOLI?
FEEDING FRENZIES ARE RARELY INTERRUPTED ON ACCOUNT OF BROCCOLI.

HI HONEY... WE'RE JUST FINISHING UP LUNCH.

THE GOOD NEWS IS HIS OBSESSION WITH SHARKS HAS MADE IT SO I DON'T HAVE ANY TROUBLE GETTING HIM TO BRUSH HIS TEETH.

THE BAD NEWS...?

WE NEED TO START BUYING TOOTHBRUSHES IN BULK.

IT DOESN'T SOUNDS AS IF MISS MATCH WAS ABLE TO FIND OUT VERY MUCH ABOUT WHAT THE GREEN DOT STOOD FOR.

I WAS ABOUT TO ASK FOR DETAILS, BUT SHE HAD TO TAKE A TELEPHONE CALL. AND, OF COURSE, MY PHONE RINGS CONSTANTLY.

EVIL INC., HOW MAY I MISDIRECT YOUR CALL?

I JUST SIGNED A CONTRACT WITH THE DEVIL, BUT I CHANGED MY MIND. HOW CAN I GET OUT OF IT?

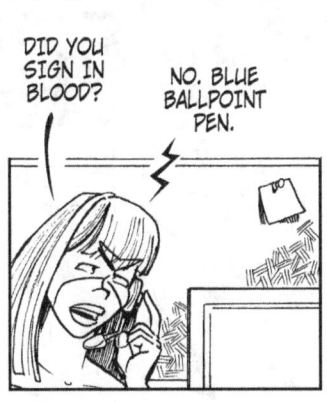

DID YOU SIGN IN BLOOD?

NO. BLUE BALLPOINT PEN.

DID YOU SMELL BRIMSTONE?

NO. "RIGHT GUARD."

DID YOU GET YOUR FONDEST WISH?

NO. ACCESS TO SOME TREAD-MILLS AND A YUCKY POOL.

SIR... YOU DIDN'T SIGN A DEAL WITH THE DEVIL — YOU SIGNED A MEMBERSHIP AT A GYM!

HOW DO I GET OUT?

PRICK YOUR FINGER AND PRACTICE YOUR PEN-MANSHIP...

EVIL INC., HOW MAY I MISDIRECT YOUR CALL?

YOU ACCIDENTALLY PULLED THE PIN ON ONE OF OUR ATOMIC HAND GRENADES?! OK. STAY CALM. IT WON'T EXPLODE AS LONG AS YOUR HAND IS ON THE SAFETY LEVER.

I'M GOING TO CONNECT YOU WITH ONE OF OUR EMERGENCY TECHNICIANS. THEY'LL WALK YOU THROUGH A DISARMAMENT PROCEDURE.

PLEASE HOLD.
...
TIGHTLY.

EVIL INCORPORATED... HOW MAY I MISDIRECT YOUR CALL?

ARE THERE ANY JOB OPEN-INGS THERE?

I CAN TAKE YOUR INFORMATION, MISTER...

AMAZO... I READ MINDS... AND AMAZO IS A PERFECTLY GOOD NAME FOR A PSYCHIC!

WOW! YOU ARE GOOD! YOU READ MY MIND!

I CAN START NEXT WEEK... AND IT'S "PSYCHIC" -- NOT "PSYCHOTIC!"

OK... THAT TIME I WASN'T THINKING ANYTHING.

OOPS. SORRY. OK... MAYBE IT'S A LITTLE OF BOTH.

SOMETIMES MY PHONE ACTUALLY STOPS RINGING.

I LIVE FOR THAT.

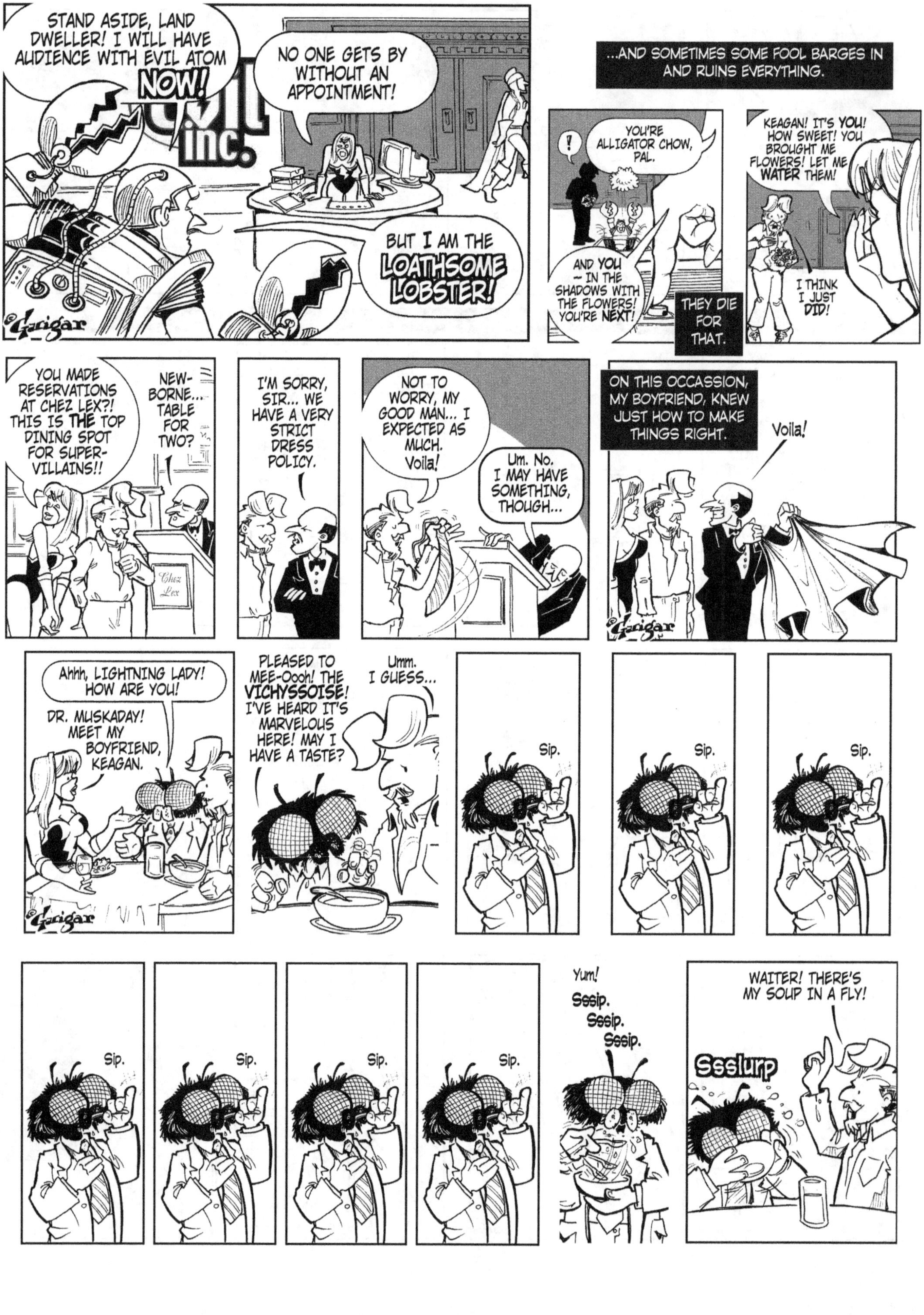

STAND ASIDE, LAND DWELLER! I WILL HAVE AUDIENCE WITH EVIL ATOM NOW!
NO ONE GETS BY WITHOUT AN APPOINTMENT!
Evil inc.
BUT I AM THE LOATHSOME LOBSTER!
©Garigar
...AND SOMETIMES SOME FOOL BARGES IN AND RUINS EVERYTHING.
!
YOU'RE ALLIGATOR CHOW, PAL.
AND YOU – IN THE SHADOWS WITH THE FLOWERS! YOU'RE NEXT!
THEY DIE FOR THAT.
KEAGAN! IT'S YOU! HOW SWEET! YOU BROUGHT ME FLOWERS! LET ME WATER THEM!
I THINK I JUST DID!
YOU MADE RESERVATIONS AT CHEZ LEX?! THIS IS THE TOP DINING SPOT FOR SUPER-VILLAINS!!
NEW-BORNE... TABLE FOR TWO?
Chez Lex
I'M SORRY, SIR... WE HAVE A VERY STRICT DRESS POLICY.
NOT TO WORRY, MY GOOD MAN... I EXPECTED AS MUCH. Voila!
Um. No. I MAY HAVE SOMETHING, THOUGH...
ON THIS OCCASSION, MY BOYFRIEND, KNEW JUST HOW TO MAKE THINGS RIGHT.
Voila!
©Garigar
Ahhh, LIGHTNING LADY! HOW ARE YOU!
DR. MUSKADAY! MEET MY BOYFRIEND, KEAGAN.
©Garigar
PLEASED TO MEE-Oooh! THE VICHYSSOISE! I'VE HEARD IT'S MARVELOUS HERE! MAY I HAVE A TASTE?
Umm. I GUESS...
Sip.
Sip.
Sip.
Sip.
Sip.
Sip.
Sip.
Yum!
Sssip.
Sssip.
Sssip.
Ssslurp
WAITER! THERE'S MY SOUP IN A FLY!

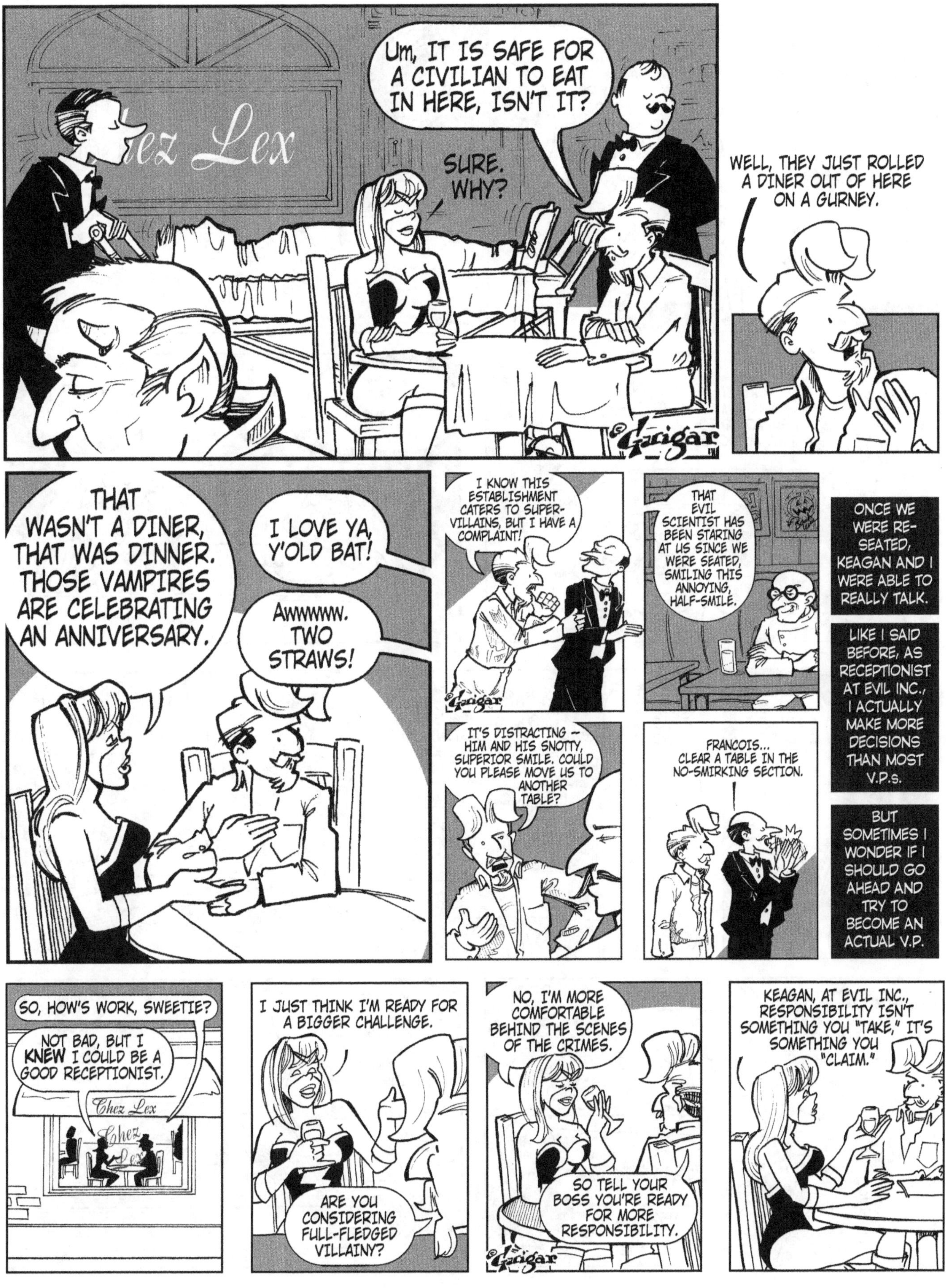
Chez Lex
SURE. WHY?
Um, IT IS SAFE FOR A CIVILIAN TO EAT IN HERE, ISN'T IT?
WELL, THEY JUST ROLLED A DINER OUT OF HERE ON A GURNEY.
THAT WASN'T A DINER, THAT WAS DINNER. THOSE VAMPIRES ARE CELEBRATING AN ANNIVERSARY.
I LOVE YA, Y'OLD BAT!
Awwwww. TWO STRAWS!
I KNOW THIS ESTABLISHMENT CATERS TO SUPER-VILLAINS, BUT I HAVE A COMPLAINT!
THAT EVIL SCIENTIST HAS BEEN STARING AT US SINCE WE WERE SEATED, SMILING THIS ANNOYING, HALF-SMILE.
IT'S DISTRACTING -- HIM AND HIS SNOTTY, SUPERIOR SMILE. COULD YOU PLEASE MOVE US TO ANOTHER TABLE?
FRANCOIS... CLEAR A TABLE IN THE NO-SMIRKING SECTION.
ONCE WE WERE RE-SEATED, KEAGAN AND I WERE ABLE TO REALLY TALK.
LIKE I SAID BEFORE, AS RECEPTIONIST AT EVIL INC., I ACTUALLY MAKE MORE DECISIONS THAN MOST V.P.s.
BUT SOMETIMES I WONDER IF I SHOULD GO AHEAD AND TRY TO BECOME AN ACTUAL V.P.
SO, HOW'S WORK, SWEETIE?
NOT BAD, BUT I KNEW I COULD BE A GOOD RECEPTIONIST.
Chez Lex
I JUST THINK I'M READY FOR A BIGGER CHALLENGE.
ARE YOU CONSIDERING FULL-FLEDGED VILLAINY?
NO, I'M MORE COMFORTABLE BEHIND THE SCENES OF THE CRIMES.
SO TELL YOUR BOSS YOU'RE READY FOR MORE RESPONSIBILITY.
KEAGAN, AT EVIL INC., RESPONSIBILITY ISN'T SOMETHING YOU "TAKE," IT'S SOMETHING YOU "CLAIM."

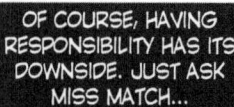

OF COURSE, HAVING RESPONSIBILITY HAS ITS DOWNSIDE. JUST ASK MISS MATCH...

WELL... HAVE YOU COME UP WITH A SCHEME FOR DR. HAYNUS?

HUH? WHA-?

YOU HEARD ME, MATCH.

I HATE WHEN YOU DO THAT. I DESIGNED A BATTLE TANK. THEY'RE TESTING IT NOW.

IS HE HAPPY?

I'LL CALL...

I DUNNO. HE'S STILL TINKLING ON THE TIRES.

WE'VE HAD A SET-BACK. DR. HAYNUS DOESN'T HAVE OPPOSABLE THUMBS, SO HE CAN'T DRIVE THE TANK.

GREAT! WHAT AM I SUPPOSED TO TELL MY BOSS?

DON'T WORRY! WE FOUND HIM A DESIGNATED DRIVER!

EVIL INC. MECHANICAL ENGINEERING

⸮sigh⸮ NOW WHAT?

I CAN'T DRIVE STICK SHIFT.

OK, MUSKIDAY, LET'S PUT THIS BATTLE TANK TO THE TEST.

SURE. JUST AS SOON AS I ADJUST THE MIRROR AND FASTEN MY SEAT-BELT.

YOU'RE A VILLAIN. PLEASE ACT LIKE IT.

♪ Popular! You're gonna be Pop-uUUU-Lar! ♪

PLEASE TELL ME WE'RE NOT LISTENING TO SHOW TUNES.

IT'S THE CAST RECORDING OF "WICKED."

IT DOESN'T SOUND EVIL.

$180 PER SEAT... AND I'M NOT SURE IF SOME OF IT ISN'T LIP-SYNCED.

GOT IT.

WE'RE TRAVELLING AT A PERFECTLY REASONABLE SPEED.

WE'RE GETTING PASSED BY OCTOGENARIANS.

MANIACS. FLOOR IT!

OKAY. I'LL PUT THE HAMMER DOWN... a little.

VrrroOOoom

Weee-oooh-wee

WHAT'S THAT?

GOOD AFTERNOON, OFFICER... DO I HAVE A TAILLIGHT OUT?

THAT... AND YOU'RE DRIVING A BATTLE TANK IN A RESIDENTIAL AREA...

Ahhhh... IF YOU WOULD JUST KINDLY POINT US TO THE HIGHWAY, THEN...

DRIVERS WANTED: DEAD OR ALIVE

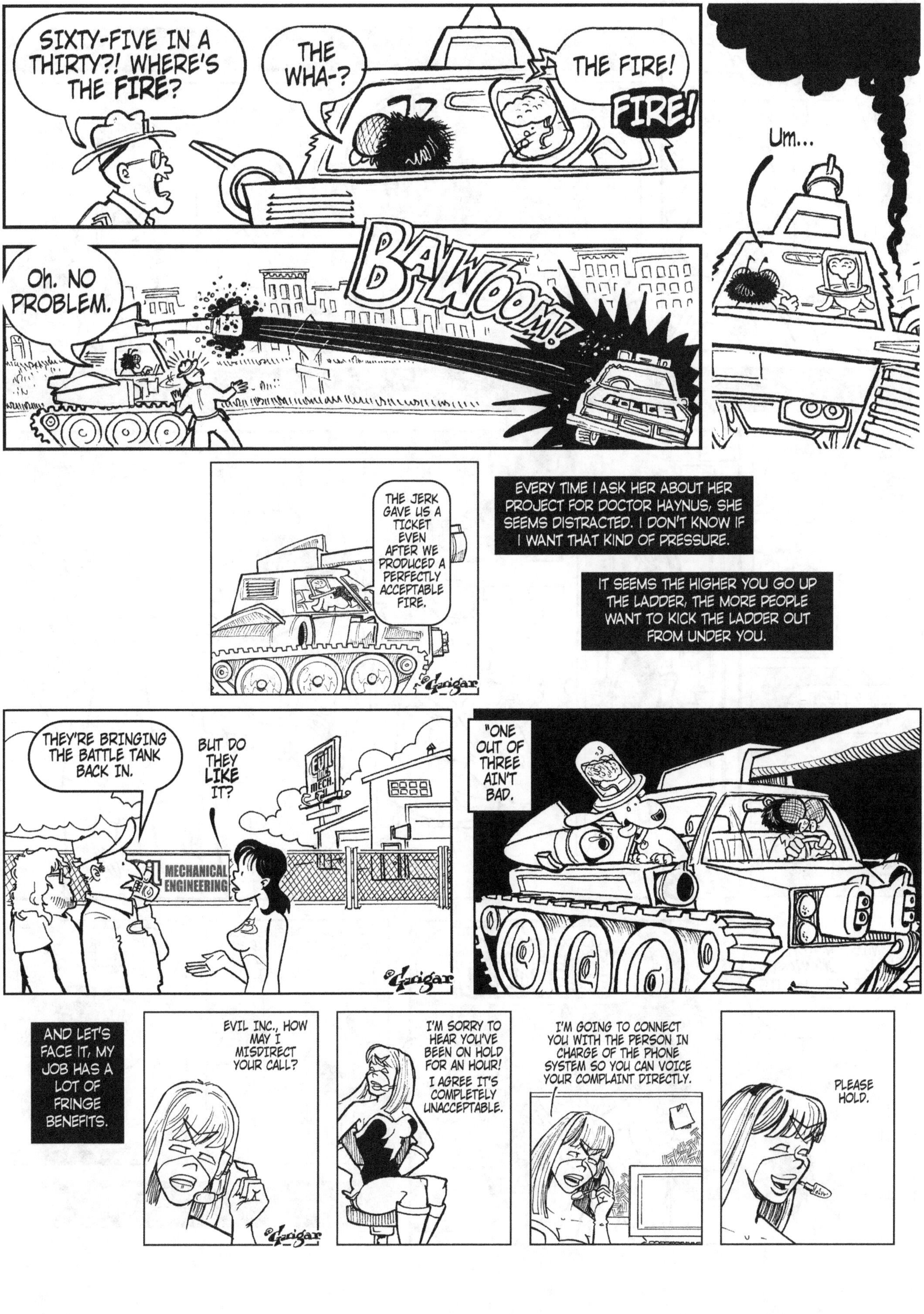

SIXTY-FIVE IN A THIRTY?! WHERE'S THE FIRE?
THE WHA-?
THE FIRE! FIRE!
Um...
Oh. NO PROBLEM.
BAWOOOM!
THE JERK GAVE US A TICKET EVEN AFTER WE PRODUCED A PERFECTLY ACCEPTABLE FIRE.
EVERY TIME I ASK HER ABOUT HER PROJECT FOR DOCTOR HAYNUS, SHE SEEMS DISTRACTED. I DON'T KNOW IF I WANT THAT KIND OF PRESSURE.
IT SEEMS THE HIGHER YOU GO UP THE LADDER, THE MORE PEOPLE WANT TO KICK THE LADDER OUT FROM UNDER YOU.
THEY'RE BRINGING THE BATTLE TANK BACK IN.
BUT DO THEY LIKE IT?
MECHANICAL ENGINEERING
"ONE OUT OF THREE AIN'T BAD.
AND LET'S FACE IT, MY JOB HAS A LOT OF FRINGE BENEFITS.
EVIL INC., HOW MAY I MISDIRECT YOUR CALL?
I'M SORRY TO HEAR YOU'VE BEEN ON HOLD FOR AN HOUR!
I AGREE IT'S COMPLETELY UNACCEPTABLE.
I'M GOING TO CONNECT YOU WITH THE PERSON IN CHARGE OF THE PHONE SYSTEM SO YOU CAN VOICE YOUR COMPLAINT DIRECTLY.
PLEASE HOLD.

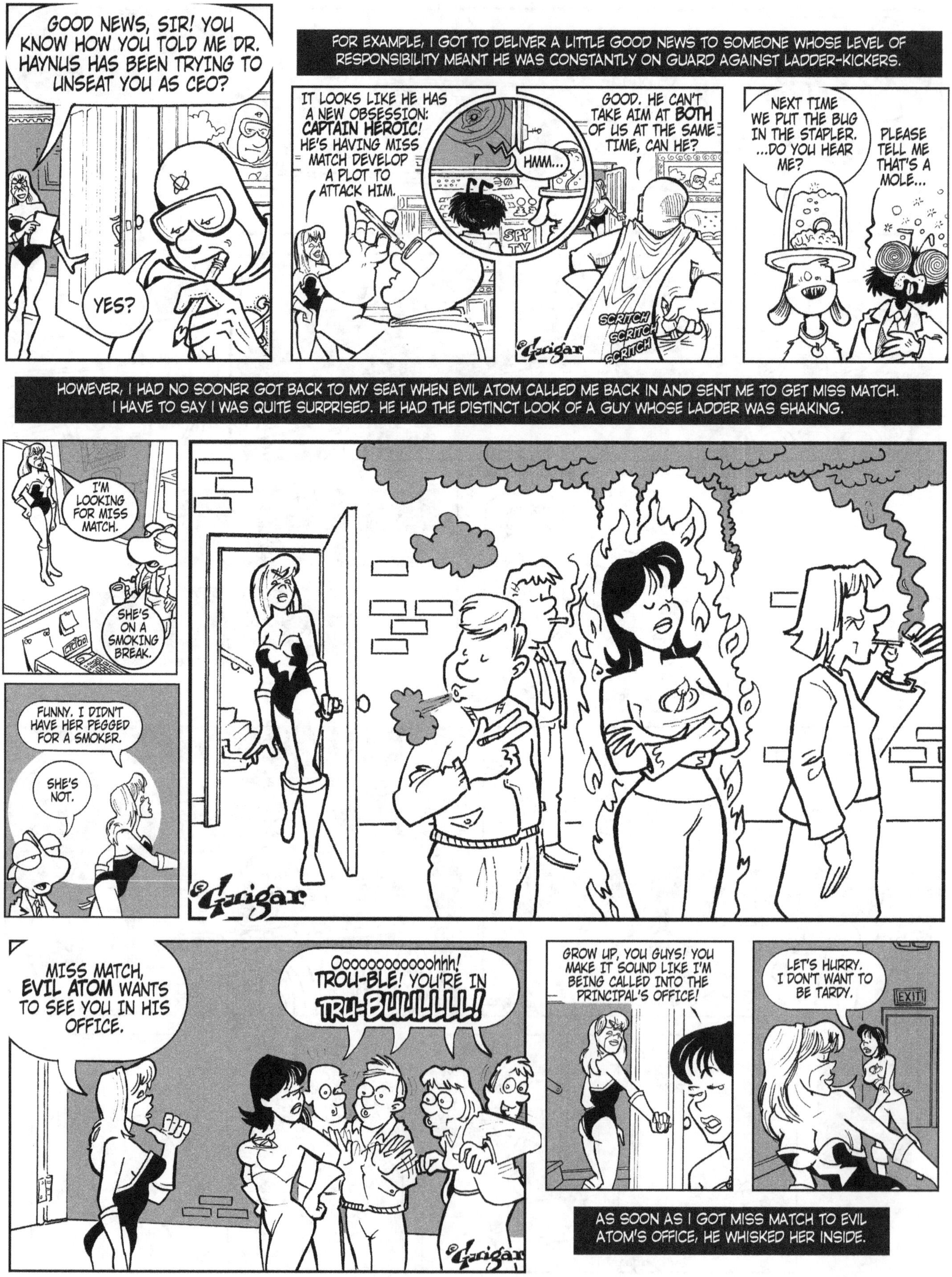
GOOD NEWS, SIR! YOU KNOW HOW YOU TOLD ME DR. HAYNUS HAS BEEN TRYING TO UNSEAT YOU AS CEO?
YES?
FOR EXAMPLE, I GOT TO DELIVER A LITTLE GOOD NEWS TO SOMEONE WHOSE LEVEL OF RESPONSIBILITY MEANT HE WAS CONSTANTLY ON GUARD AGAINST LADDER-KICKERS.
IT LOOKS LIKE HE HAS A NEW OBSESSION: CAPTAIN HEROIC! HE'S HAVING MISS MATCH DEVELOP A PLOT TO ATTACK HIM.
HMM...
SPY TV
GOOD. HE CAN'T TAKE AIM AT BOTH OF US AT THE SAME TIME, CAN HE?
SCRITCH SCRITCH SCRITCH
NEXT TIME WE PUT THE BUG IN THE STAPLER. ...DO YOU HEAR ME?
PLEASE TELL ME THAT'S A MOLE...
HOWEVER, I HAD NO SOONER GOT BACK TO MY SEAT WHEN EVIL ATOM CALLED ME BACK IN AND SENT ME TO GET MISS MATCH. I HAVE TO SAY I WAS QUITE SURPRISED. HE HAD THE DISTINCT LOOK OF A GUY WHOSE LADDER WAS SHAKING.
I'M LOOKING FOR MISS MATCH.
SHE'S ON A SMOKING BREAK.
FUNNY. I DIDN'T HAVE HER PEGGED FOR A SMOKER.
SHE'S NOT.
MISS MATCH, EVIL ATOM WANTS TO SEE YOU IN HIS OFFICE.
Oooooooooooohhh! TROU-BLE! YOU'RE IN TRU-BUULLLLL!
GROW UP, YOU GUYS! YOU MAKE IT SOUND LIKE I'M BEING CALLED INTO THE PRINCIPAL'S OFFICE!
LET'S HURRY. I DON'T WANT TO BE TARDY.
EXIT
AS SOON AS I GOT MISS MATCH TO EVIL ATOM'S OFFICE, HE WHISKED HER INSIDE.

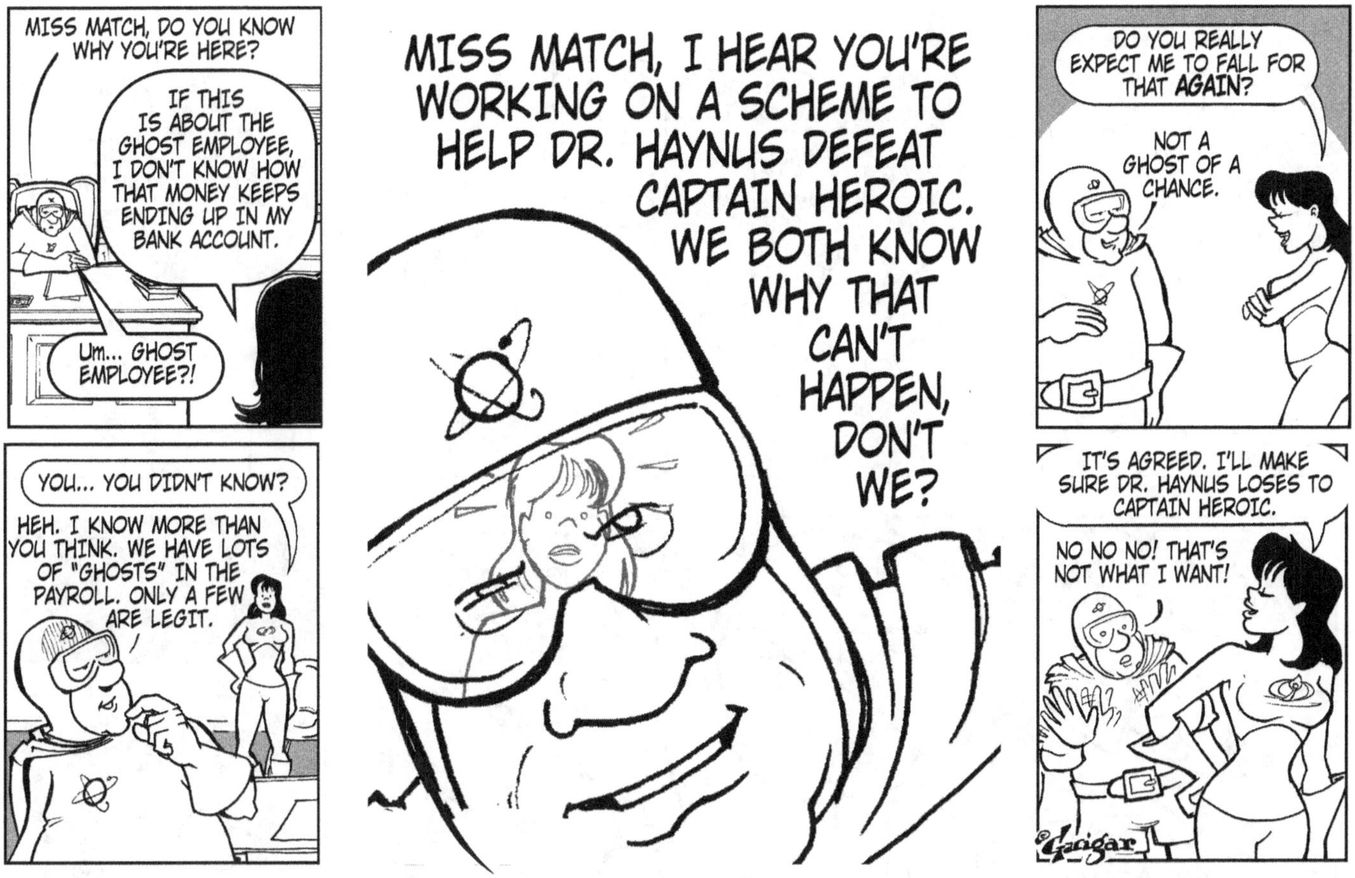

MISS MATCH, DO YOU KNOW WHY YOU'RE HERE?
IF THIS IS ABOUT THE GHOST EMPLOYEE, I DON'T KNOW HOW THAT MONEY KEEPS ENDING UP IN MY BANK ACCOUNT.
Um... GHOST EMPLOYEE?!
YOU... YOU DIDN'T KNOW?
HEH. I KNOW MORE THAN YOU THINK. WE HAVE LOTS OF "GHOSTS" IN THE PAYROLL. ONLY A FEW ARE LEGIT.
MISS MATCH, I HEAR YOU'RE WORKING ON A SCHEME TO HELP DR. HAYNUS DEFEAT CAPTAIN HEROIC. WE BOTH KNOW WHY THAT CAN'T HAPPEN, DON'T WE?
DO YOU REALLY EXPECT ME TO FALL FOR THAT AGAIN?
NOT A GHOST OF A CHANCE.
IT'S AGREED. I'LL MAKE SURE DR. HAYNUS LOSES TO CAPTAIN HEROIC.
NO NO NO! THAT'S NOT WHAT I WANT!
©Garigar

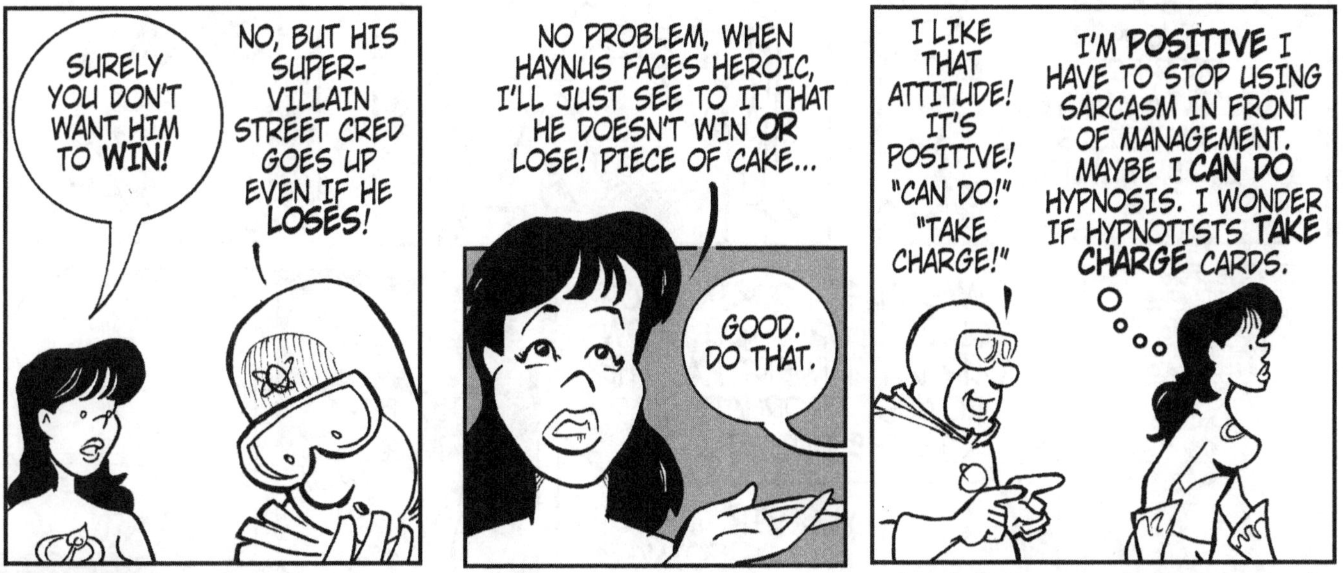

SURELY YOU DON'T WANT HIM TO WIN!
NO, BUT HIS SUPER-VILLAIN STREET CRED GOES UP EVEN IF HE LOSES!
NO PROBLEM, WHEN HAYNUS FACES HEROIC, I'LL JUST SEE TO IT THAT HE DOESN'T WIN OR LOSE! PIECE OF CAKE...
GOOD. DO THAT.
I LIKE THAT ATTITUDE! IT'S POSITIVE! "CAN DO!" "TAKE CHARGE!"
I'M POSITIVE I HAVE TO STOP USING SARCASM IN FRONT OF MANAGEMENT. MAYBE I CAN DO HYPNOSIS. I WONDER IF HYPNOTISTS TAKE CHARGE CARDS.

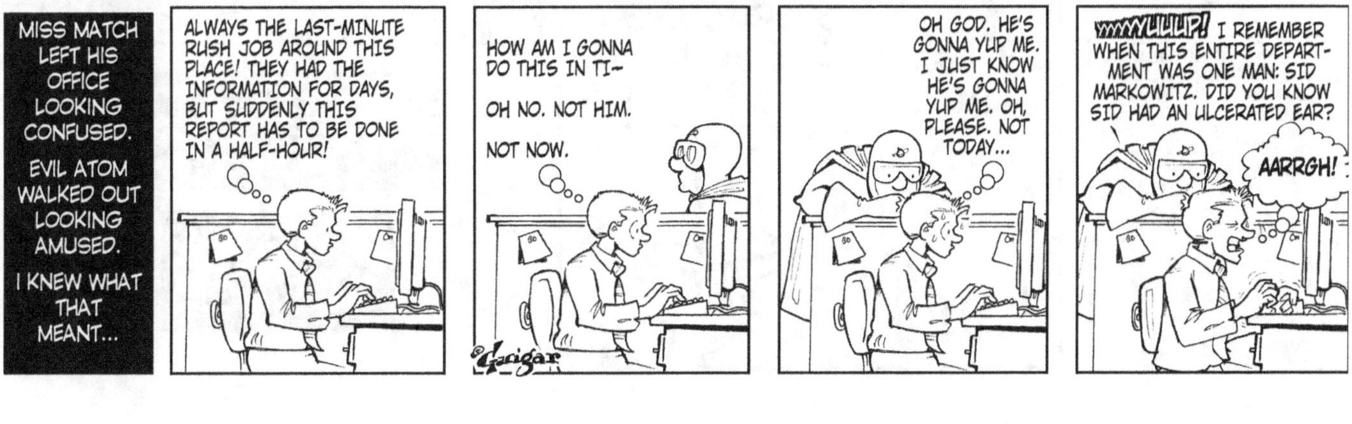

MISS MATCH LEFT HIS OFFICE LOOKING CONFUSED.
EVIL ATOM WALKED OUT LOOKING AMUSED.
I KNEW WHAT THAT MEANT...
ALWAYS THE LAST-MINUTE RUSH JOB AROUND THIS PLACE! THEY HAD THE INFORMATION FOR DAYS, BUT SUDDENLY THIS REPORT HAS TO BE DONE IN A HALF-HOUR!
HOW AM I GONNA DO THIS IN TI–
OH NO. NOT HIM.
NOT NOW.
OH GOD. HE'S GONNA YUP ME. I JUST KNOW HE'S GONNA YUP ME. OH, PLEASE. NOT TODAY...
YYYYYYULLUP! I REMEMBER WHEN THIS ENTIRE DEPART-MENT WAS ONE MAN: SID MARKOWITZ. DID YOU KNOW SID HAD AN ULCERATED EAR?
AARRGH!
©Garigar

... SOMEONE WAS GOING TO GET ABUSED.

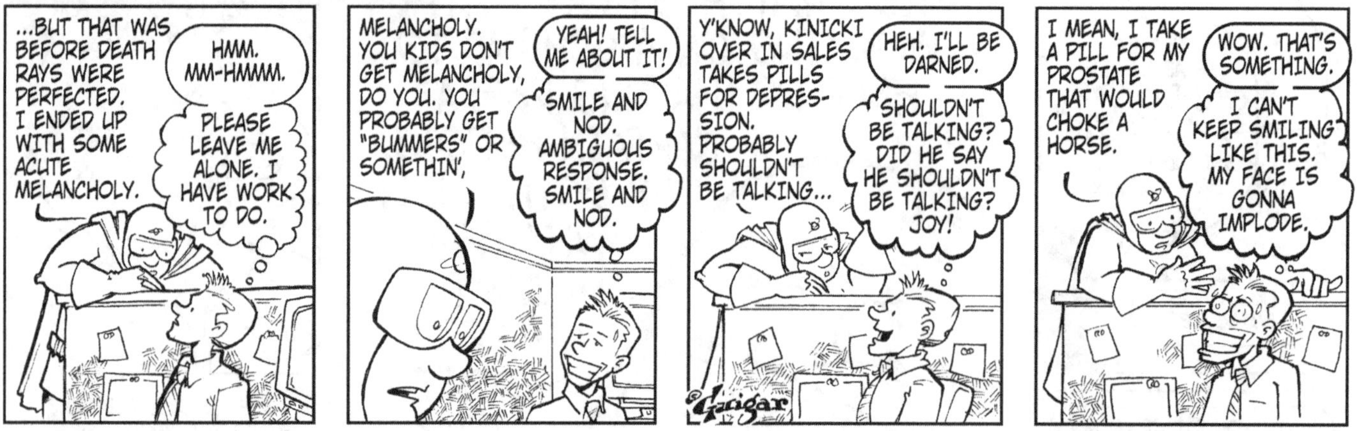
...BUT THAT WAS BEFORE DEATH RAYS WERE PERFECTED. I ENDED UP WITH SOME ACUTE MELANCHOLY.
HMM. MM-HMMM.
PLEASE LEAVE ME ALONE. I HAVE WORK TO DO.
MELANCHOLY. YOU KIDS DON'T GET MELANCHOLY, DO YOU. YOU PROBABLY GET "BUMMERS" OR SOMETHIN',
YEAH! TELL ME ABOUT IT!
SMILE AND NOD. AMBIGUOUS RESPONSE. SMILE AND NOD.
Y'KNOW, KINICKI OVER IN SALES TAKES PILLS FOR DEPRES-SION. PROBABLY SHOULDN'T BE TALKING...
HEH. I'LL BE DARNED.
SHOULDN'T BE TALKING? DID HE SAY HE SHOULDN'T BE TALKING? JOY!
I MEAN, I TAKE A PILL FOR MY PROSTATE THAT WOULD CHOKE A HORSE.
WOW. THAT'S SOMETHING.
I CAN'T KEEP SMILING LIKE THIS. MY FACE IS GONNA IMPLODE.

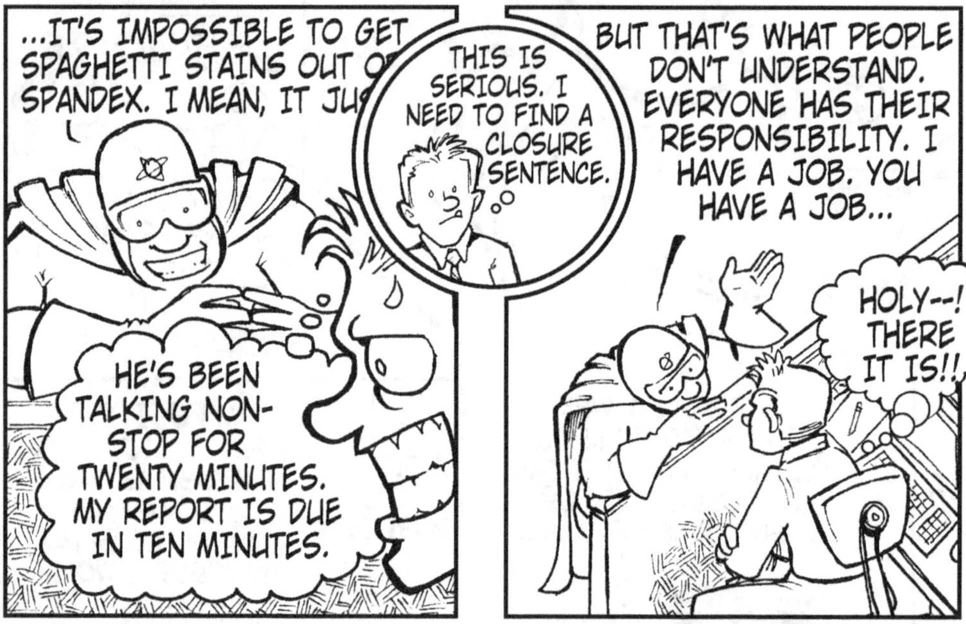
...IT'S IMPOSSIBLE TO GET SPAGHETTI STAINS OUT OF SPANDEX. I MEAN, IT JUS
THIS IS SERIOUS. I NEED TO FIND A CLOSURE SENTENCE.
HE'S BEEN TALKING NON-STOP FOR TWENTY MINUTES. MY REPORT IS DUE IN TEN MINUTES.
BUT THAT'S WHAT PEOPLE DON'T UNDERSTAND. EVERYONE HAS THEIR RESPONSIBILITY. I HAVE A JOB. YOU HAVE A JOB...
HOLY--! THERE IT IS!!

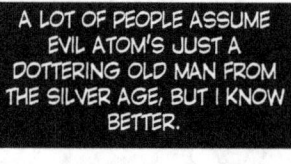

A LOT OF PEOPLE ASSUME EVIL ATOM'S JUST A DOTTERING OLD MAN FROM THE SILVER AGE, BUT I KNOW BETTER.

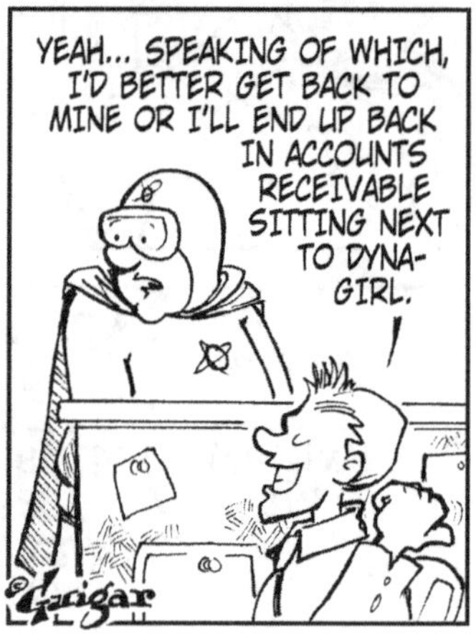
YEAH... SPEAKING OF WHICH, I'D BETTER GET BACK TO MINE OR I'LL END UP BACK IN ACCOUNTS RECEIVABLE SITTING NEXT TO DYNA-GIRL.

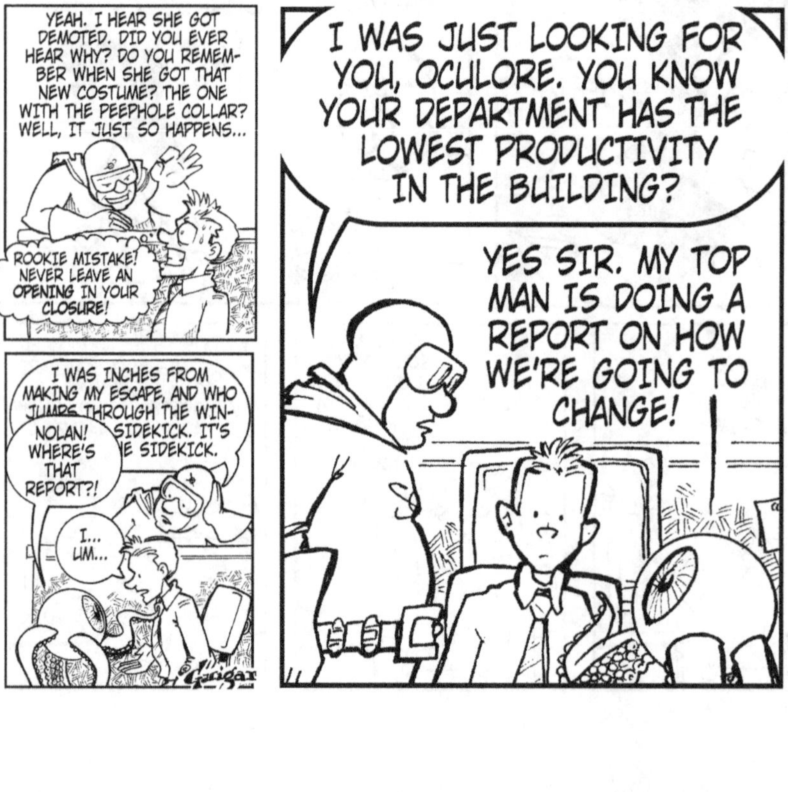
YEAH. I HEAR SHE GOT DEMOTED. DID YOU EVER HEAR WHY? DO YOU REMEM-BER WHEN SHE GOT THAT NEW COSTUME? THE ONE WITH THE PEEPHOLE COLLAR? WELL, IT JUST SO HAPPENS...
ROOKIE MISTAKE! NEVER LEAVE AN OPENING IN YOUR CLOSURE!
I WAS INCHES FROM MAKING MY ESCAPE, AND WHO JUMPS THROUGH THE WIN-
SIDEKICK. IT'S
E SIDEKICK.
NOLAN! WHERE'S THAT REPORT?!
I... UM...
I WAS JUST LOOKING FOR YOU, OCULORE. YOU KNOW YOUR DEPARTMENT HAS THE LOWEST PRODUCTIVITY IN THE BUILDING?
YES SIR. MY TOP MAN IS DOING A REPORT ON HOW WE'RE GOING TO CHANGE!

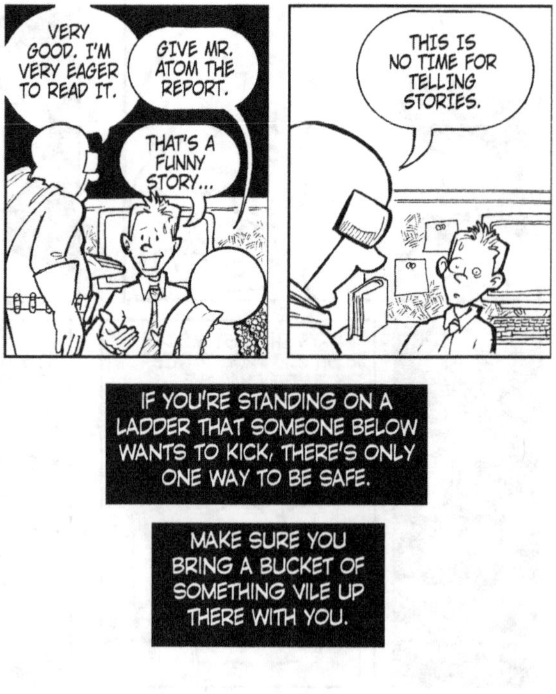
VERY GOOD. I'M VERY EAGER TO READ IT.
GIVE MR. ATOM THE REPORT.
THAT'S A FUNNY STORY...
THIS IS NO TIME FOR TELLING STORIES.

IF YOU'RE STANDING ON A LADDER THAT SOMEONE BELOW WANTS TO KICK, THERE'S ONLY ONE WAY TO BE SAFE.

MAKE SURE YOU BRING A BUCKET OF SOMETHING VILE UP THERE WITH YOU.

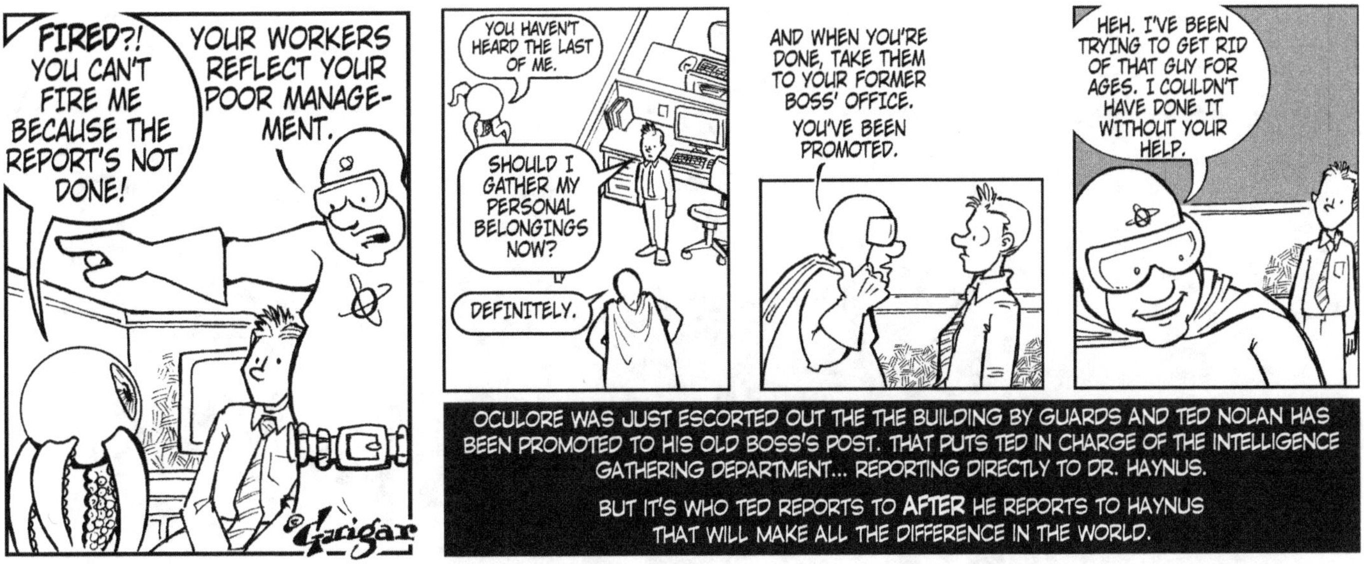

FIRED?! YOU CAN'T FIRE ME BECAUSE THE REPORT'S NOT DONE!
YOUR WORKERS REFLECT YOUR POOR MANAGEMENT.
YOU HAVEN'T HEARD THE LAST OF ME.
SHOULD I GATHER MY PERSONAL BELONGINGS NOW?
DEFINITELY.
AND WHEN YOU'RE DONE, TAKE THEM TO YOUR FORMER BOSS' OFFICE.
YOU'VE BEEN PROMOTED.
HEH. I'VE BEEN TRYING TO GET RID OF THAT GUY FOR AGES. I COULDN'T HAVE DONE IT WITHOUT YOUR HELP.
OCULORE WAS JUST ESCORTED OUT THE THE BUILDING BY GUARDS AND TED NOLAN HAS BEEN PROMOTED TO HIS OLD BOSS'S POST. THAT PUTS TED IN CHARGE OF THE INTELLIGENCE GATHERING DEPARTMENT... REPORTING DIRECTLY TO DR. HAYNUS.
BUT IT'S WHO TED REPORTS TO AFTER HE REPORTS TO HAYNUS THAT WILL MAKE ALL THE DIFFERENCE IN THE WORLD.
©Garigar

Intermission: Your call is very important to us...

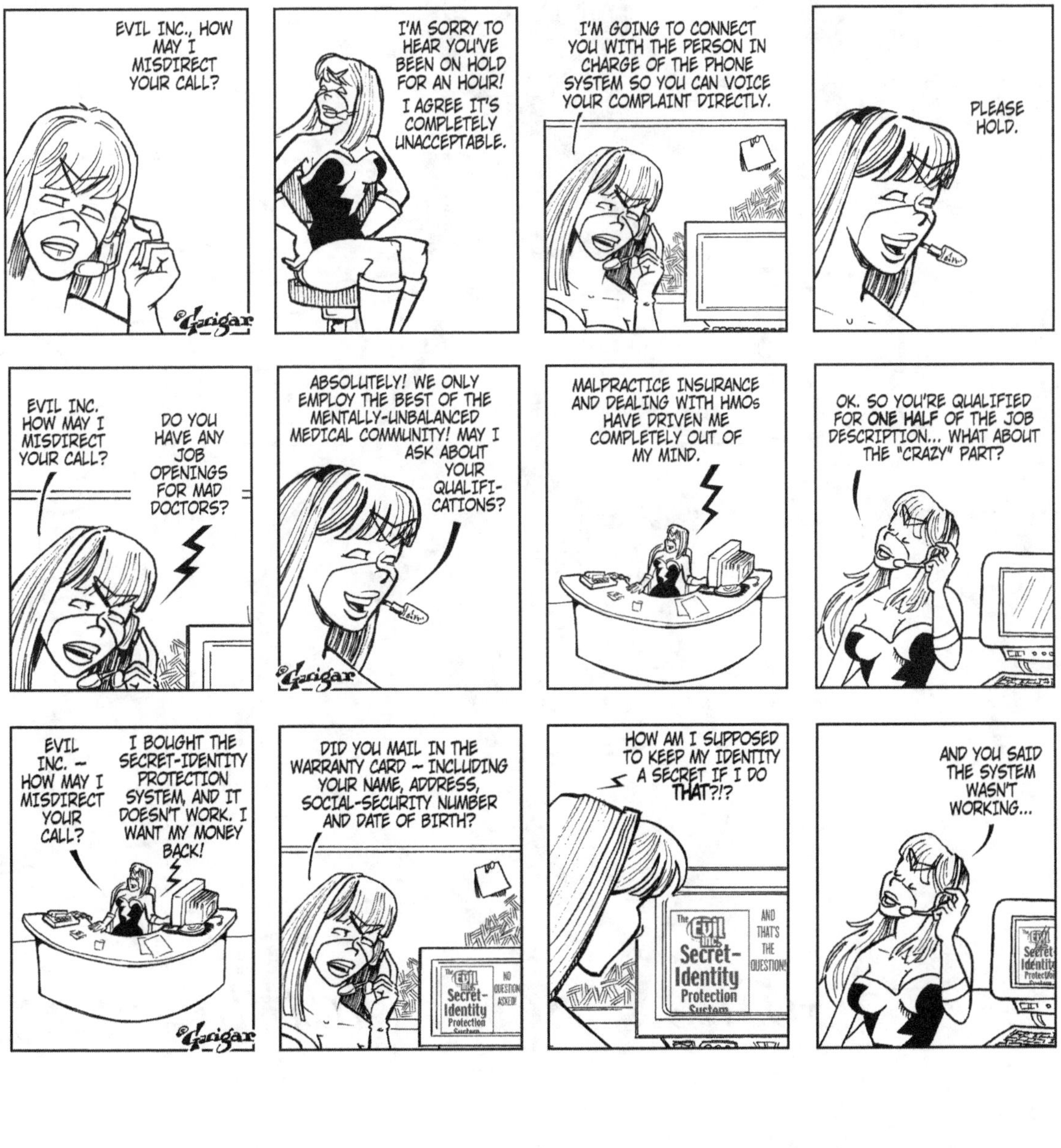

EVIL INC., HOW MAY I MISDIRECT YOUR CALL?
I'M SORRY TO HEAR YOU'VE BEEN ON HOLD FOR AN HOUR! I AGREE IT'S COMPLETELY UNACCEPTABLE.
I'M GOING TO CONNECT YOU WITH THE PERSON IN CHARGE OF THE PHONE SYSTEM SO YOU CAN VOICE YOUR COMPLAINT DIRECTLY.
PLEASE HOLD.
©Garigar
EVIL INC. HOW MAY I MISDIRECT YOUR CALL?
DO YOU HAVE ANY JOB OPENINGS FOR MAD DOCTORS?
ABSOLUTELY! WE ONLY EMPLOY THE BEST OF THE MENTALLY-UNBALANCED MEDICAL COMMUNITY! MAY I ASK ABOUT YOUR QUALIFICATIONS?
MALPRACTICE INSURANCE AND DEALING WITH HMOs HAVE DRIVEN ME COMPLETELY OUT OF MY MIND.
OK. SO YOU'RE QUALIFIED FOR ONE HALF OF THE JOB DESCRIPTION... WHAT ABOUT THE "CRAZY" PART?
©Garigar
EVIL INC. ~ HOW MAY I MISDIRECT YOUR CALL?
I BOUGHT THE SECRET-IDENTITY PROTECTION SYSTEM, AND IT DOESN'T WORK. I WANT MY MONEY BACK!
DID YOU MAIL IN THE WARRANTY CARD ~ INCLUDING YOUR NAME, ADDRESS, SOCIAL-SECURITY NUMBER AND DATE OF BIRTH?
NO QUESTIONS ASKED!
HOW AM I SUPPOSED TO KEEP MY IDENTITY A SECRET IF I DO THAT?!?
The Evil Inc. Secret-Identity Protection System
AND THAT'S THE QUESTION!
AND YOU SAID THE SYSTEM WASN'T WORKING...
©Garigar

Chapter 2

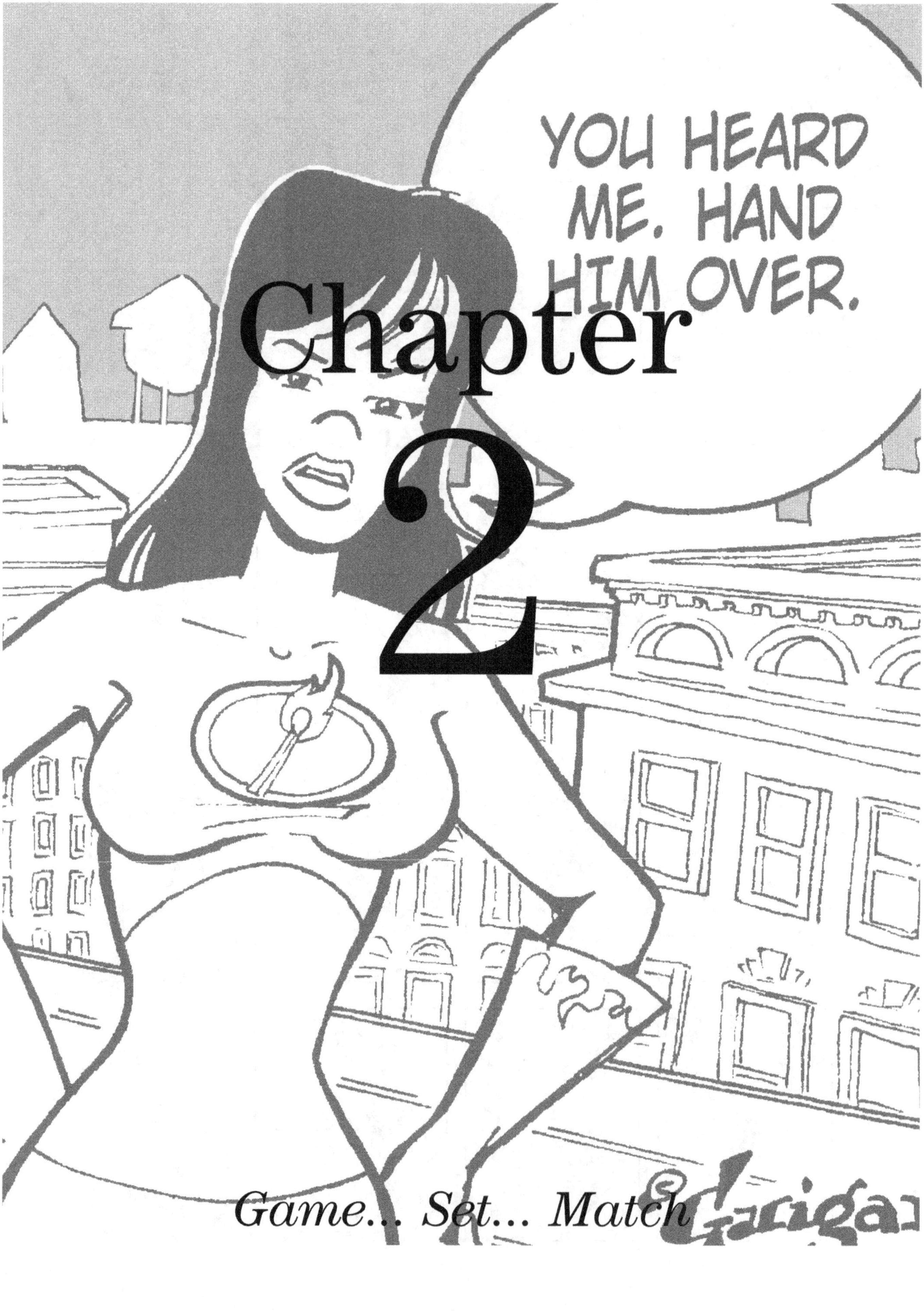
YOU HEARD ME. HAND HIM OVER.
Garigan

Game... Set... Match

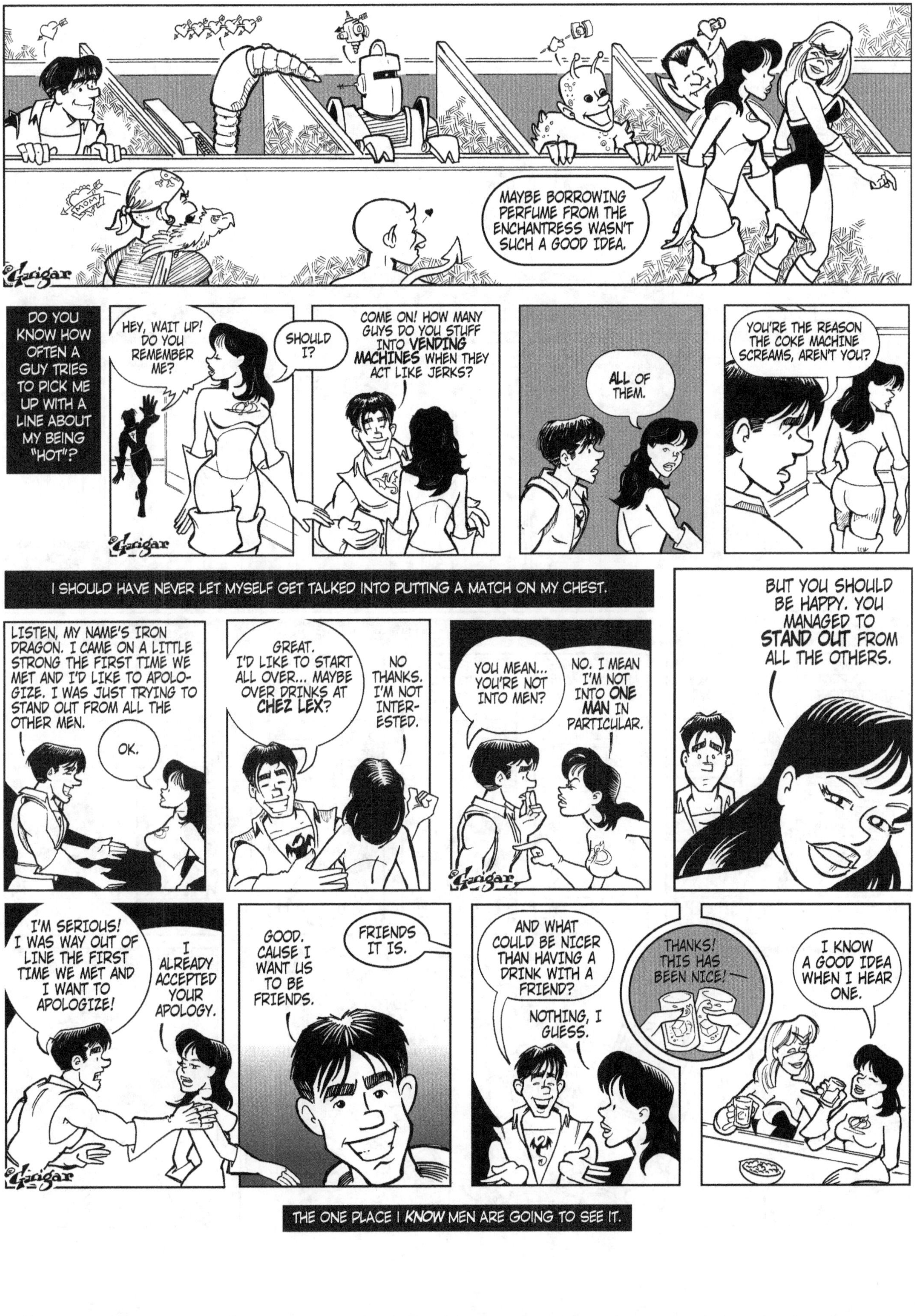
MOM
MAYBE BORROWING PERFUME FROM THE ENCHANTRESS WASN'T SUCH A GOOD IDEA.
DO YOU KNOW HOW OFTEN A GUY TRIES TO PICK ME UP WITH A LINE ABOUT MY BEING "HOT"?
HEY, WAIT UP! DO YOU REMEMBER ME?
SHOULD I?
COME ON! HOW MANY GUYS DO YOU STUFF INTO VENDING MACHINES WHEN THEY ACT LIKE JERKS?
ALL OF THEM.
YOU'RE THE REASON THE COKE MACHINE SCREAMS, AREN'T YOU?
I SHOULD HAVE NEVER LET MYSELF GET TALKED INTO PUTTING A MATCH ON MY CHEST.
LISTEN, MY NAME'S IRON DRAGON. I CAME ON A LITTLE STRONG THE FIRST TIME WE MET AND I'D LIKE TO APOLOGIZE. I WAS JUST TRYING TO STAND OUT FROM ALL THE OTHER MEN.
OK.
GREAT. I'D LIKE TO START ALL OVER... MAYBE OVER DRINKS AT CHEZ LEX?
NO THANKS. I'M NOT INTERESTED.
YOU MEAN... YOU'RE NOT INTO MEN?
NO. I MEAN I'M NOT INTO ONE MAN IN PARTICULAR.
BUT YOU SHOULD BE HAPPY. YOU MANAGED TO STAND OUT FROM ALL THE OTHERS.
I'M SERIOUS! I WAS WAY OUT OF LINE THE FIRST TIME WE MET AND I WANT TO APOLOGIZE!
I ALREADY ACCEPTED YOUR APOLOGY.
GOOD. CAUSE I WANT US TO BE FRIENDS.
FRIENDS IT IS.
AND WHAT COULD BE NICER THAN HAVING A DRINK WITH A FRIEND?
NOTHING, I GUESS.
THANKS! THIS HAS BEEN NICE!
I KNOW A GOOD IDEA WHEN I HEAR ONE.
THE ONE PLACE I KNOW MEN ARE GOING TO SEE IT.

EXCUSE ME. MY NAME'S IRON DRAGON YOU KNOW MISS MATCH, RIGHT? YOU'RE FRIENDS? DOES SHE EVER MENTION ME?

SHE MENTIONED WHAT SHE'D LOVE TO DO TO YOU.

R-REALLY?

YEAH. SHE SAID SHE'D LOVE TO WIPE THAT FRATBOY SMIRK OFF YOUR FACE.

REALLY? ARE YOU SURE IT WASN'T "LIKE"? SHE SAID "LOVE"?

LISTEN, JUST GIVE ME THE "DO YOU LIKE ME ☐YES ☐NO" NOTE AND I'LL GIVE IT TO HER IN HOMEROOM.

VERY FUNNY.

RIIIPP

THEY JUST DON'T GET IT. THERE'S NOT A MAN AT EVIL INC THAT INTERESTS ME. -- AND BEFORE YOU GET EXCITED, I'M NOT INTO WOMEN EITHER.

NOT THAT MY CHOICES END THERE ...

...BUT YOU GET THE PICTURE...

THERE'S NO GOOD PLACE TO START EXPLAINING MY SITUATION, SO I'LL START WITH TV NEWS... A VERY NO-GOOD PLACE...

WAL-MART MISSED PROFIT EXPECTATIONS...

EFD EIC EP
21.30 60.33 11.33

FUELING FEARS OF AN ECONOMIC SLOWDOWN.

EFD ⅃I...ᴄEP
21.30 60.33 11.33

AND HIGH GAS PRICES HAVE HURT SPENDING.

EFD ⅃I FP
21.30 60.33 7.33

BUT THERE'S ONE WINNER ON WALL STREET...

EFD ⅃I EP
21.30 60.33

SHARES OF EVIL INC. INCREASED

EFD ⅃I EP
21 30 60.33

...A WHOMPING $11.30!!

EW EFD ⅃IC E
42.01 21 60.63

...THE HARD WAY.

BURP!

EW EFD EIC
42.01 21 71.63

ATOM! IS YOUR TV ON?!

IT IS... AND I'M APPALLED.

Evil Inc. HOSTILE TAKEOVER?

THIS IS AN OUT-RAGE!

IT'S ATROCIOUS!

YOU HAVE TO DO SOMETHING! THIS DEMANDS IMMEDIATE ACTION ON YOUR PART!

YOU'RE RIGHT!

THAT'S THE LAST TIME I TAPE "LAGUNA BEACH!" KRISTIN IS SUCH A LITTLE BRAT!

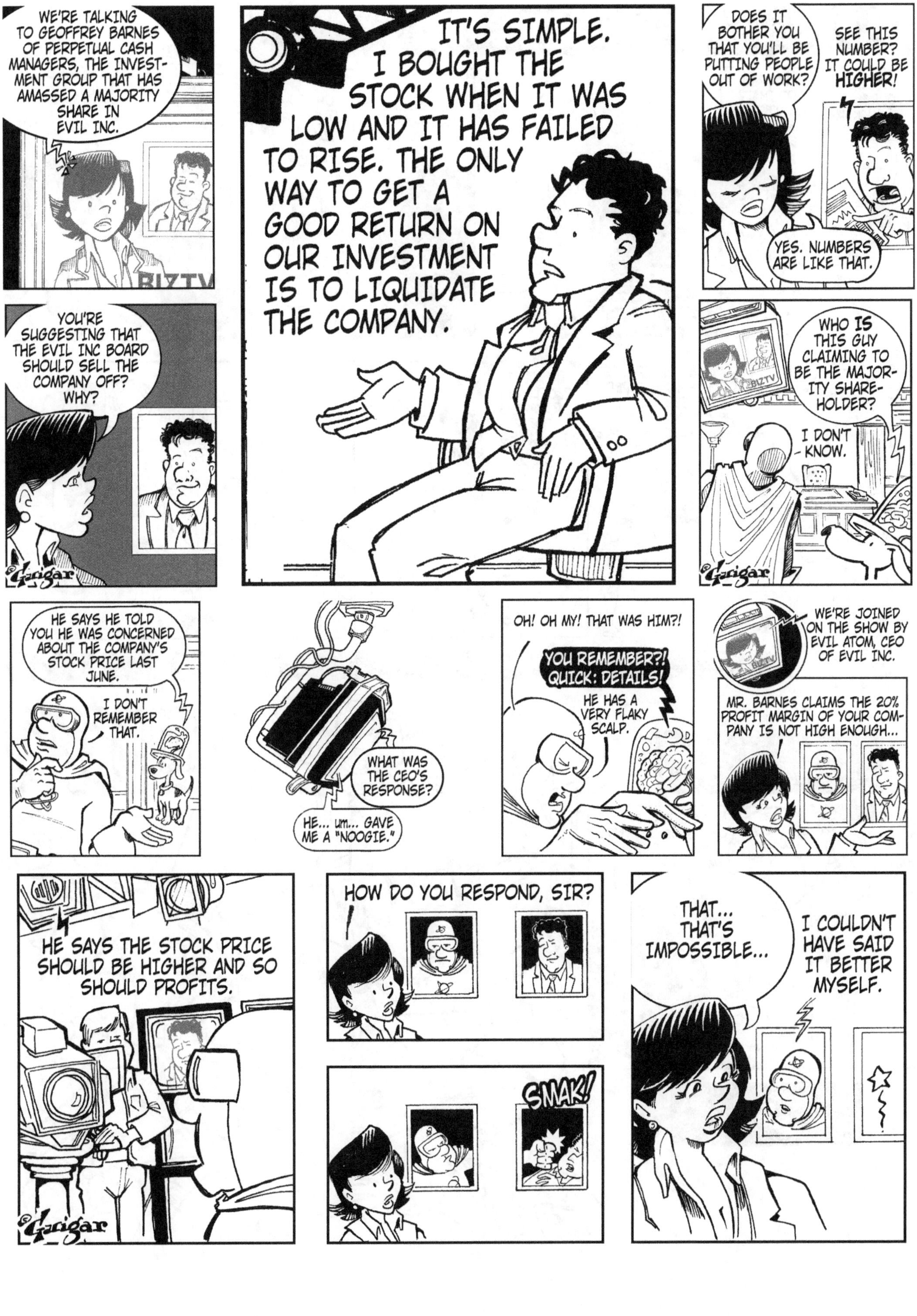

WE'RE TALKING TO GEOFFREY BARNES OF PERPETUAL CASH MANAGERS, THE INVESTMENT GROUP THAT HAS AMASSED A MAJORITY SHARE IN EVIL INC.
BIZTV
IT'S SIMPLE. I BOUGHT THE STOCK WHEN IT WAS LOW AND IT HAS FAILED TO RISE. THE ONLY WAY TO GET A GOOD RETURN ON OUR INVESTMENT IS TO LIQUIDATE THE COMPANY.
DOES IT BOTHER YOU THAT YOU'LL BE PUTTING PEOPLE OUT OF WORK?
SEE THIS NUMBER? IT COULD BE HIGHER!
YES. NUMBERS ARE LIKE THAT.
YOU'RE SUGGESTING THAT THE EVIL INC BOARD SHOULD SELL THE COMPANY OFF? WHY?
©Garigar
WHO IS THIS GUY CLAIMING TO BE THE MAJORITY SHAREHOLDER?
I DON'T KNOW.
©Garigar
HE SAYS HE TOLD YOU HE WAS CONCERNED ABOUT THE COMPANY'S STOCK PRICE LAST JUNE.
I DON'T REMEMBER THAT.
WHAT WAS THE CEO'S RESPONSE?
HE... um... GAVE ME A "NOOGIE."
OH! OH MY! THAT WAS HIM?!
YOU REMEMBER?! QUICK: DETAILS!
HE HAS A VERY FLAKY SCALP.
WE'RE JOINED ON THE SHOW BY EVIL ATOM, CEO OF EVIL INC.
MR. BARNES CLAIMS THE 20% PROFIT MARGIN OF YOUR COMPANY IS NOT HIGH ENOUGH...
HE SAYS THE STOCK PRICE SHOULD BE HIGHER AND SO SHOULD PROFITS.
©Garigar
HOW DO YOU RESPOND, SIR?
SMAK!
THAT... THAT'S IMPOSSIBLE...
I COULDN'T HAVE SAID IT BETTER MYSELF.

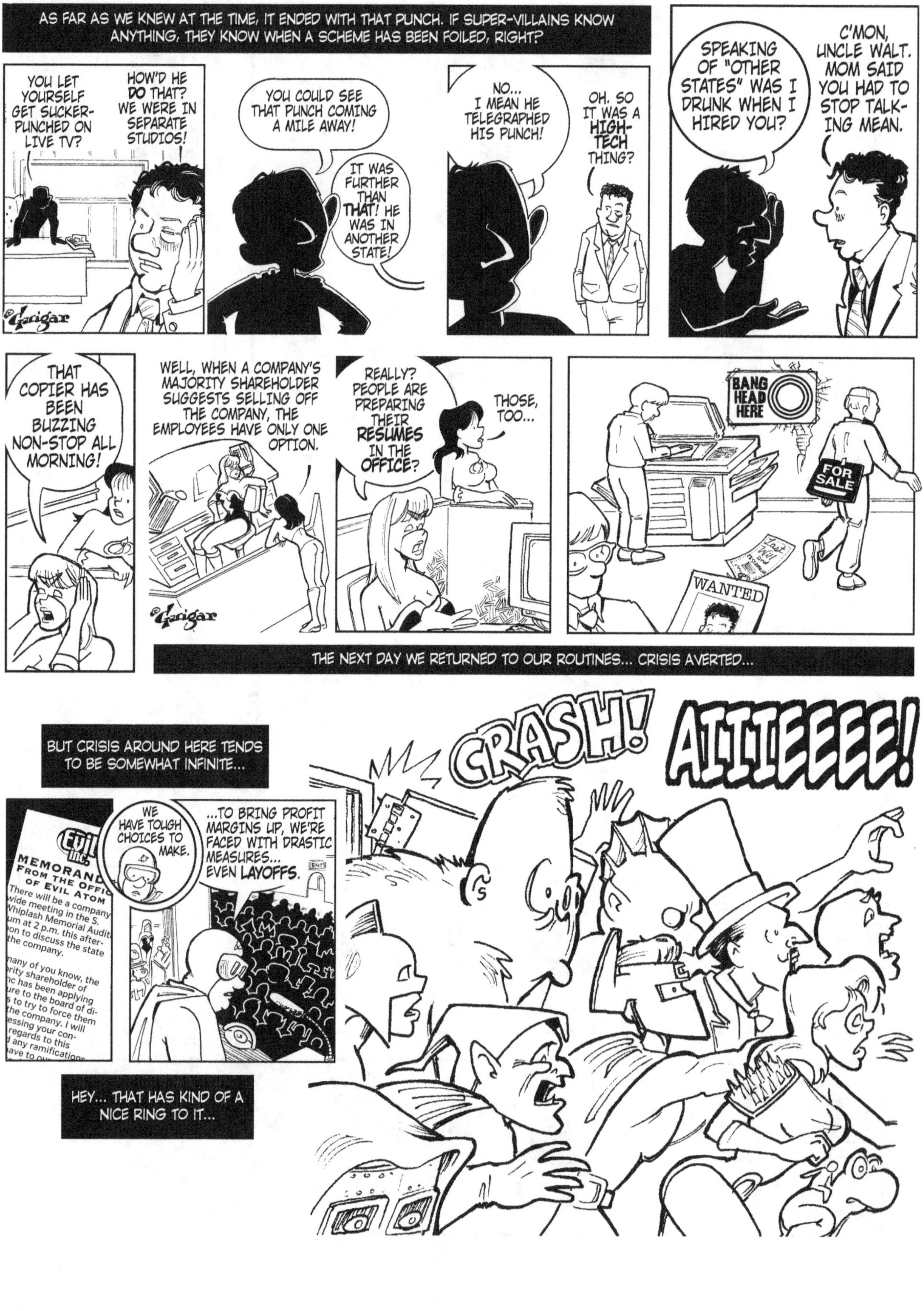
AS FAR AS WE KNEW AT THE TIME, IT ENDED WITH THAT PUNCH. IF SUPER-VILLAINS KNOW ANYTHING, THEY KNOW WHEN A SCHEME HAS BEEN FOILED, RIGHT?
YOU LET YOURSELF GET SUCKER-PUNCHED ON LIVE TV?
HOW'D HE **DO** THAT? WE WERE IN SEPARATE STUDIOS!
YOU COULD SEE THAT PUNCH COMING A MILE AWAY!
IT WAS FURTHER THAN **THAT**! HE WAS IN ANOTHER STATE!
NO... I MEAN HE TELEGRAPHED HIS PUNCH!
OH. SO IT WAS A **HIGH-TECH** THING?
SPEAKING OF "OTHER STATES" WAS I DRUNK WHEN I HIRED YOU?
C'MON, UNCLE WALT. MOM SAID YOU HAD TO STOP TALKING MEAN.
THAT COPIER HAS BEEN BUZZING NON-STOP ALL MORNING!
WELL, WHEN A COMPANY'S MAJORITY SHAREHOLDER SUGGESTS SELLING OFF THE COMPANY, THE EMPLOYEES HAVE ONLY ONE OPTION.
REALLY? PEOPLE ARE PREPARING THEIR **RESUMES** IN THE **OFFICE**?
THOSE, TOO...
BANG HEAD HERE
FOR SALE
WANTED
THE NEXT DAY WE RETURNED TO OUR ROUTINES... CRISIS AVERTED...
BUT CRISIS AROUND HERE TENDS TO BE SOMEWHAT INFINITE...
WE HAVE TOUGH CHOICES TO MAKE.
...TO BRING PROFIT MARGINS UP, WE'RE FACED WITH DRASTIC MEASURES... EVEN **LAYOFFS**.
HEY... THAT HAS KIND OF A NICE RING TO IT...
CRASH!
AIIIEEEE!

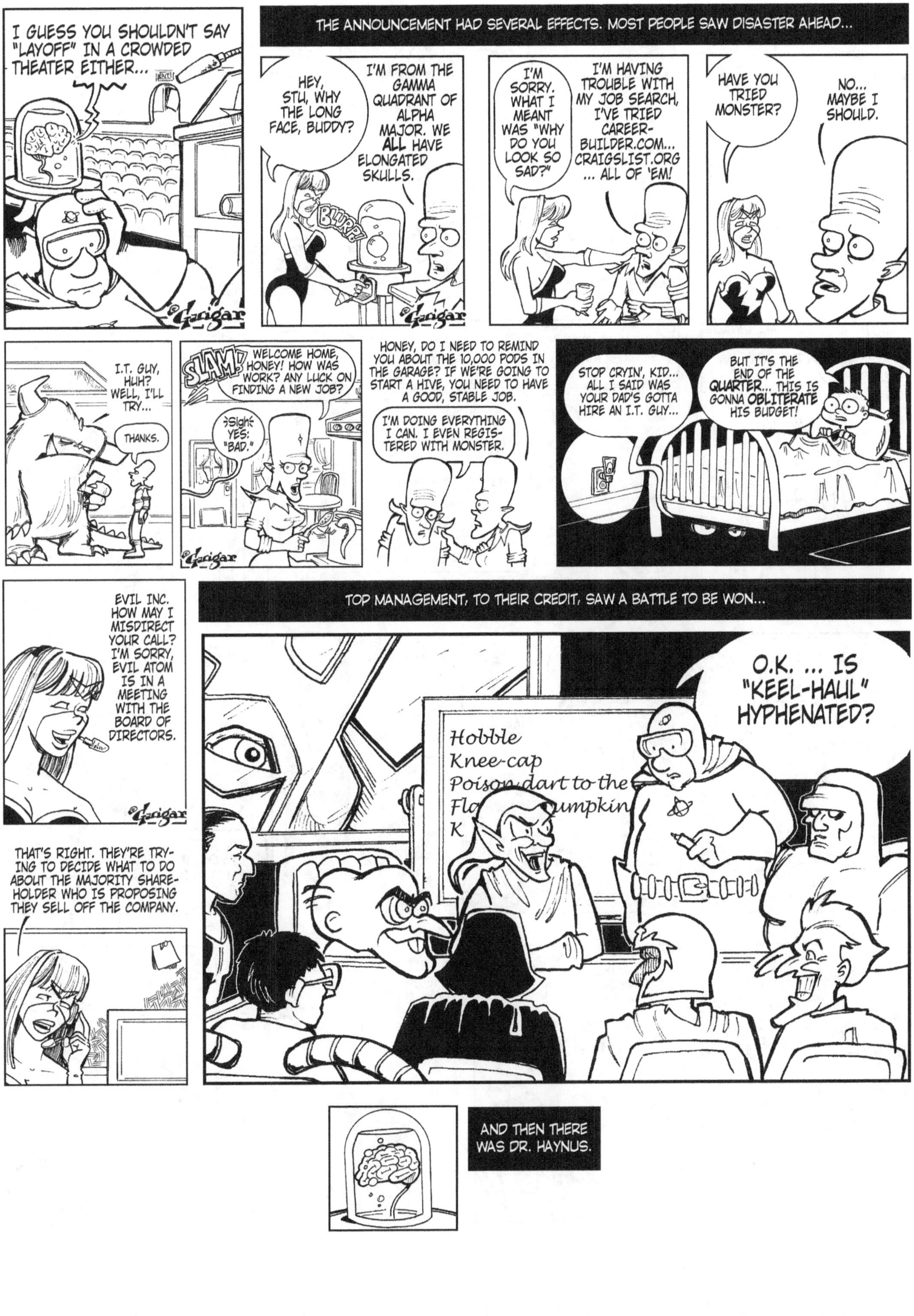

I GUESS YOU SHOULDN'T SAY "LAYOFF" IN A CROWDED THEATER EITHER...
THE ANNOUNCEMENT HAD SEVERAL EFFECTS. MOST PEOPLE SAW DISASTER AHEAD...
HEY, STU, WHY THE LONG FACE, BUDDY?
I'M FROM THE GAMMA QUADRANT OF ALPHA MAJOR. WE ALL HAVE ELONGATED SKULLS.
BLURP!
I'M SORRY. WHAT I MEANT WAS "WHY DO YOU LOOK SO SAD?"
I'M HAVING TROUBLE WITH MY JOB SEARCH, I'VE TRIED CAREER-BUILDER.COM... CRAIGSLIST.ORG ... ALL OF 'EM!
HAVE YOU TRIED MONSTER?
NO... MAYBE I SHOULD.
I.T. GUY, HUH? WELL, I'LL TRY...
THANKS.
SLAM!
WELCOME HOME, HONEY! HOW WAS WORK? ANY LUCK ON FINDING A NEW JOB?
Sigh YES: "BAD."
HONEY, DO I NEED TO REMIND YOU ABOUT THE 10,000 PODS IN THE GARAGE? IF WE'RE GOING TO START A HIVE, YOU NEED TO HAVE A GOOD, STABLE JOB.
I'M DOING EVERYTHING I CAN. I EVEN REGISTERED WITH MONSTER.
STOP CRYIN', KID... ALL I SAID WAS YOUR DAD'S GOTTA HIRE AN I.T. GUY...
BUT IT'S THE END OF THE QUARTER... THIS IS GONNA OBLITERATE HIS BUDGET!
EVIL INC. HOW MAY I MISDIRECT YOUR CALL? I'M SORRY, EVIL ATOM IS IN A MEETING WITH THE BOARD OF DIRECTORS.
THAT'S RIGHT. THEY'RE TRYING TO DECIDE WHAT TO DO ABOUT THE MAJORITY SHAREHOLDER WHO IS PROPOSING THEY SELL OFF THE COMPANY.
TOP MANAGEMENT, TO THEIR CREDIT, SAW A BATTLE TO BE WON...
Hobble
Knee-cap
Poison dart to the
O.K. ... IS "KEEL-HAUL" HYPHENATED?
AND THEN THERE WAS DR. HAYNUS.

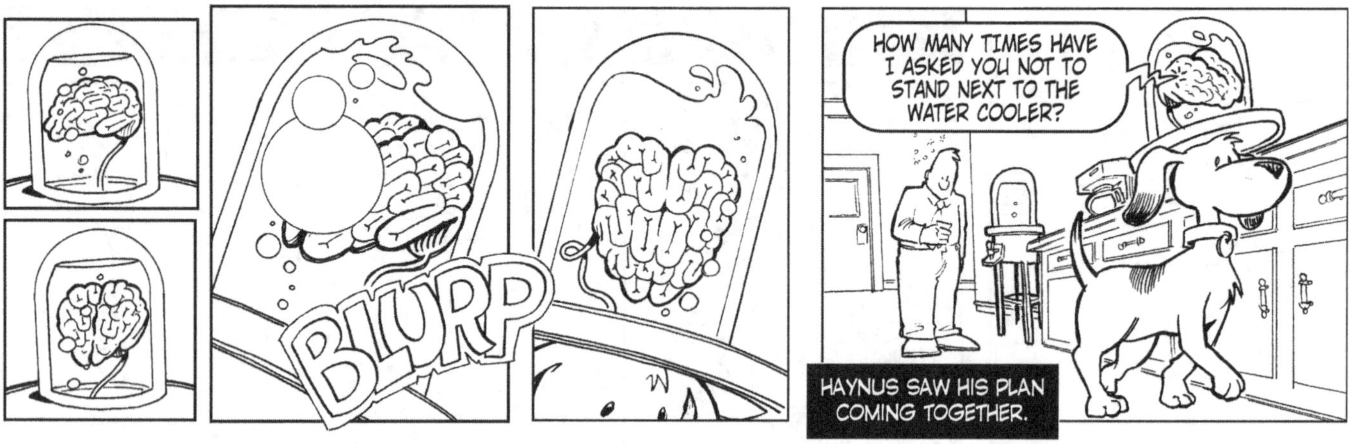
BLURP
HOW MANY TIMES HAVE I ASKED YOU NOT TO STAND NEXT TO THE WATER COOLER?
HAYNUS SAW HIS PLAN COMING TOGETHER.

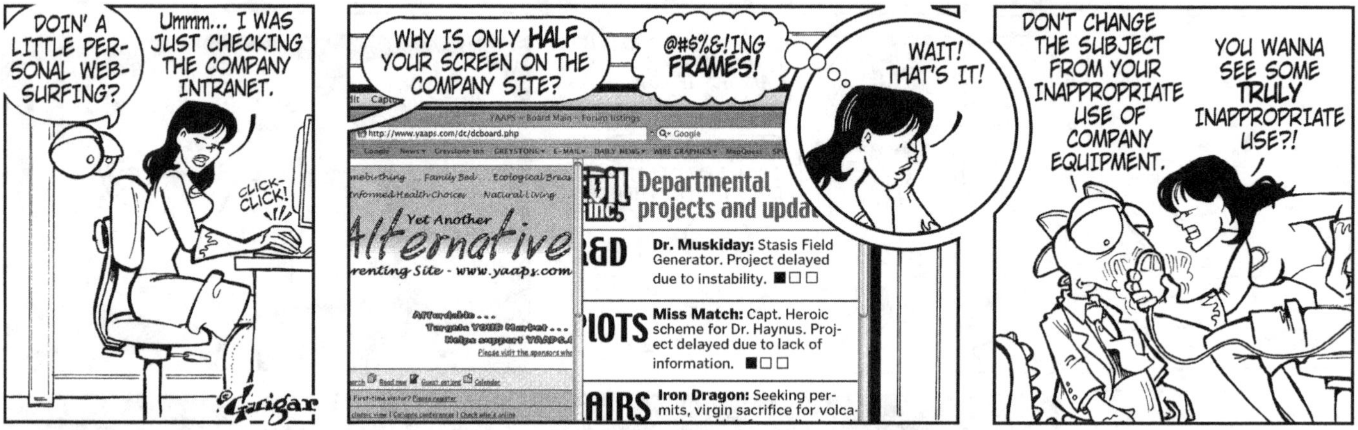
DOIN' A LITTLE PERSONAL WEB-SURFING?
Ummm... I WAS JUST CHECKING THE COMPANY INTRANET.
CLICK-CLICK!
WHY IS ONLY HALF YOUR SCREEN ON THE COMPANY SITE?
@#$%&!ING FRAMES!
WAIT! THAT'S IT!
Yet Another Alternative Parenting Site - www.yaaps.com
Departmental projects and upda
R&D
Dr. Muskiday: Stasis Field Generator. Project delayed due to instability.
PLOTS
Miss Match: Capt. Heroic scheme for Dr. Haynus. Project delayed due to lack of information.
AIRS
Iron Dragon: Seeking permits, virgin sacrifice for volca-
DON'T CHANGE THE SUBJECT FROM YOUR INAPPROPRIATE USE OF COMPANY EQUIPMENT.
YOU WANNA SEE SOME TRULY INAPPROPRIATE USE?!

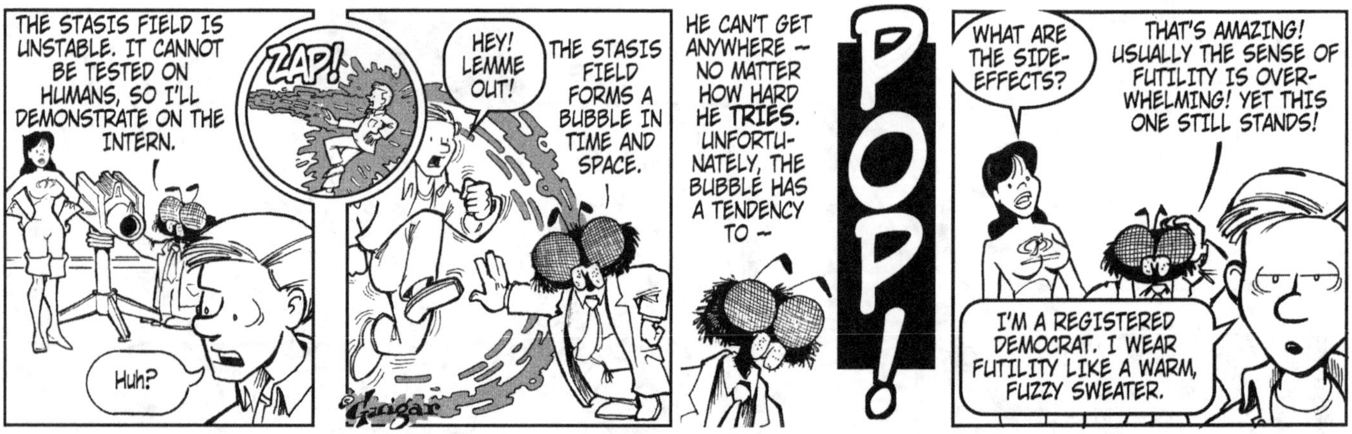
THE STASIS FIELD IS UNSTABLE. IT CANNOT BE TESTED ON HUMANS, SO I'LL DEMONSTRATE ON THE INTERN.
Huh?
ZAP!
HEY! LEMME OUT!
THE STASIS FIELD FORMS A BUBBLE IN TIME AND SPACE.
HE CAN'T GET ANYWHERE -- NO MATTER HOW HARD HE TRIES. UNFORTUNATELY, THE BUBBLE HAS A TENDENCY TO --
POP!
WHAT ARE THE SIDE-EFFECTS?
THAT'S AMAZING! USUALLY THE SENSE OF FUTILITY IS OVERWHELMING! YET THIS ONE STILL STANDS!
I'M A REGISTERED DEMOCRAT. I WEAR FUTILITY LIKE A WARM, FUZZY SWEATER.

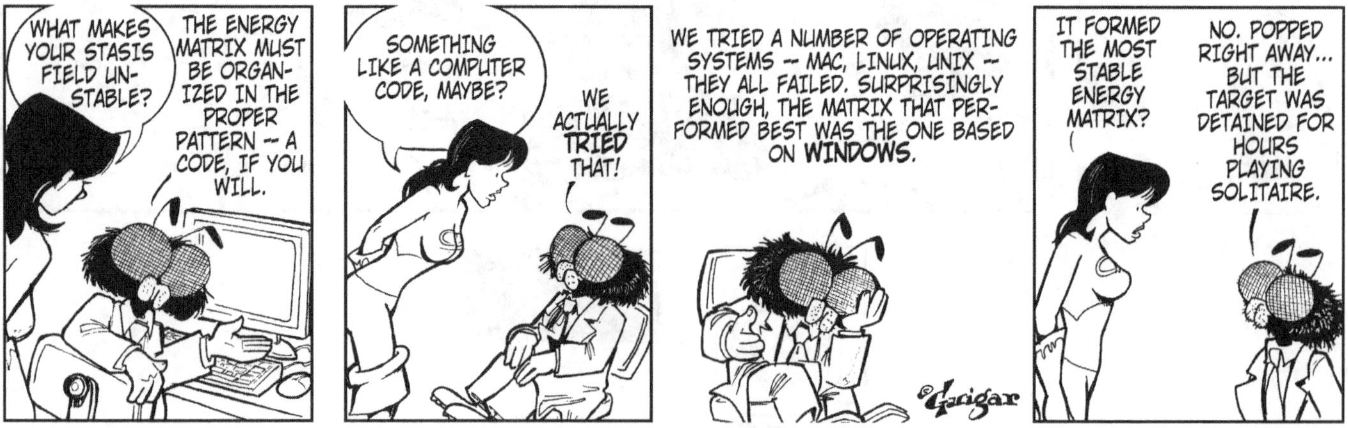
WHAT MAKES YOUR STASIS FIELD UNSTABLE?
THE ENERGY MATRIX MUST BE ORGANIZED IN THE PROPER PATTERN -- A CODE, IF YOU WILL.
SOMETHING LIKE A COMPUTER CODE, MAYBE?
WE ACTUALLY TRIED THAT!
WE TRIED A NUMBER OF OPERATING SYSTEMS -- MAC, LINUX, UNIX -- THEY ALL FAILED. SURPRISINGLY ENOUGH, THE MATRIX THAT PERFORMED BEST WAS THE ONE BASED ON WINDOWS.
IT FORMED THE MOST STABLE ENERGY MATRIX?
NO. POPPED RIGHT AWAY... BUT THE TARGET WAS DETAINED FOR HOURS PLAYING SOLITAIRE.

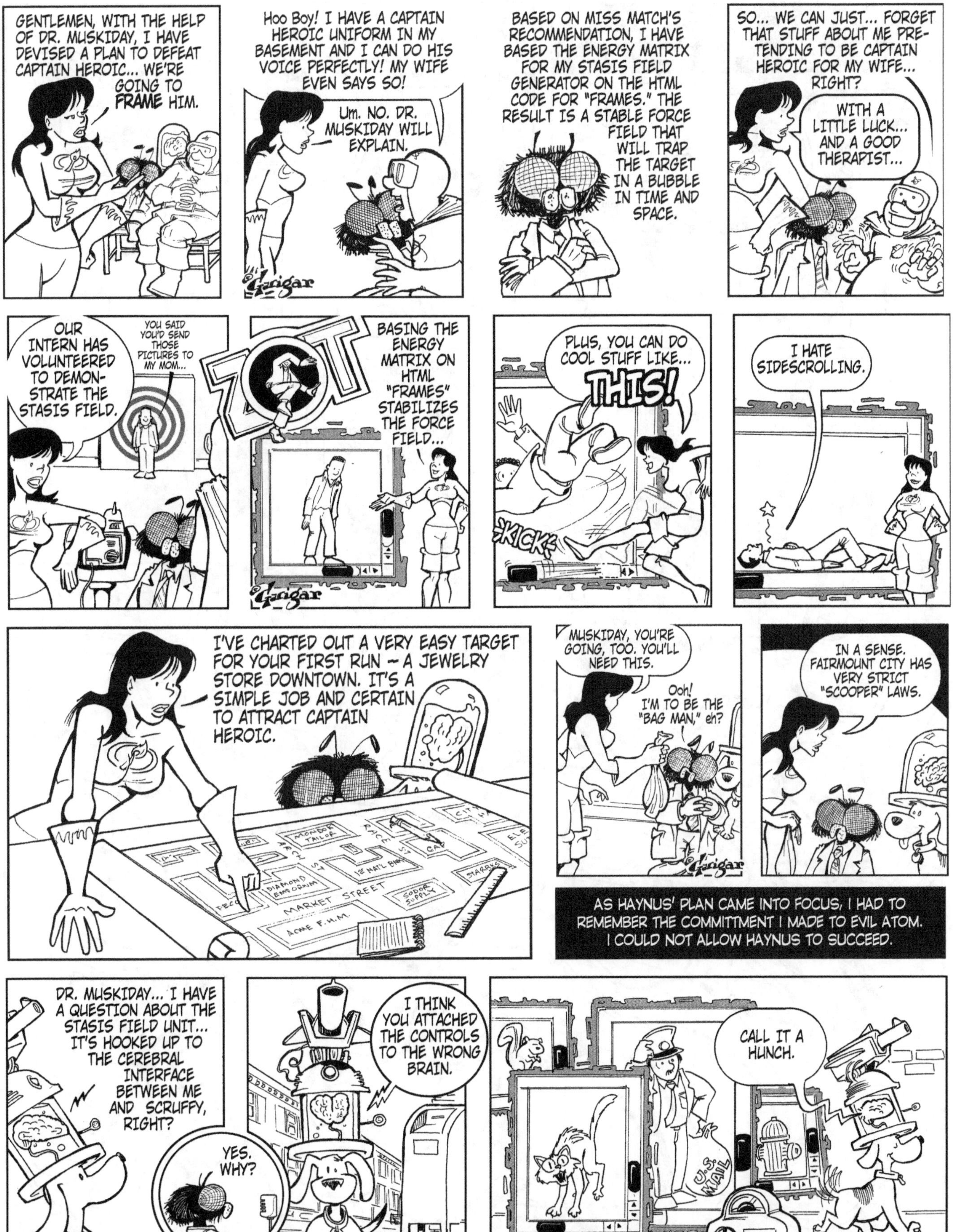
GENTLEMEN, WITH THE HELP OF DR. MUSKIDAY, I HAVE DEVISED A PLAN TO DEFEAT CAPTAIN HEROIC... WE'RE GOING TO FRAME HIM.
Hoo Boy! I HAVE A CAPTAIN HEROIC UNIFORM IN MY BASEMENT AND I CAN DO HIS VOICE PERFECTLY! MY WIFE EVEN SAYS SO!
Um. NO. DR. MUSKIDAY WILL EXPLAIN.
BASED ON MISS MATCH'S RECOMMENDATION, I HAVE BASED THE ENERGY MATRIX FOR MY STASIS FIELD GENERATOR ON THE HTML CODE FOR "FRAMES." THE RESULT IS A STABLE FORCE FIELD THAT WILL TRAP THE TARGET IN A BUBBLE IN TIME AND SPACE.
SO... WE CAN JUST... FORGET THAT STUFF ABOUT ME PRETENDING TO BE CAPTAIN HEROIC FOR MY WIFE... RIGHT?
WITH A LITTLE LUCK... AND A GOOD THERAPIST...
OUR INTERN HAS VOLUNTEERED TO DEMONSTRATE THE STASIS FIELD.
YOU SAID YOU'D SEND THOSE PICTURES TO MY MOM...
ZOT
BASING THE ENERGY MATRIX ON HTML "FRAMES" STABILIZES THE FORCE FIELD...
PLUS, YOU CAN DO COOL STUFF LIKE... THIS!
KICK
I HATE SIDESCROLLING.
I'VE CHARTED OUT A VERY EASY TARGET FOR YOUR FIRST RUN ~ A JEWELRY STORE DOWNTOWN. IT'S A SIMPLE JOB AND CERTAIN TO ATTRACT CAPTAIN HEROIC.
MONDOR TAILOR
RACE ST
ARCH ST
1ST NAT'L BANK
DIAMOND EMPORIUM
MARKET STREET
SODOR SUPPLY
ACME F.H.M.
MUSKIDAY, YOU'RE GOING, TOO. YOU'LL NEED THIS.
Ooh! I'M TO BE THE "BAG MAN," eh?
IN A SENSE. FAIRMOUNT CITY HAS VERY STRICT "SCOOPER" LAWS.
AS HAYNUS' PLAN CAME INTO FOCUS, I HAD TO REMEMBER THE COMMITTMENT I MADE TO EVIL ATOM. I COULD NOT ALLOW HAYNUS TO SUCCEED.
DR. MUSKIDAY... I HAVE A QUESTION ABOUT THE STASIS FIELD UNIT... IT'S HOOKED UP TO THE CEREBRAL INTERFACE BETWEEN ME AND SCRUFFY, RIGHT?
YES. WHY?
I THINK YOU ATTACHED THE CONTROLS TO THE WRONG BRAIN.
CALL IT A HUNCH.
U.S. MAIL
OF COURSE, MAYBE I WOULDN'T HAVE TO WORRY ABOUT IT.

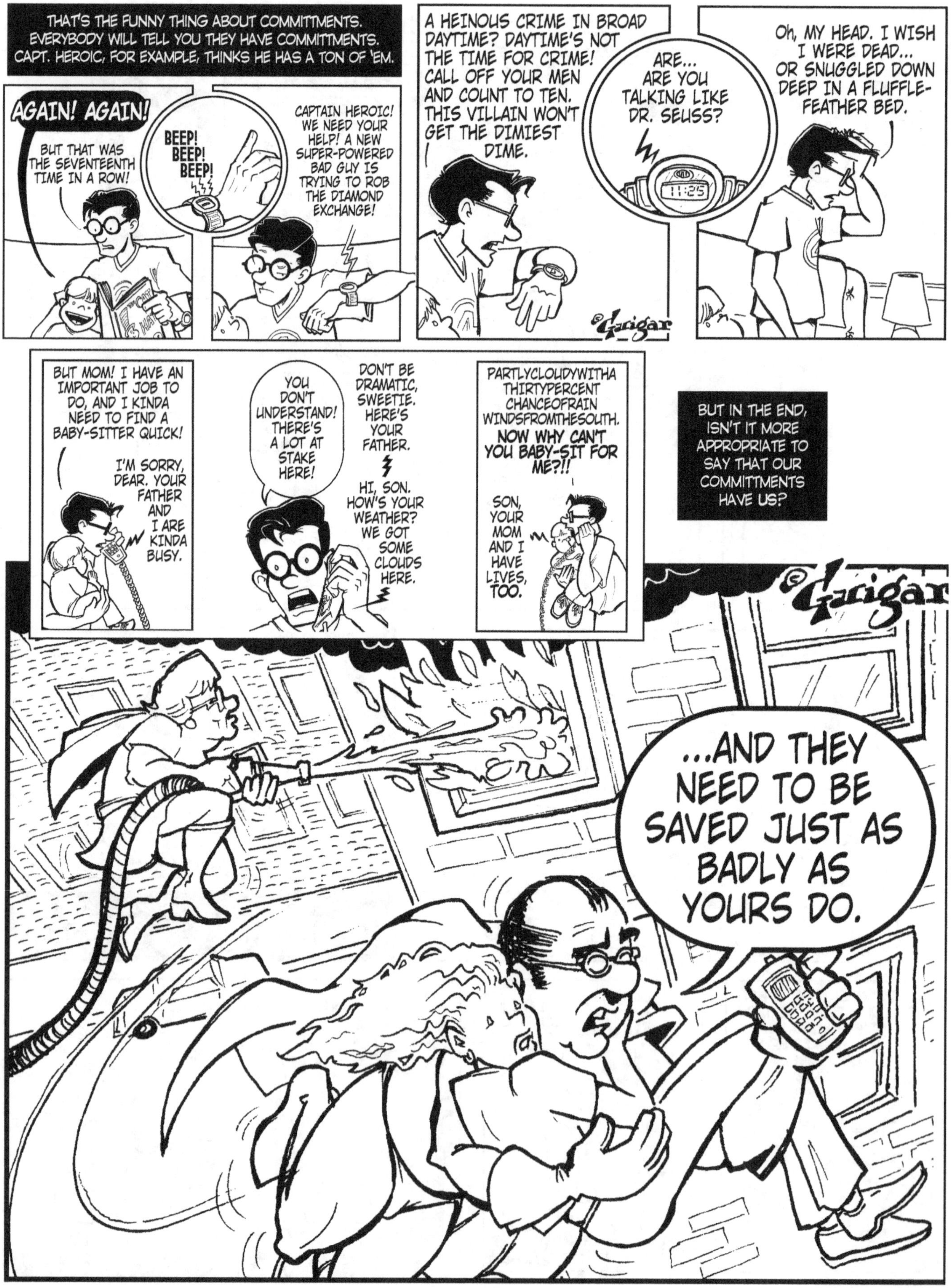

THAT'S THE FUNNY THING ABOUT COMMITTMENTS. EVERYBODY WILL TELL YOU THEY HAVE COMMITTMENTS. CAPT. HEROIC, FOR EXAMPLE, THINKS HE HAS A TON OF 'EM.
AGAIN! AGAIN!
BUT THAT WAS THE SEVENTEENTH TIME IN A ROW!
BEEP! BEEP! BEEP!
CAPTAIN HEROIC! WE NEED YOUR HELP! A NEW SUPER-POWERED BAD GUY IS TRYING TO ROB THE DIAMOND EXCHANGE!
A HEINOUS CRIME IN BROAD DAYTIME? DAYTIME'S NOT THE TIME FOR CRIME! CALL OFF YOUR MEN AND COUNT TO TEN. THIS VILLAIN WON'T GET THE DIMIEST DIME.
ARE... ARE YOU TALKING LIKE DR. SEUSS?
11:25
Oh, MY HEAD. I WISH I WERE DEAD... OR SNUGGLED DOWN DEEP IN A FLUFFLE-FEATHER BED.
©Garigar
BUT MOM! I HAVE AN IMPORTANT JOB TO DO, AND I KINDA NEED TO FIND A BABY-SITTER QUICK!
I'M SORRY, DEAR. YOUR FATHER AND I ARE KINDA BUSY.
YOU DON'T UNDERSTAND! THERE'S A LOT AT STAKE HERE!
DON'T BE DRAMATIC, SWEETIE. HERE'S YOUR FATHER.
HI, SON. HOW'S YOUR WEATHER? WE GOT SOME CLOUDS HERE.
PARTLYCLOUDYWITHA THIRTYPERCENT CHANCEOFRAIN WINDSFROMTHESOUTH. NOW WHY CAN'T YOU BABY-SIT FOR ME?!!
SON, YOUR MOM AND I HAVE LIVES, TOO.
BUT IN THE END, ISN'T IT MORE APPROPRIATE TO SAY THAT OUR COMMITTMENTS HAVE US?
©Garigar
...AND THEY NEED TO BE SAVED JUST AS BADLY AS YOURS DO.

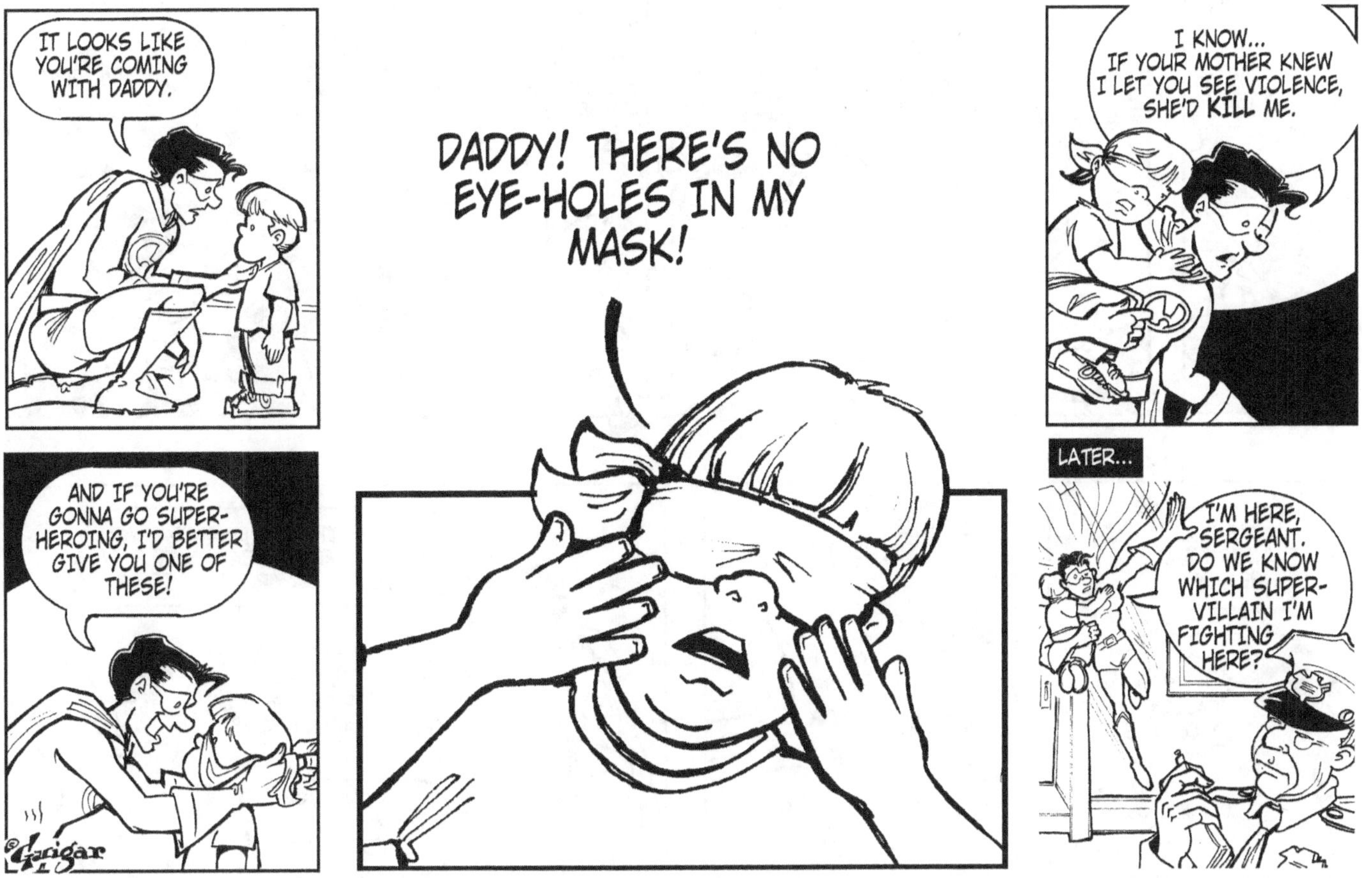
IT LOOKS LIKE YOU'RE COMING WITH DADDY.
AND IF YOU'RE GONNA GO SUPER-HEROING, I'D BETTER GIVE YOU ONE OF THESE!
DADDY! THERE'S NO EYE-HOLES IN MY MASK!
I KNOW... IF YOUR MOTHER KNEW I LET YOU SEE VIOLENCE, SHE'D **KILL** ME.
LATER...
I'M HERE, SERGEANT. DO WE KNOW WHICH SUPER-VILLAIN I'M FIGHTING HERE?

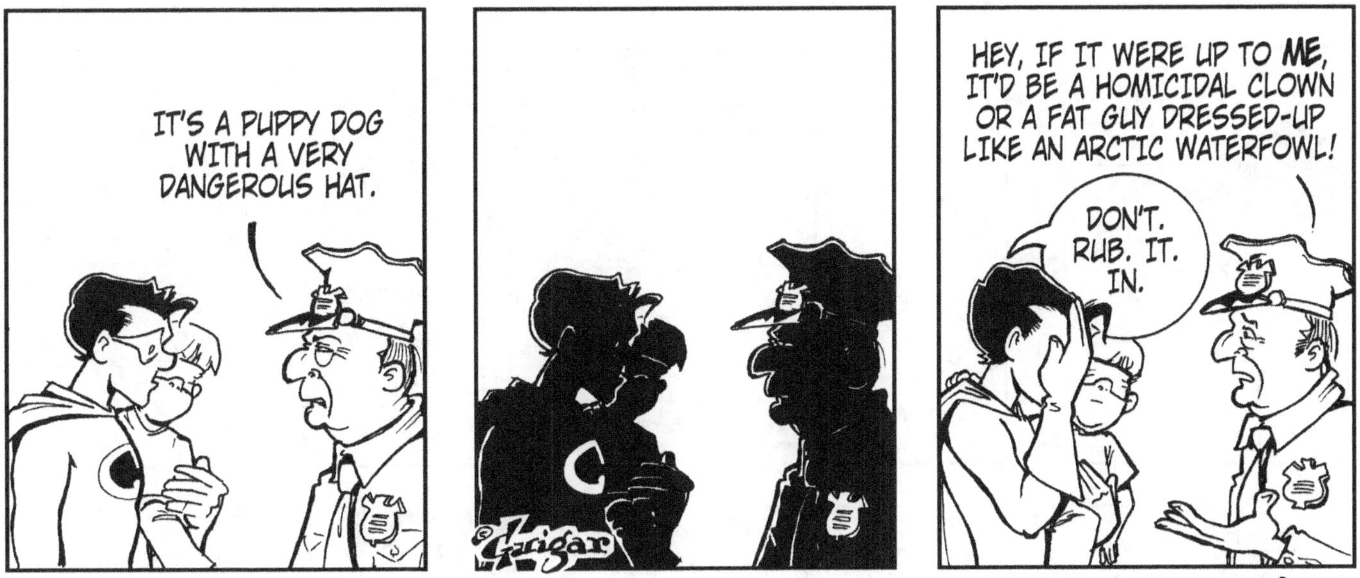
IT'S A PUPPY DOG WITH A VERY DANGEROUS HAT.
HEY, IF IT WERE UP TO **ME**, IT'D BE A HOMICIDAL CLOWN OR A FAT GUY DRESSED-UP LIKE AN ARCTIC WATERFOWL!
DON'T. RUB. IT. IN.

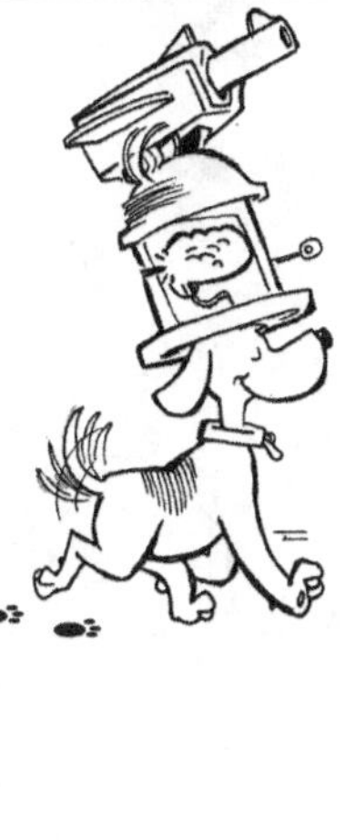

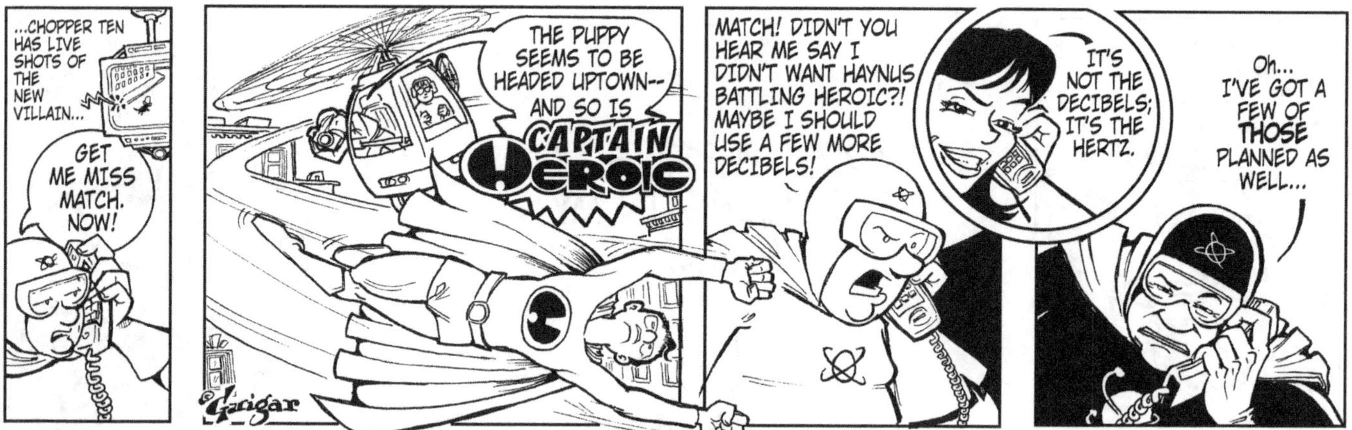

...CHOPPER TEN HAS LIVE SHOTS OF THE NEW VILLAIN...
GET ME MISS MATCH. NOW!
THE PUPPY SEEMS TO BE HEADED UPTOWN-- AND SO IS
CAPTAIN HEROIC
MATCH! DIDN'T YOU HEAR ME SAY I DIDN'T WANT HAYNUS BATTLING HEROIC?! MAYBE I SHOULD USE A FEW MORE DECIBELS!
IT'S NOT THE DECIBELS; IT'S THE HERTZ.
Oh... I'VE GOT A FEW OF THOSE PLANNED AS WELL...

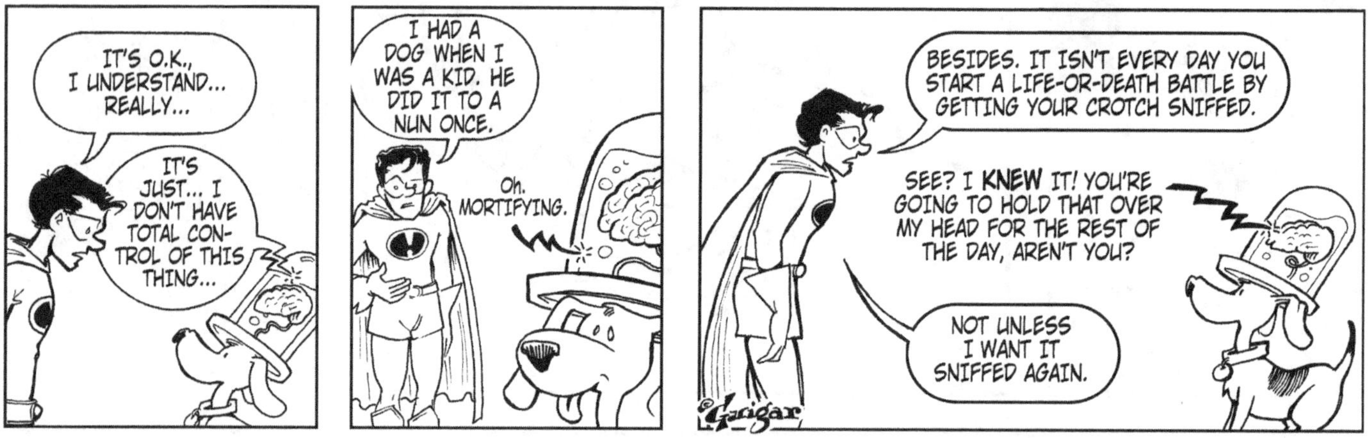

IT'S O.K., I UNDERSTAND... REALLY...
IT'S JUST... I DON'T HAVE TOTAL CONTROL OF THIS THING...
I HAD A DOG WHEN I WAS A KID. HE DID IT TO A NUN ONCE.
Oh. MORTIFYING.
BESIDES. IT ISN'T EVERY DAY YOU START A LIFE-OR-DEATH BATTLE BY GETTING YOUR CROTCH SNIFFED.
SEE? I KNEW IT! YOU'RE GOING TO HOLD THAT OVER MY HEAD FOR THE REST OF THE DAY, AREN'T YOU?
NOT UNLESS I WANT IT SNIFFED AGAIN.

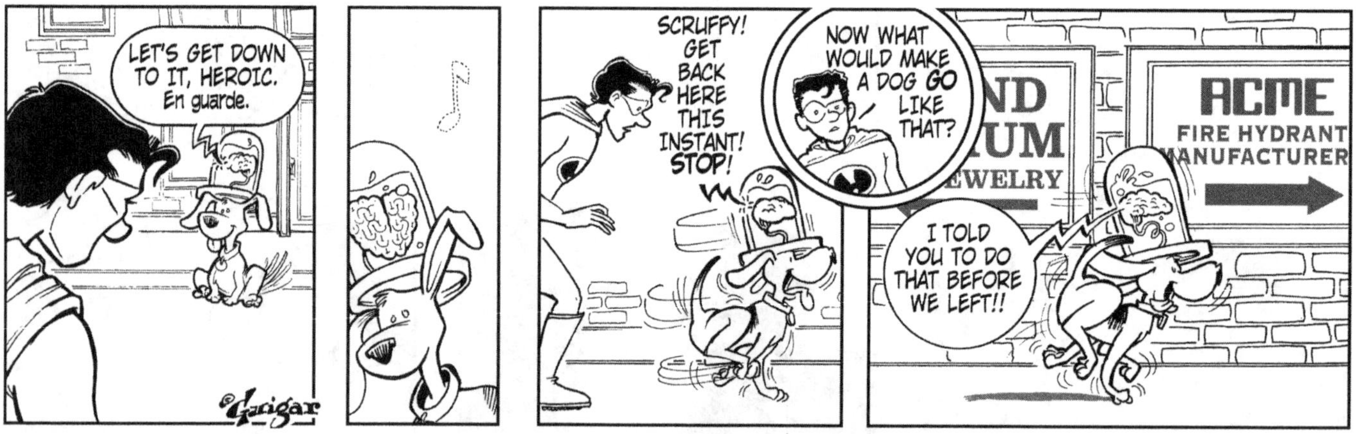

LET'S GET DOWN TO IT, HEROIC. En guarde.
SCRUFFY! GET BACK HERE THIS INSTANT! STOP!
NOW WHAT WOULD MAKE A DOG GO LIKE THAT?
ACME
FIRE HYDRANT MANUFACTURER
I TOLD YOU TO DO THAT BEFORE WE LEFT!!

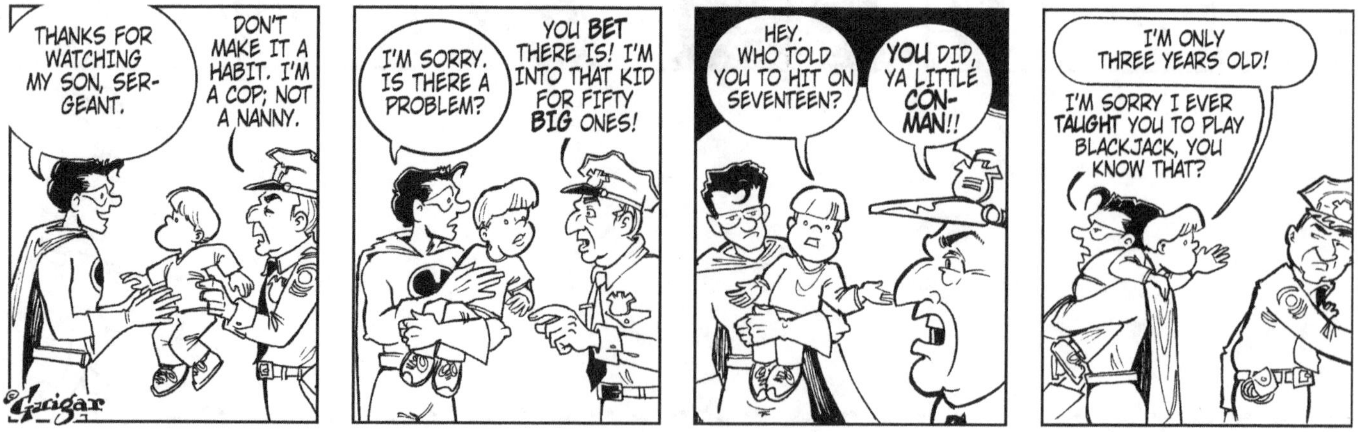

THANKS FOR WATCHING MY SON, SERGEANT.
DON'T MAKE IT A HABIT. I'M A COP; NOT A NANNY.
I'M SORRY. IS THERE A PROBLEM?
YOU BET THERE IS! I'M INTO THAT KID FOR FIFTY BIG ONES!
HEY. WHO TOLD YOU TO HIT ON SEVENTEEN?
YOU DID, YA LITTLE CON-MAN!!
I'M ONLY THREE YEARS OLD!
I'M SORRY I EVER TAUGHT YOU TO PLAY BLACKJACK, YOU KNOW THAT?

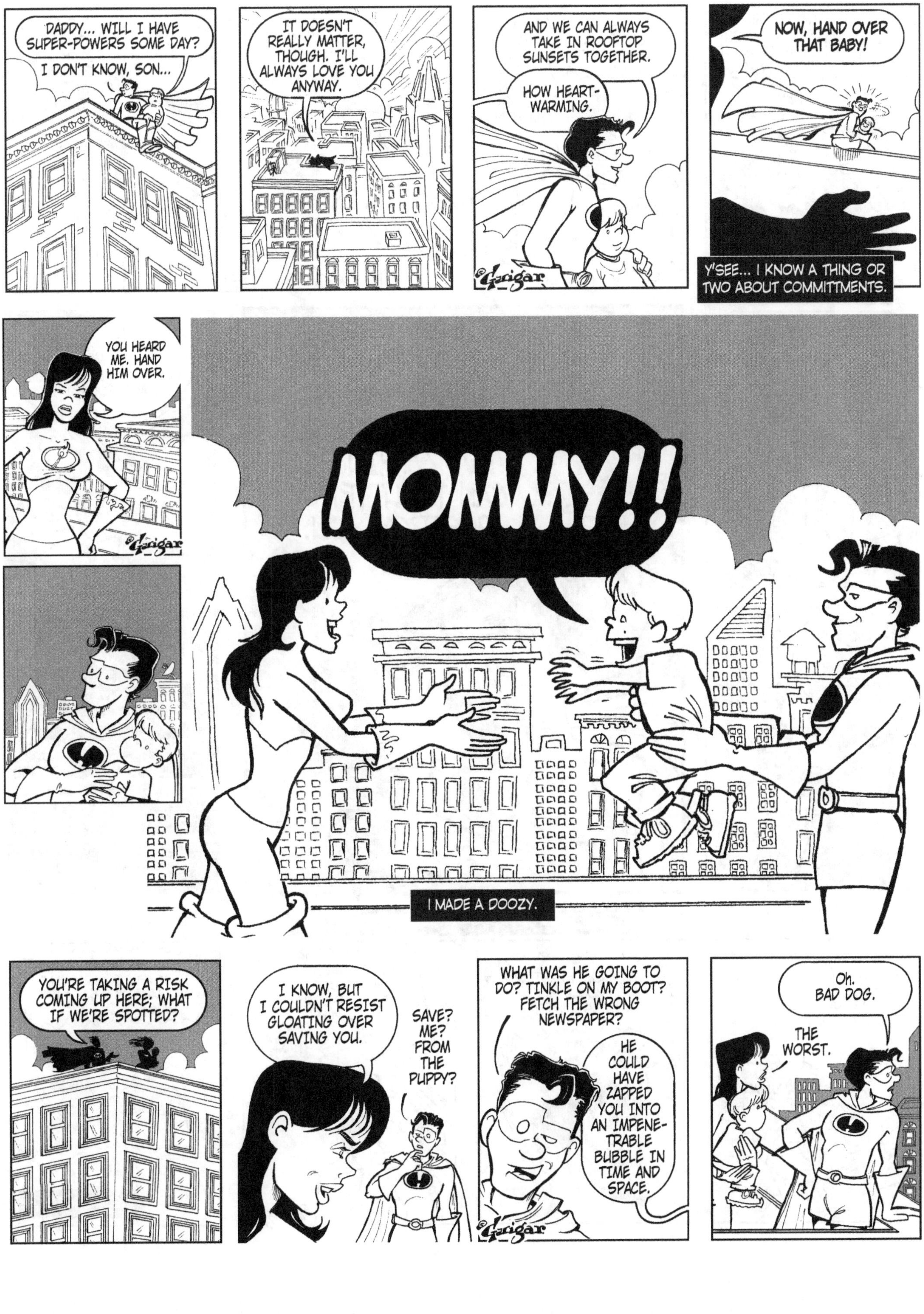
DADDY... WILL I HAVE SUPER-POWERS SOME DAY?
I DON'T KNOW, SON...
IT DOESN'T REALLY MATTER, THOUGH. I'LL ALWAYS LOVE YOU ANYWAY.
AND WE CAN ALWAYS TAKE IN ROOFTOP SUNSETS TOGETHER.
HOW HEART-WARMING.
NOW, HAND OVER THAT BABY!
Y'SEE... I KNOW A THING OR TWO ABOUT COMMITTMENTS.
YOU HEARD ME. HAND HIM OVER.
MOMMY!!
I MADE A DOOZY.
YOU'RE TAKING A RISK COMING UP HERE; WHAT IF WE'RE SPOTTED?
I KNOW, BUT I COULDN'T RESIST GLOATING OVER SAVING YOU.
SAVE? ME? FROM THE PUPPY?
WHAT WAS HE GOING TO DO? TINKLE ON MY BOOT? FETCH THE WRONG NEWSPAPER?
HE COULD HAVE ZAPPED YOU INTO AN IMPENE-TRABLE BUBBLE IN TIME AND SPACE.
THE WORST.
Oh. BAD DOG.

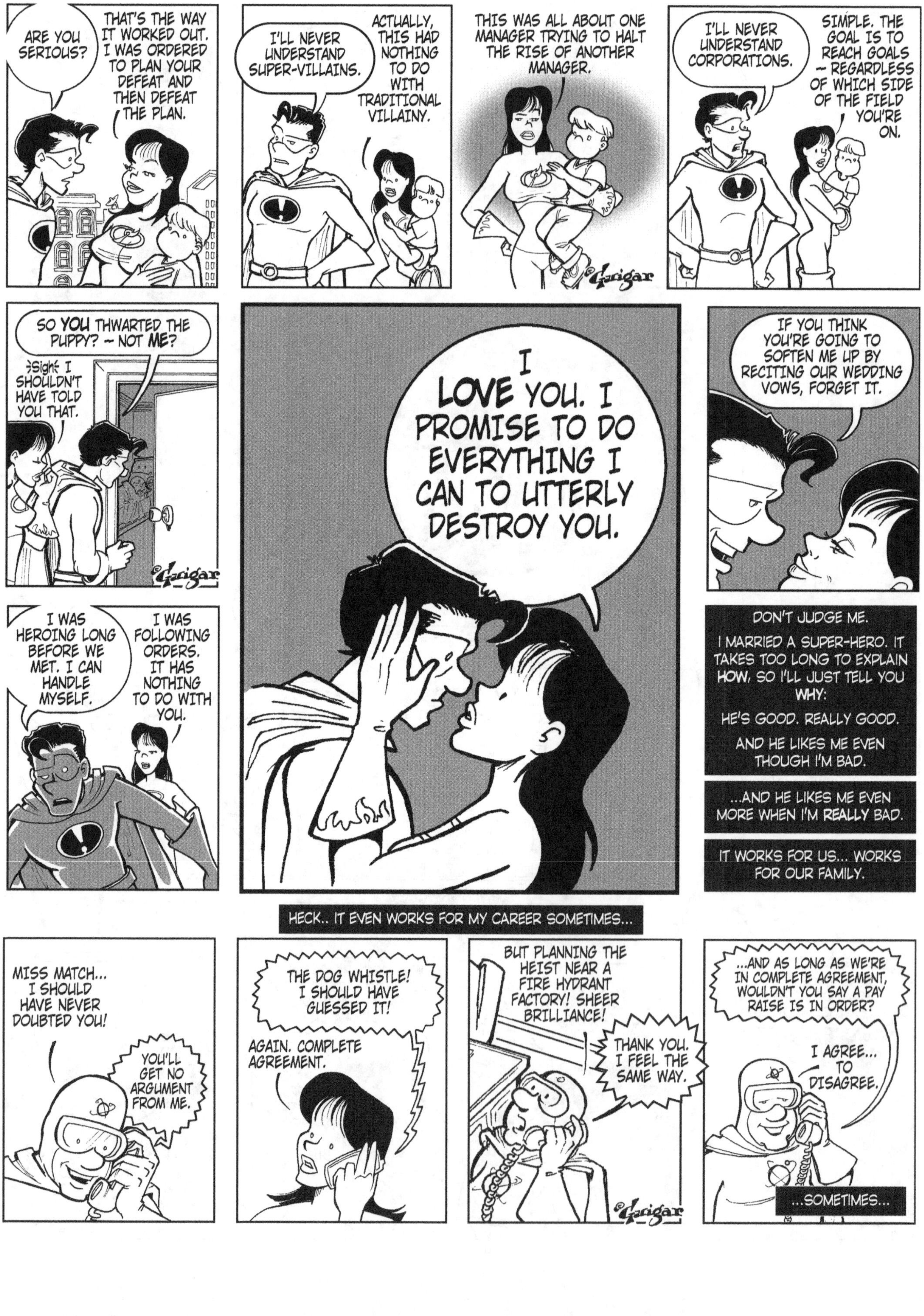

ARE YOU SERIOUS?
THAT'S THE WAY IT WORKED OUT. I WAS ORDERED TO PLAN YOUR DEFEAT AND THEN DEFEAT THE PLAN.
I'LL NEVER UNDERSTAND SUPER-VILLAINS.
ACTUALLY, THIS HAD NOTHING TO DO WITH TRADITIONAL VILLAINY.
THIS WAS ALL ABOUT ONE MANAGER TRYING TO HALT THE RISE OF ANOTHER MANAGER.
I'LL NEVER UNDERSTAND CORPORATIONS.
SIMPLE. THE GOAL IS TO REACH GOALS – REGARDLESS OF WHICH SIDE OF THE FIELD YOU'RE ON.
©Gorigar
SO YOU THWARTED THE PUPPY? – NOT ME?
Sigh I SHOULDN'T HAVE TOLD YOU THAT.
©Gorigar
I WAS HEROING LONG BEFORE WE MET. I CAN HANDLE MYSELF.
I WAS FOLLOWING ORDERS. IT HAS NOTHING TO DO WITH YOU.
I LOVE YOU. I PROMISE TO DO EVERYTHING I CAN TO UTTERLY DESTROY YOU.
IF YOU THINK YOU'RE GOING TO SOFTEN ME UP BY RECITING OUR WEDDING VOWS, FORGET IT.
DON'T JUDGE ME.
I MARRIED A SUPER-HERO. IT TAKES TOO LONG TO EXPLAIN HOW, SO I'LL JUST TELL YOU WHY:
HE'S GOOD. REALLY GOOD.
AND HE LIKES ME EVEN THOUGH I'M BAD.
...AND HE LIKES ME EVEN MORE WHEN I'M REALLY BAD.
IT WORKS FOR US... WORKS FOR OUR FAMILY.
HECK.. IT EVEN WORKS FOR MY CAREER SOMETIMES...
MISS MATCH... I SHOULD HAVE NEVER DOUBTED YOU!
YOU'LL GET NO ARGUMENT FROM ME.
THE DOG WHISTLE! I SHOULD HAVE GUESSED IT!
AGAIN. COMPLETE AGREEMENT.
BUT PLANNING THE HEIST NEAR A FIRE HYDRANT FACTORY! SHEER BRILLIANCE!
THANK YOU. I FEEL THE SAME WAY.
©Gorigar
...AND AS LONG AS WE'RE IN COMPLETE AGREEMENT, WOULDN'T YOU SAY A PAY RAISE IS IN ORDER?
I AGREE... TO DISAGREE.
...SOMETIMES...

Chapter 3

I'll Get You Next Time... Next Time...

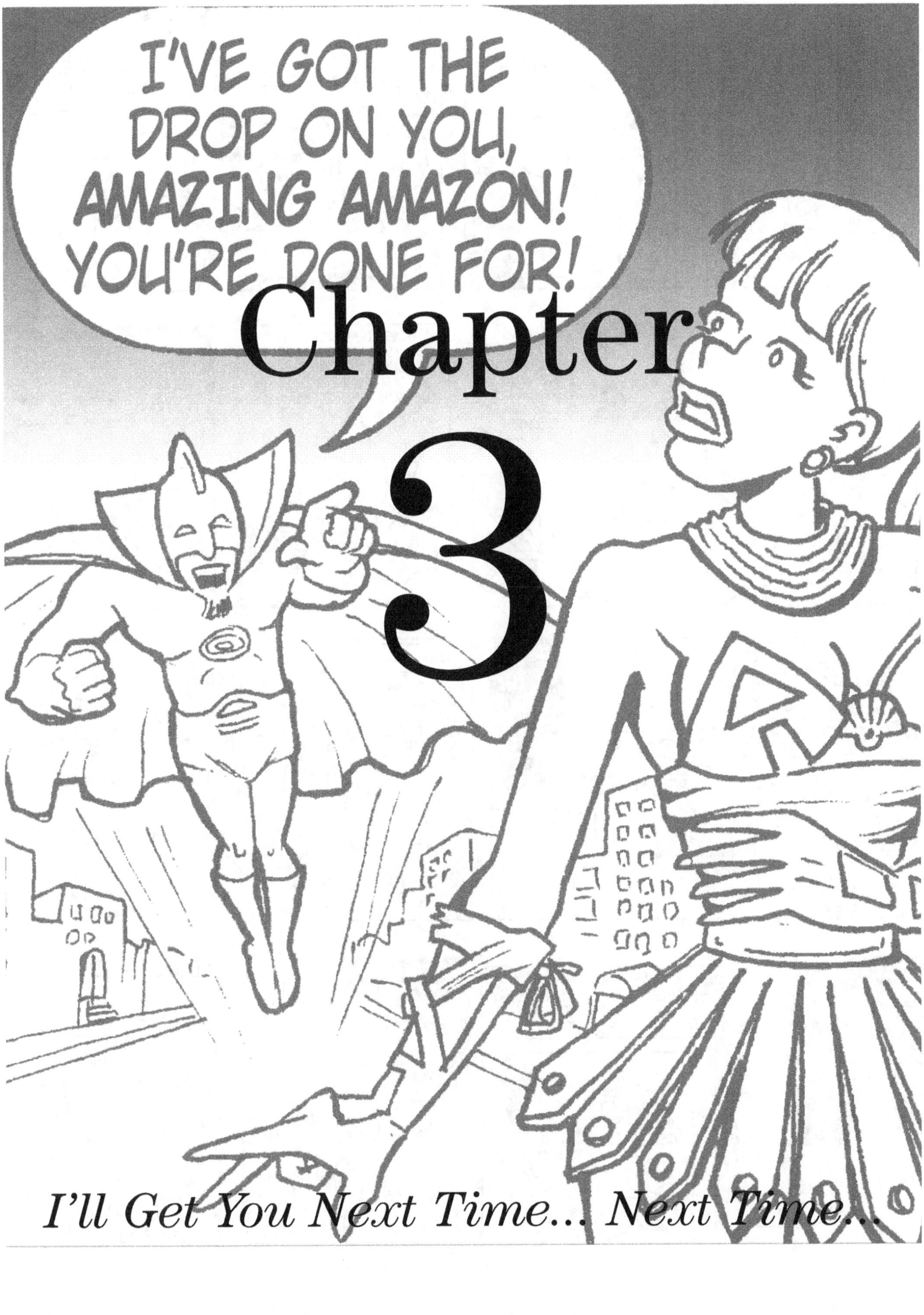
I'VE GOT THE DROP ON YOU, AMAZING AMAZON! YOU'RE DONE FOR!

I'VE GOT THE DROP ON YOU, **AMAZING AMAZON**! YOU'RE DONE FOR!
EXCUSE ME, SIR. DID YOU JUST SAY "DONE FOR?"
EH?! WHAT'S THE MEANING OF THIS?
I DON'T KNOW THIS GUY, ED.
I'M FROM "VIMA" -- THE VILLAINOUS IDIOM MANAGEMENT AGENCY. I'M TAKING YOU IN ON AN 11-13: MEANINGLESS AND OUT-DATED PHRASEOLOGY.
CURSES!
YOU'RE JUST MAKING IT HARDER ON YOURSELF, SIR.
SO WHERE ARE YOU TAKING ME?
WE HAVE A REMEDIAL EDUCATION PROGRAM FOR GUYS LIKE YOU.
GUYS LIKE ME?
VILLAINS WHO INSIST ON USING DATED, MEANINGLESS PHRASES AND MELODRAMATIC CLICHES.
BLAST IT! BLAST IT TO **OBLIVION**! I HAD YOU IN MY CLUTCHES, AMAZING AMAZON, MY OLD FRIEND... VICTORY WAS MINE! BUT I'LL BE BACK -- oh yes... I'LL BE BACK.
HOW LONG DOES THIS PROGRAM TAKE?
IN **YOUR** CASE? WE'VE RESERVED THE RICARDO MONTALBAN "WRATH OF KHAN" SUITE.
THIS IS A SPECIAL CLASS FOR EXTRA-TERRESTRIAL VILLAINS.
VILLAINOUS IDIOM MANAGEMENT AGENCY
TAKE ME TO YOUR LEADER.
CAN ANYONE TELL ME WHAT'S WRONG WITH THIS SENTENCE?
THERE'S NO SINGLE, CENTRAL LEADER ON EARTH.
VERY GOOD, MONDOK!
MAY I GO BACK TO ENSLAVING EARTHLINGS NOW? I HAVE AN ENTIRE PLANET TO MINE.
ENSLAVING WHOM?
OH! I **KNOW** THIS ONE! "TERRESTRIALS!" NO-NO-NO! "**EARTHERS!**" NO! "EARTH-DWELLERS!"
IS **THAT** HOW YOU'LL ENSLAVE PEOPLE? BY **GUESSING** THEM INTO SUBMISSION?!
IT TOOK ME TWELVE ~~OF YOUR EARTH~~ YEARS TO GET HERE.
VERY GOOD, N'TUK.
WHEN ADDRESSING A HUMAN, IT IS UNNECESSARY TO EXPLAIN THE CONCEPT OF "YEARS."
N'TUK, I THINK YOU'RE READY TO GRADUATE. YOU MAY BE DISMISSED.
<FREE! I'M FREE!>
HOW LONG WERE YOU **IN** FOR?
ONLY THREE DAYS... BUT THAT'S 12 ZEEBLOKS ON **MY** PLANET.
N'TUK! GET BACK HERE!
CLASS, CAN YOU HELP N'TUK?
DON'T OFFER MEASUREMENT CONVERSIONS TO A RACE IN WHICH MANY MEMBERS STILL MEASURE IN INCHES.

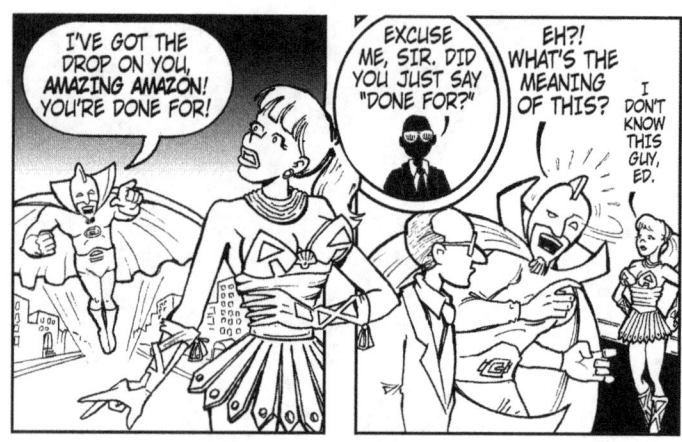

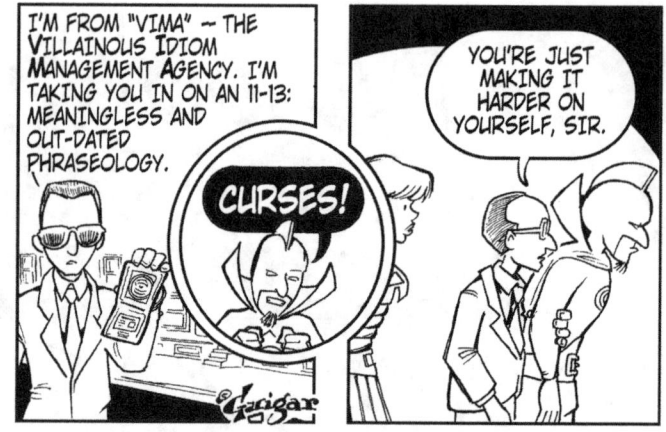

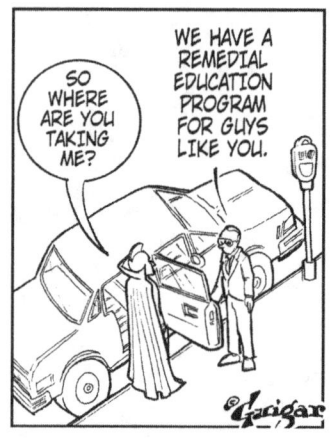

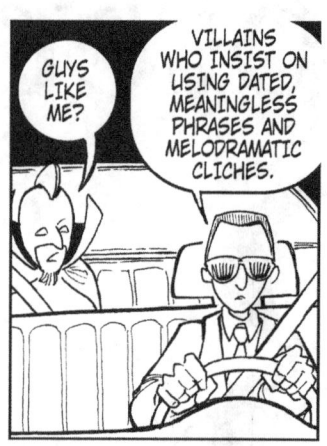

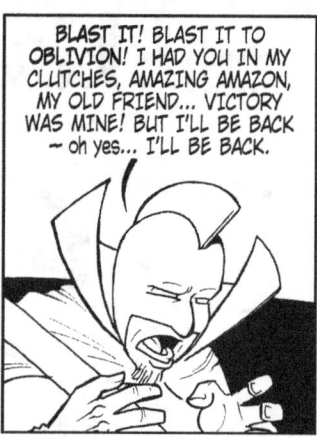

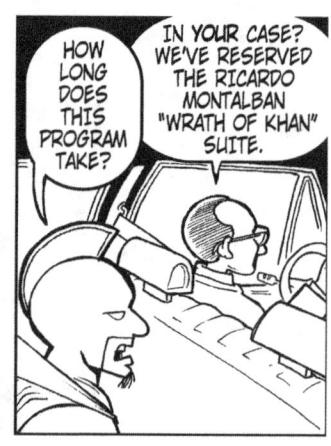

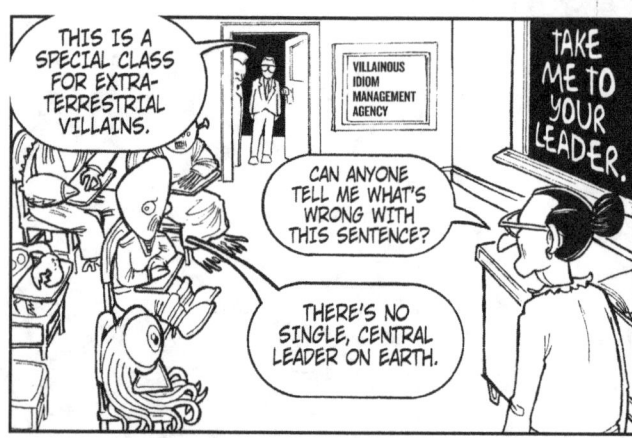

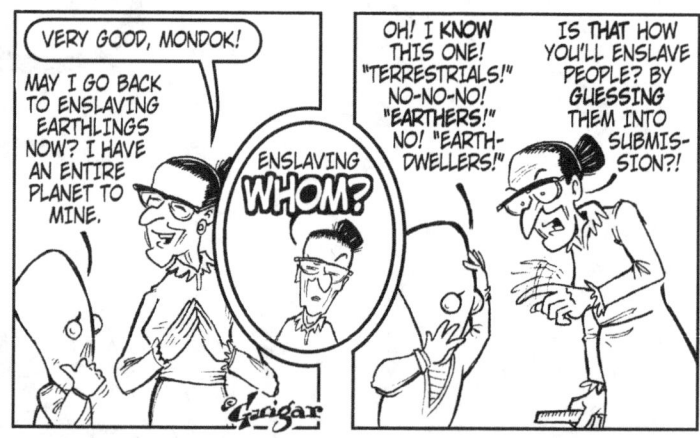

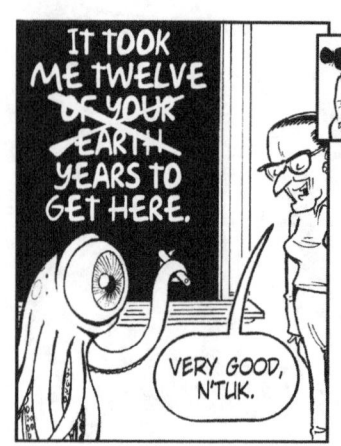

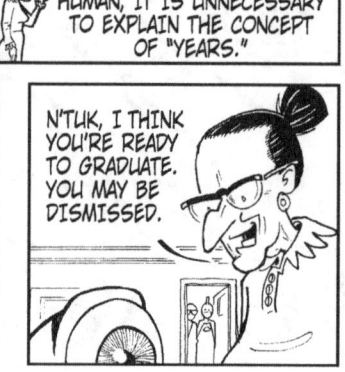

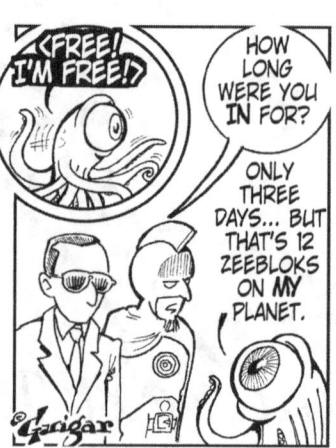

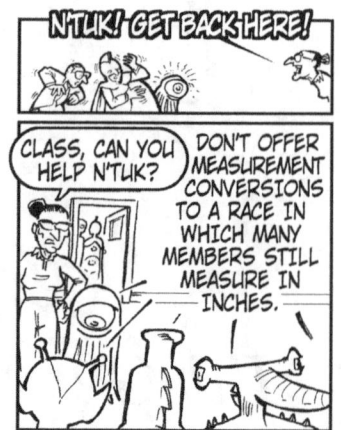

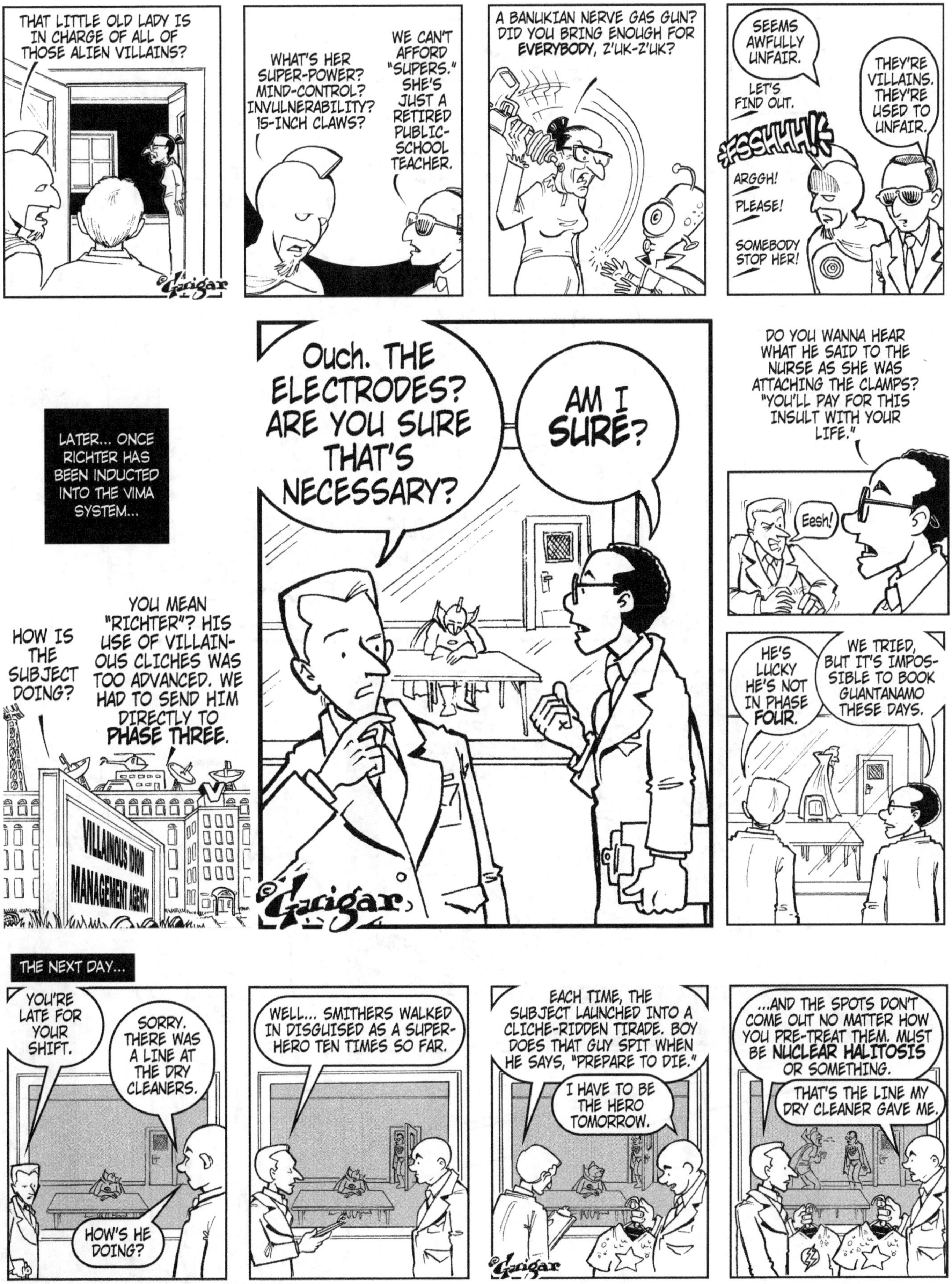
THAT LITTLE OLD LADY IS IN CHARGE OF ALL OF THOSE ALIEN VILLAINS?
WHAT'S HER SUPER-POWER? MIND-CONTROL? INVULNERABILITY? 15-INCH CLAWS?
WE CAN'T AFFORD "SUPERS." SHE'S JUST A RETIRED PUBLIC-SCHOOL TEACHER.
A BANUKIAN NERVE GAS GUN? DID YOU BRING ENOUGH FOR EVERYBODY, Z'UK-Z'UK?
SEEMS AWFULLY UNFAIR.
LET'S FIND OUT.
THEY'RE VILLAINS. THEY'RE USED TO UNFAIR.
FSSHHH!
ARGGH!
PLEASE!
SOMEBODY STOP HER!
LATER... ONCE RICHTER HAS BEEN INDUCTED INTO THE VIMA SYSTEM...
HOW IS THE SUBJECT DOING?
YOU MEAN "RICHTER"? HIS USE OF VILLAIN-OUS CLICHES WAS TOO ADVANCED. WE HAD TO SEND HIM DIRECTLY TO PHASE THREE.
VILLAINOUS IDIOM MANAGEMENT AGENCY
Ouch. THE ELECTRODES? ARE YOU SURE THAT'S NECESSARY?
AM I SURE?
DO YOU WANNA HEAR WHAT HE SAID TO THE NURSE AS SHE WAS ATTACHING THE CLAMPS? "YOU'LL PAY FOR THIS INSULT WITH YOUR LIFE."
Eesh!
HE'S LUCKY HE'S NOT IN PHASE FOUR.
WE TRIED, BUT IT'S IMPOS-SIBLE TO BOOK GUANTANAMO THESE DAYS.
THE NEXT DAY...
YOU'RE LATE FOR YOUR SHIFT.
SORRY. THERE WAS A LINE AT THE DRY CLEANERS.
HOW'S HE DOING?
WELL... SMITHERS WALKED IN DISGUISED AS A SUPER-HERO TEN TIMES SO FAR.
EACH TIME, THE SUBJECT LAUNCHED INTO A CLICHE-RIDDEN TIRADE. BOY DOES THAT GUY SPIT WHEN HE SAYS, "PREPARE TO DIE."
I HAVE TO BE THE HERO TOMORROW.
...AND THE SPOTS DON'T COME OUT NO MATTER HOW YOU PRE-TREAT THEM. MUST BE NUCLEAR HALITOSIS OR SOMETHING.
THAT'S THE LINE MY DRY CLEANER GAVE ME.
©Garigar

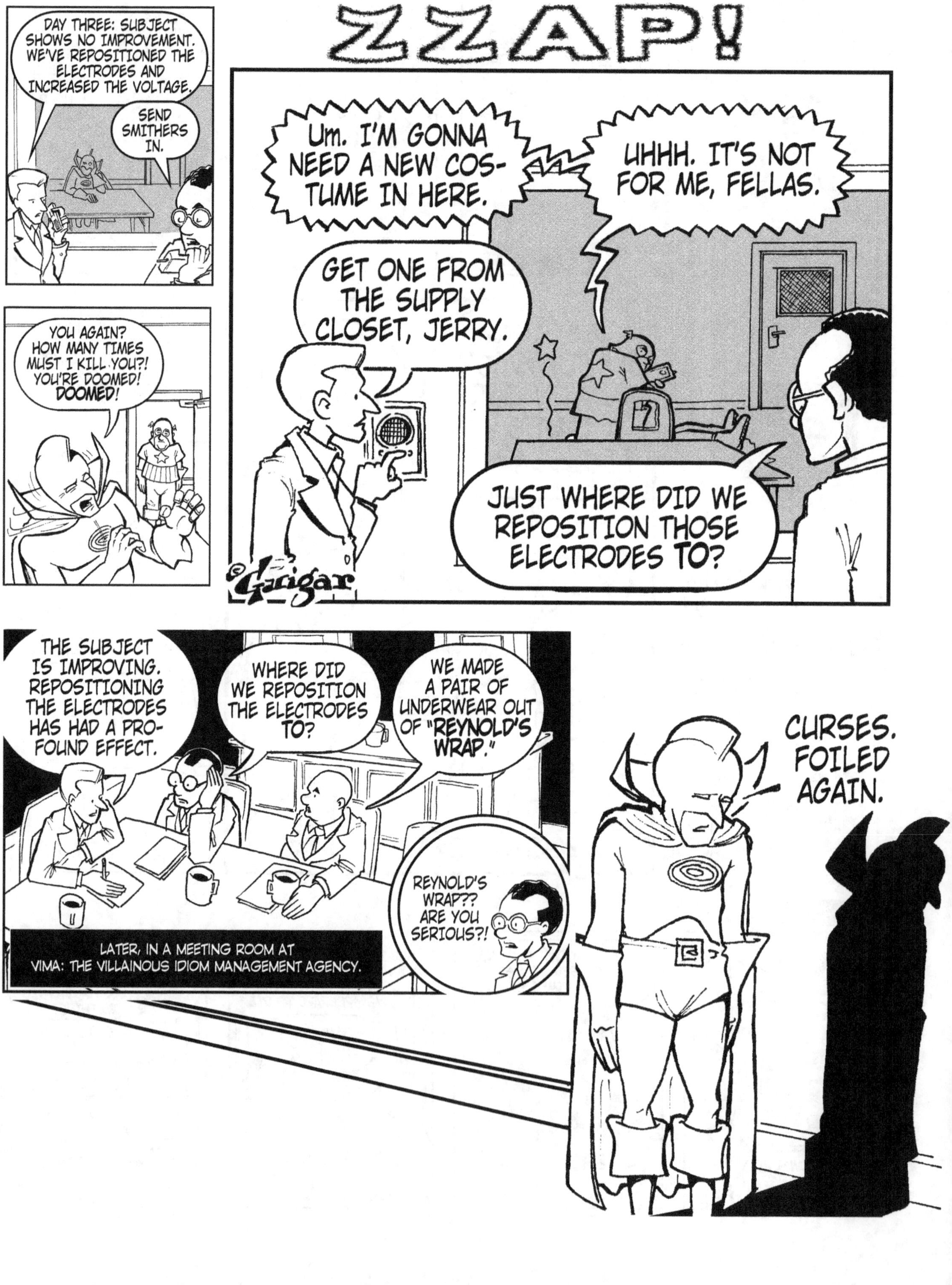
DAY THREE: SUBJECT SHOWS NO IMPROVEMENT. WE'VE REPOSITIONED THE ELECTRODES AND INCREASED THE VOLTAGE.
SEND SMITHERS IN.
YOU AGAIN? HOW MANY TIMES MUST I KILL YOU?! YOU'RE DOOMED! DOOMED!
ZZAP!
Um. I'M GONNA NEED A NEW COS-TUME IN HERE.
UHHH. IT'S NOT FOR ME, FELLAS.
GET ONE FROM THE SUPPLY CLOSET, JERRY.
JUST WHERE DID WE REPOSITION THOSE ELECTRODES TO?
© Garigar
THE SUBJECT IS IMPROVING. REPOSITIONING THE ELECTRODES HAS HAD A PRO-FOUND EFFECT.
WHERE DID WE REPOSITION THE ELECTRODES TO?
WE MADE A PAIR OF UNDERWEAR OUT OF "REYNOLD'S WRAP."
REYNOLD'S WRAP?? ARE YOU SERIOUS?!
LATER, IN A MEETING ROOM AT VIMA: THE VILLAINOUS IDIOM MANAGEMENT AGENCY.
CURSES. FOILED AGAIN.

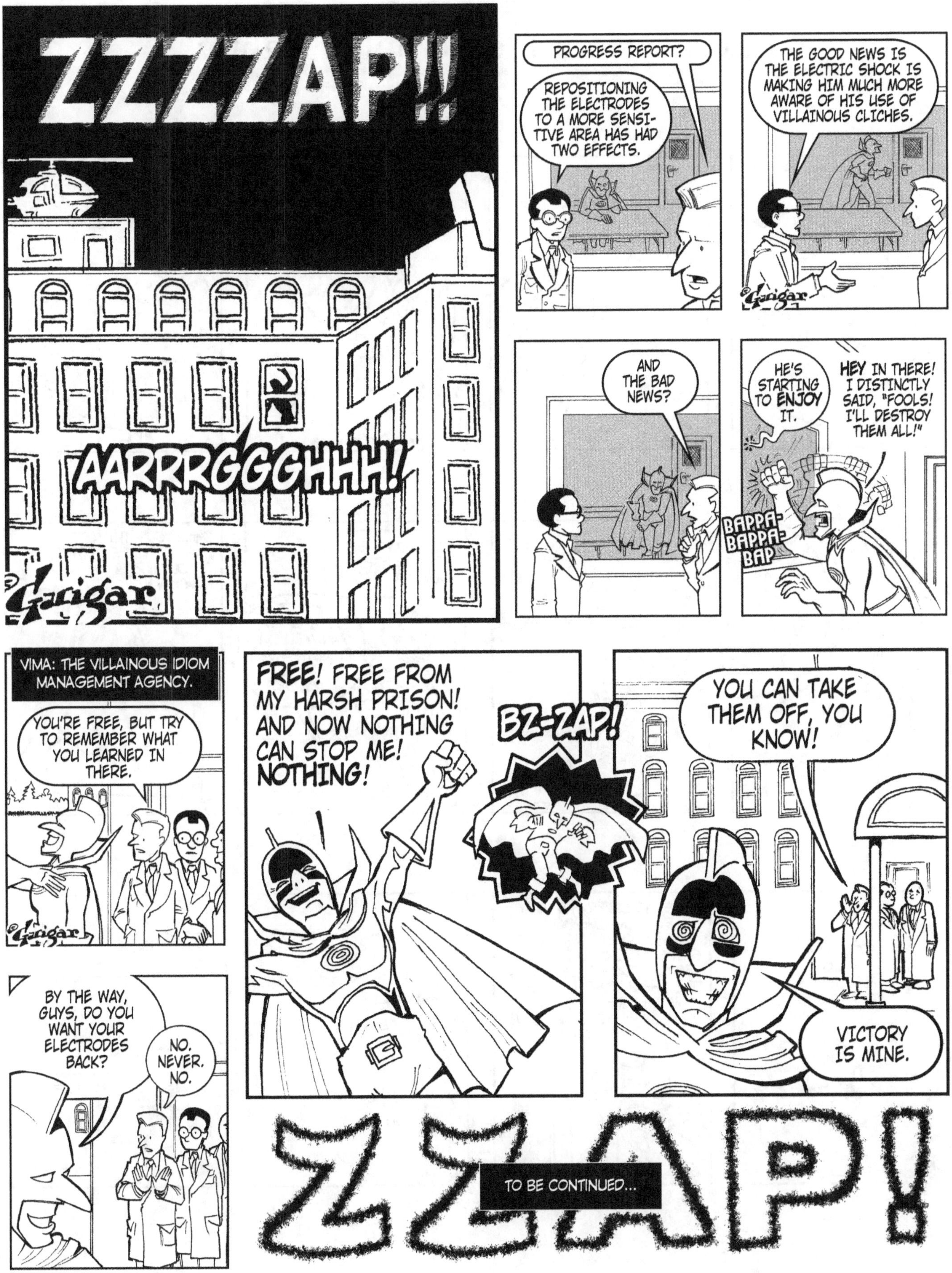

ZZZZAP!!
AARRRGGGHHH!
PROGRESS REPORT?
REPOSITIONING THE ELECTRODES TO A MORE SENSI-TIVE AREA HAS HAD TWO EFFECTS.
THE GOOD NEWS IS THE ELECTRIC SHOCK IS MAKING HIM MUCH MORE AWARE OF HIS USE OF VILLAINOUS CLICHES.
AND THE BAD NEWS?
HE'S STARTING TO ENJOY IT.
HEY IN THERE! I DISTINCTLY SAID, "FOOLS! I'LL DESTROY THEM ALL!"
BAPPA-BAPPA-BAP
VIMA: THE VILLAINOUS IDIOM MANAGEMENT AGENCY.
YOU'RE FREE, BUT TRY TO REMEMBER WHAT YOU LEARNED IN THERE.
BY THE WAY, GUYS, DO YOU WANT YOUR ELECTRODES BACK?
NO. NEVER. NO.
FREE! FREE FROM MY HARSH PRISON! AND NOW NOTHING CAN STOP ME! NOTHING!
BZ-ZAP!
YOU CAN TAKE THEM OFF, YOU KNOW!
VICTORY IS MINE.
ZZAP!
TO BE CONTINUED...

Intermission: Please hold. Tightly...

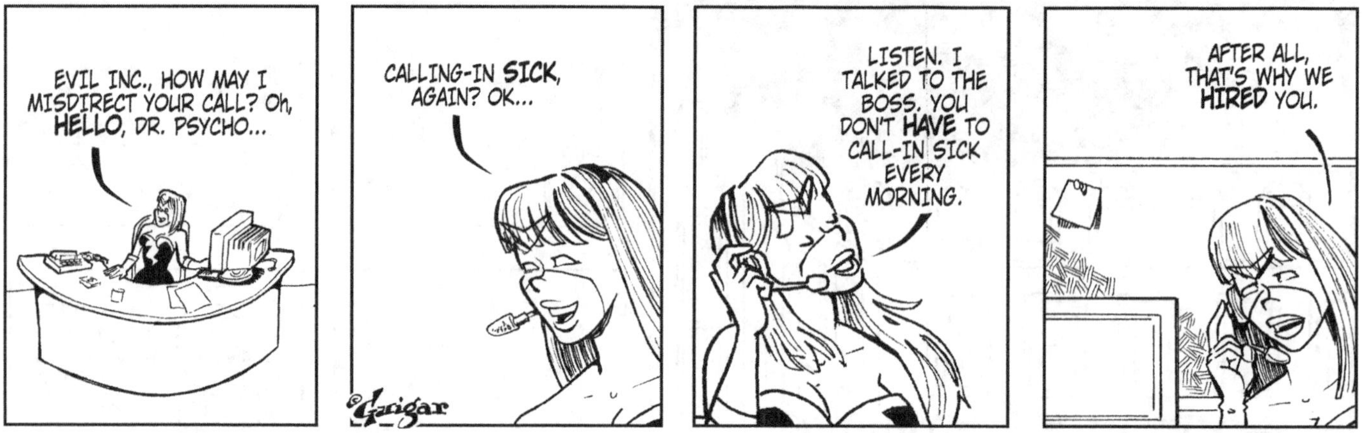
EVIL INC., HOW MAY I MISDIRECT YOUR CALL? Oh, **HELLO**, DR. PSYCHO...
CALLING-IN **SICK**, AGAIN? OK...
LISTEN. I TALKED TO THE BOSS. YOU DON'T **HAVE** TO CALL-IN SICK EVERY MORNING.
AFTER ALL, THAT'S WHY WE **HIRED** YOU.

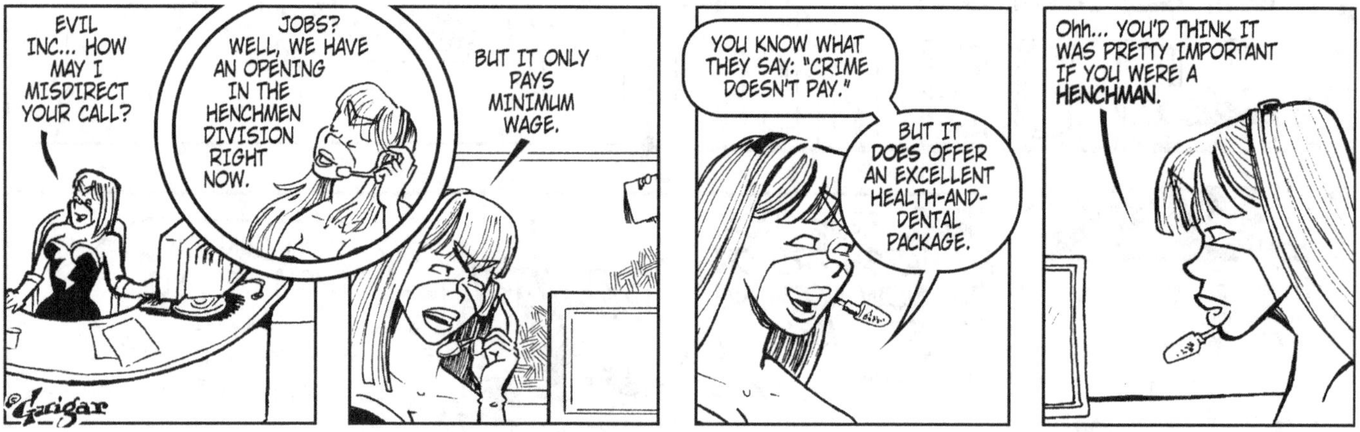
EVIL INC... HOW MAY I MISDIRECT YOUR CALL?
JOBS? WELL, WE HAVE AN OPENING IN THE HENCHMEN DIVISION RIGHT NOW.
BUT IT ONLY PAYS MINIMUM WAGE.
YOU KNOW WHAT THEY SAY: "CRIME DOESN'T PAY."
BUT IT **DOES** OFFER AN EXCELLENT HEALTH-AND-DENTAL PACKAGE.
Ohh... YOU'D THINK IT WAS PRETTY IMPORTANT IF YOU WERE A **HENCHMAN**.

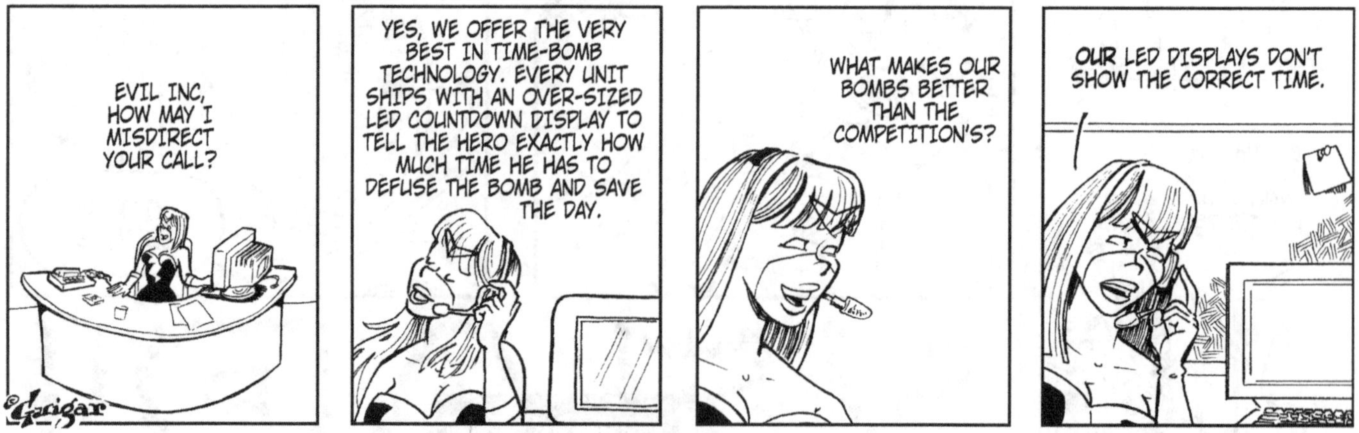
EVIL INC, HOW MAY I MISDIRECT YOUR CALL?
YES, WE OFFER THE VERY BEST IN TIME-BOMB TECHNOLOGY. EVERY UNIT SHIPS WITH AN OVER-SIZED LED COUNTDOWN DISPLAY TO TELL THE HERO EXACTLY HOW MUCH TIME HE HAS TO DEFUSE THE BOMB AND SAVE THE DAY.
WHAT MAKES OUR BOMBS BETTER THAN THE COMPETITION'S?
OUR LED DISPLAYS DON'T SHOW THE CORRECT TIME.

Epilogue

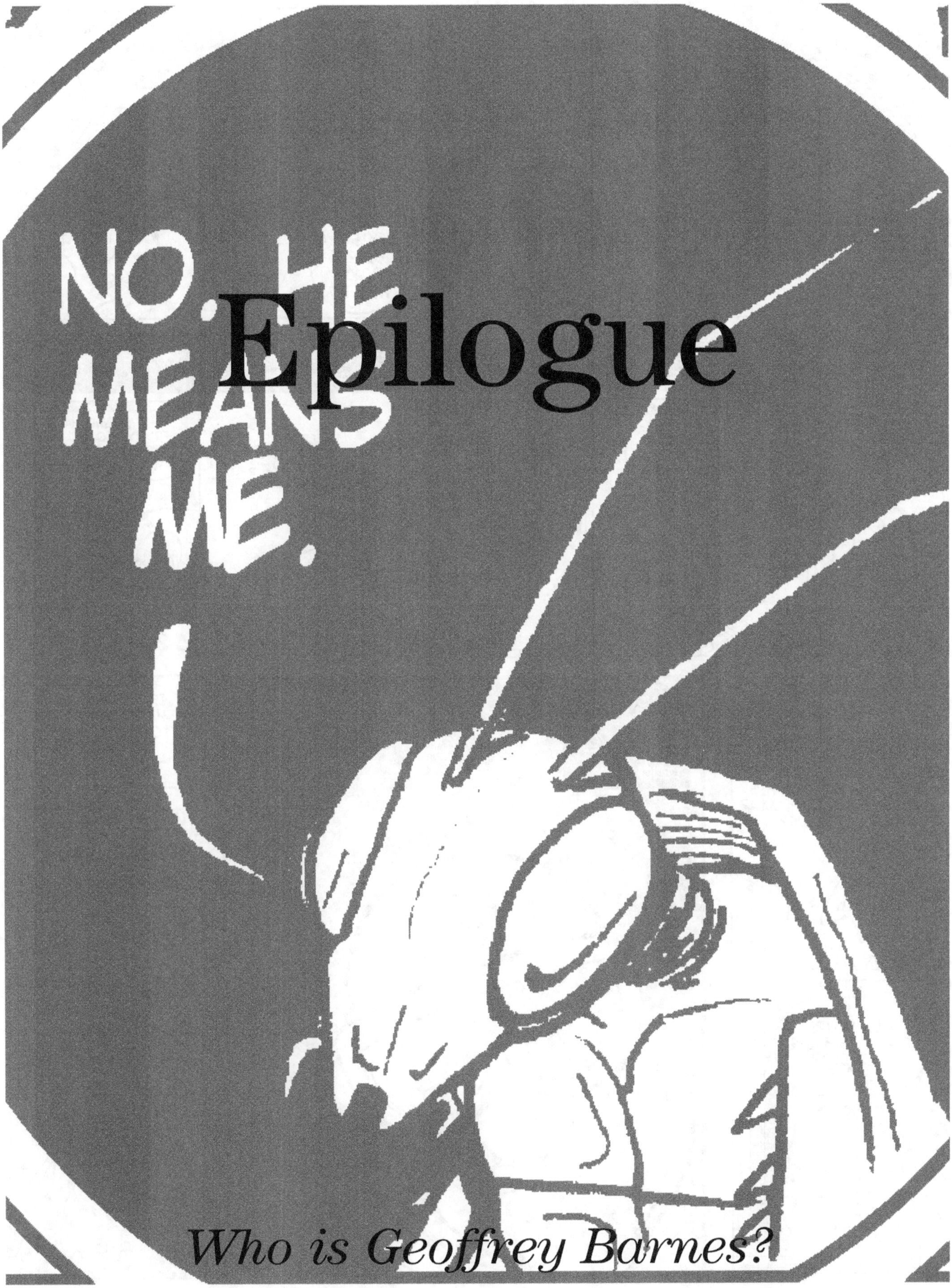
NO. HE MEANS ME.

Who is Geoffrey Barnes?

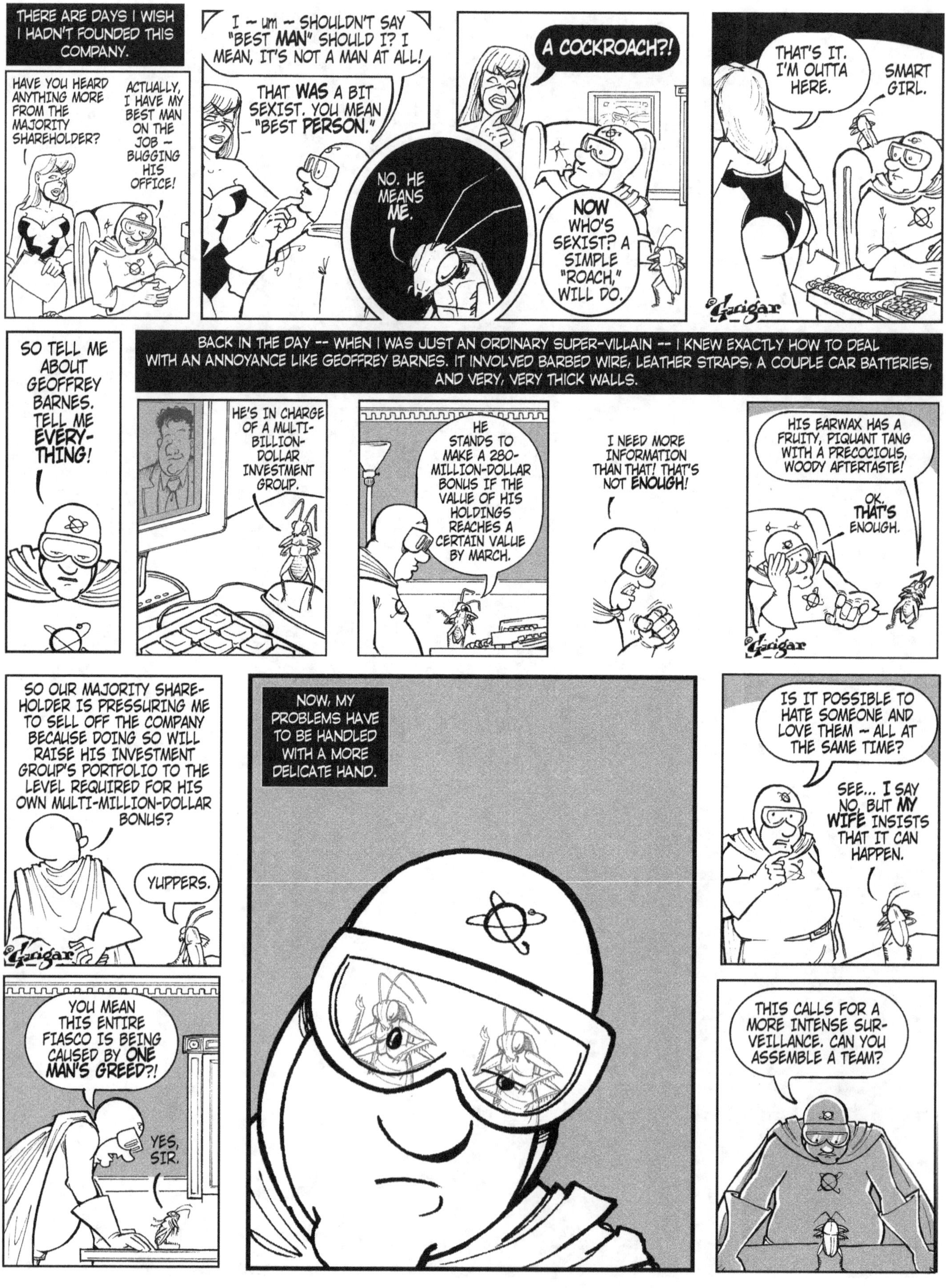
THERE ARE DAYS I WISH I HADN'T FOUNDED THIS COMPANY.
HAVE YOU HEARD ANYTHING MORE FROM THE MAJORITY SHAREHOLDER?
ACTUALLY, I HAVE MY BEST MAN ON THE JOB -- BUGGING HIS OFFICE!
I -- um -- SHOULDN'T SAY "BEST MAN" SHOULD I? I MEAN, IT'S NOT A MAN AT ALL!
THAT WAS A BIT SEXIST. YOU MEAN "BEST PERSON."
NO. HE MEANS ME.
A COCKROACH?!
NOW WHO'S SEXIST? A SIMPLE "ROACH," WILL DO.
THAT'S IT. I'M OUTTA HERE.
SMART GIRL.
SO TELL ME ABOUT GEOFFREY BARNES. TELL ME EVERY-THING!
BACK IN THE DAY -- WHEN I WAS JUST AN ORDINARY SUPER-VILLAIN -- I KNEW EXACTLY HOW TO DEAL WITH AN ANNOYANCE LIKE GEOFFREY BARNES. IT INVOLVED BARBED WIRE, LEATHER STRAPS, A COUPLE CAR BATTERIES, AND VERY, VERY THICK WALLS.
HE'S IN CHARGE OF A MULTI-BILLION-DOLLAR INVESTMENT GROUP.
HE STANDS TO MAKE A 280-MILLION-DOLLAR BONUS IF THE VALUE OF HIS HOLDINGS REACHES A CERTAIN VALUE BY MARCH.
I NEED MORE INFORMATION THAN THAT! THAT'S NOT ENOUGH!
HIS EARWAX HAS A FRUITY, PIQUANT TANG WITH A PRECOCIOUS, WOODY AFTERTASTE!
OK. THAT'S ENOUGH.
SO OUR MAJORITY SHARE-HOLDER IS PRESSURING ME TO SELL OFF THE COMPANY BECAUSE DOING SO WILL RAISE HIS INVESTMENT GROUP'S PORTFOLIO TO THE LEVEL REQUIRED FOR HIS OWN MULTI-MILLION-DOLLAR BONUS?
YUPPERS.
YOU MEAN THIS ENTIRE FIASCO IS BEING CAUSED BY ONE MAN'S GREED?!
YES, SIR.
NOW, MY PROBLEMS HAVE TO BE HANDLED WITH A MORE DELICATE HAND.
IS IT POSSIBLE TO HATE SOMEONE AND LOVE THEM -- ALL AT THE SAME TIME?
SEE... I SAY NO, BUT MY WIFE INSISTS THAT IT CAN HAPPEN.
THIS CALLS FOR A MORE INTENSE SUR-VEILLANCE. CAN YOU ASSEMBLE A TEAM?

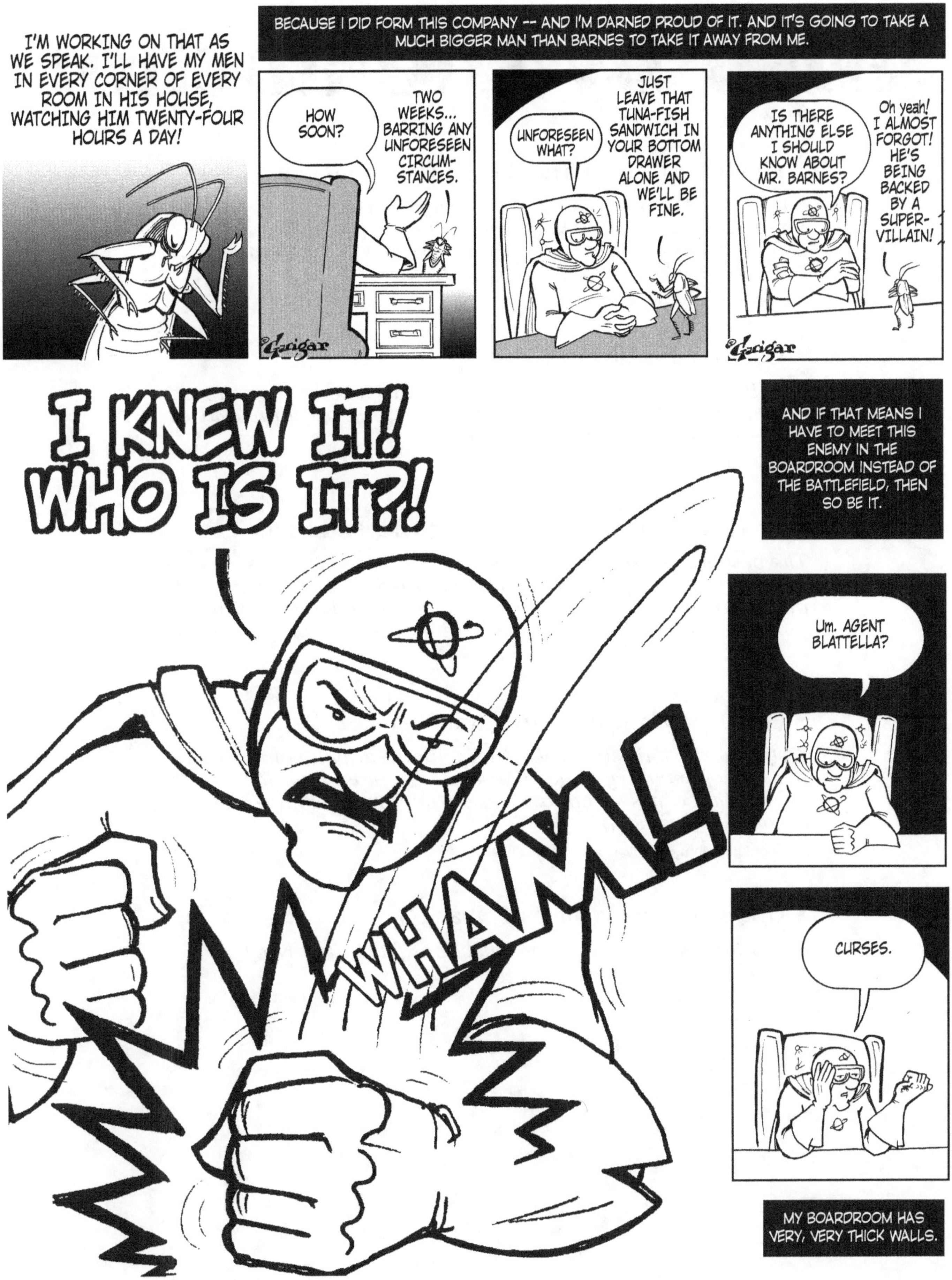

I'M WORKING ON THAT AS WE SPEAK. I'LL HAVE MY MEN IN EVERY CORNER OF EVERY ROOM IN HIS HOUSE, WATCHING HIM TWENTY-FOUR HOURS A DAY!
BECAUSE I DID FORM THIS COMPANY -- AND I'M DARNED PROUD OF IT. AND IT'S GOING TO TAKE A MUCH BIGGER MAN THAN BARNES TO TAKE IT AWAY FROM ME.
HOW SOON?
TWO WEEKS... BARRING ANY UNFORESEEN CIRCUM-STANCES.
©Garigar
UNFORESEEN WHAT?
JUST LEAVE THAT TUNA-FISH SANDWICH IN YOUR BOTTOM DRAWER ALONE AND WE'LL BE FINE.
IS THERE ANYTHING ELSE I SHOULD KNOW ABOUT MR. BARNES?
Oh yeah! I ALMOST FORGOT! HE'S BEING BACKED BY A SUPER-VILLAIN!
©Garigar
I KNEW IT! WHO IS IT?!
WHAM!
AND IF THAT MEANS I HAVE TO MEET THIS ENEMY IN THE BOARDROOM INSTEAD OF THE BATTLEFIELD, THEN SO BE IT.
Um. AGENT BLATTELLA?
CURSES.
MY BOARDROOM HAS VERY, VERY THICK WALLS.

Also by the author

- ## Lightning Lady — The Best of Greystone Inn

The best of the Greystone Inn comics featuring Lightning Lady. Like this book, it takes the comic strip panels and re-assembles them into a continuous-narrative graphic novel. This is considered a pre-history to Evil Inc.

To order: www.lulu.com/guigar

- ## Courting Disaster, vol. 1

A collection of the single-panel comics produced to accompany a weekly sex-advice column. The perfect mix og funny and sexy — you'll laugh your pants off!

To order: www.lulu.com/guigar

- ## Prodromal Teeth — The Best of Greystone Inn

The best of the Greystone Inn comics featuring Mac and Sam's experiences with pregnancy and childbirth. Also presented in graphic-novel format, like this book. Topics include positive portrayals of natural childbirth, midwives, and breastfeeding.

To order: www.lulu.com/guigar

- ## Counting Wrongs — Greystone Inn, vol. 4

A standard comic-strip collection with an added bonus — cartoonist commentary under the comics! A must-read for behind-the-scenes scoops and gossip surrounding this ground-breaking comic strip.

To order: www.lulu.com/guigar

- ## Greystone Inn, volumes 1, 2 and 3

Small-format Greystone Inn collections from Plan Nine Publishing.

To order: www.plan9.org

www.ingramcontent.com/pod-product-compliance
Lightning Source LLC
Chambersburg PA
CBHW080836250626
47160CB00008B/2953